PRAISE FOR *TROUBLE THE LIVING*

"Francesca Capossela is a startling new talent, elegant, erudite, humane, and with a true novelist's sense of form and proportion. Her debut straddles continents and generations with seemingly effortless lyricism and verve. Her exacting insight into the emotional dynamics of family is astonishing."
—Jonathan Lethem, bestselling author of *Motherless Brooklyn* and *The Fortress of Solitude*

"*Trouble the Living* is a beautiful, perceptive, heartfelt novel about family: how it shapes us, how we need it, how we struggle against it. Every page contains half a dozen perfectly captured nuances—of mood, of emotion, of weather, of politics. This is a debut by a novelist of startling gifts; Francesca Capossela's scenes come powerfully to life on the page, and she has the true writer's sense of character and place. A hugely impressive and enjoyable book."
—Kevin Power, author of *White City* and *Bad Day in Blackrock*

"Francesca Capossela's *Trouble the Living* is that rare novel that's both wonderfully propulsive and attuned to the textures of intimate exchange. An accomplished exploration of family, time, place, and autonomy by a writer of great power."
—Paul Lisicky, author of *Later: My Life at the Edge of the World*

"*Trouble the Living* is an honest portrait of mothers and daughters that spans generations and cultures, illuminating the cracks formed when lies and deception define relationships. With exquisite writing that transports the reader through time and place, Capossela explores with heart and keen insight the lengths we will go to for the ones we love and ultimately what we are willing to sacrifice to protect our own hearts."
—Melissa Payne, author of *A Light in the Forest* and *The Night of Many Endings*

TROUBLE THE LIVING

TROUBLE THE LIVING

A Novel

FRANCESCA McDONNELL CAPOSSELA

LAKE UNION
PUBLISHING

Published by Lake Union Publishing, Seattle

www.apub.com

Amazon, the Amazon logo, and Lake Union Publishing are trademarks of Amazon.com, Inc., or its affiliates.

ISBN-13: 9781662511233 (paperback)
ISBN-13: 9781662511226 (digital)

Cover design by Faceout Studio, Amanda Hudson

Cover image: ©Videophilia Stock / Stocksy United; ©Cafe Racer / Shutterstock

Printed in the United States of America

For my mother, Maura,
and for Antonia and Mino

Hearts with one purpose alone

Through summer and winter seem

Enchanted to a stone

To trouble the living stream.

  —William Butler Yeats, from "Easter, 1916"

PART ONE

Chapter One

On the first sunny day in April, when the world smelled as clean as water tastes, Ma took us to see the border.

"No boys allowed," she said, closing the door of the blue station wagon in our brother Tad's face. She had told Ina and me that we were going shopping for the wedding. In the back seat, Ina wore a bright-yellow turtleneck, her hair pinned like a halo on top of her head. She had a pimple below her left nostril; in every other regard, she was perfect.

On the motorway, Ma drove quickly. I rolled down my window and dangled my wrist out, catching the wind. She kept her gaze on the road, her body still despite the speed, but I had the feeling she was watching me.

We drove on back roads until I was sure we were not, after all, going dress shopping, until I became entirely disoriented as to our location. Only then did Ma pull onto a spot of grass and park the car by a stream. The sun was strong even though it was not warm. I opened the car door and turned my body toward the outdoors.

"Where are we?" Ina asked.

Ma got out of the car slowly, her body tensed. She was wearing black suit trousers, a white blouse, and, over it all, a long, black leather coat. In the mud, she stood in boots with three-inch heels. She towered. Ina and I followed.

We stood in the clearing, three women in boots and coats, and Ina and I looked around to see what made this spot more important than the shopping center.

"That's the border," Ma said. Her pointer finger arced in the sky, following the water until she landed on a birch tree. "Until there." The stream went north; the border went east.

"Do you see it?" she asked.

We shook our heads.

"That's because it isn't real," she said. "They drew a line on a map, and they want us to live by it."

It was not the first time I had seen the border. Not the first time I had crossed it. But it was the first time I had seen a slice of it that was not swarming with Brits. This was the border's naked underbelly, what it looked like without its armor. She was showing us its weak spots, the places where we could do damage.

We stood still, three points on a triangle, looking up at the gray-blue sky. The trees above us reached, as if to grasp each other. There was a hole between them, a space where no branches loomed. After a minute, I took off my boots.

The water was icy on my ankles. The rocks slipped under my feet. I walked in the stream up to the birch tree, stepped onto the grass, and kept walking. Trying to feel the line beneath my feet, the evidence of separation.

I looked back at my mother. There was a white scar across her stomach, hidden now beneath her blouse. The scar was raised, like braille, and it marked the place where she'd been opened when she gave birth to Ina. When it was still red and I was very small, she wouldn't let me see it. She said that that kind of pain hurt to look at. But when it healed, and only the white road of it remained, I would trace my fingers across it, the sewn-up severing of her. If she hadn't been a mother, I thought, she would have been a soldier. I saw it in her straight back, her set jaw.

"Don't tell your da," Ma said as she started the car again, her hand on the gearshift knotted and tense with her power, the machine that she controlled, the weight she wielded. "And don't tell your brothers. Girls understand these things much better than fellas."

We nodded. It did not have to be said. We did not speak of scars with our father. But we felt them, Ina and I. In different ways, we felt them.

❖   ❖   ❖

In the morning, I woke with Ma beside me in bed. Her stomach was hot on my lower back, the tuck of her knees into the backs of mine. She always slept like that, curled into herself. They must have fought again.

Outside the window, the morning was dark, except for the ribbons of pink closest to the horizon. Even with Ma beside me, I was cold. It was the time of thawing, the steady climb toward Easter. Fish and vegetables for dinner every night. All of us waiting for Him to die, to be reborn.

I rolled over and looked at Him, hanging on the wall on the left side of my bed. Body stretched out on the cross, ragged and desperate, limp as a lover. His eyes shiny as gemstones, His ribs concave with hunger, His stomach rounded the slightest bit as it led down to the vee where His loincloth bandaged Him. I touched my stomach, held the fatty bit between my pointer finger and thumb. Just to feel my own thickness. Then I crossed myself.

I got out of bed without waking Ma. Ina was still asleep in the bed across from mine. I went downstairs and put the kettle on the range. When it boiled, I held my mug with both hands to warm myself. The weather was always the worst when you expected the worst to be over. It was a quarter to seven, and I was waiting for Conor O'Malley to come for our bottles.

The car pulled into our driveway at five minutes to seven. It was an old Ford Cortina, pale green with scratched paint. Conor got out, walked toward the back door. As I went to meet him, I located Tad's hurley stick to the left of the doormat, just in case.

"Dia dhuit," I said.

He repeated the phrase, barely meeting my eye. Conor would've been handsome, despite the burn on his face, if he had not had eyes that shone so malevolently. His nose was thin and long, like a weapon, and his lips were as plush as sofa cushions. He'd graduated from secondary school two summers ago, but he'd been a volunteer even before then. I remembered him from school: the slump of his shoulders in the hallways, his gaze always fixed on some distant point. Something about him made you want to move out of his way.

The bottles were in a bag under the sink. All week, I had collected them for him, for this. They clinked quietly, full of possibility. Guinness, Magners, Coca-Cola. Giving Conor the bottles had been my job for the last year. The duty Ma had given me, both a mark of her regard and a cross I had to bear.

"Good girl." Conor smiled at me when I handed him the bag. I watched his hand as he took it, as it dangled near his knee. I could see that same hand, hours from now, dipping rags into petrol, placing them into those glass shells. The click and whoosh of a lighter igniting. The trash I'd given him turned to weapons.

He nodded at me. The bag clinked again. And then he was walking back to the car. The Cortina pulled out of the driveway, and the headlights passed through the trees. The sun was rising, the pink of dawn ascending beyond the gray-green fields. I went inside and turned on the TV to watch the morning news. I did not want to go back upstairs just yet. I wanted to stay in the new day's light and feel the promise of what I had done; I had given something secret to my motherland. The song of the empty bottles. A kiss for my country.

Ina's favorite fashion magazine lay on the coffee table, and I picked it up. A model was wearing a dark-red lipstick, almost purple. *Vendetta*, the shade was called. I studied her face, checked the skin tone of my hands against hers. I turned the page, read about blush pink and halter tops. When we were smaller, I used to kiss Ina on the lips, hoping some of her would come off on my mouth; she tasted like strawberry ChapStick.

On the TV, newsmen were discussing a bomb scare at a Liverpool horse race. Calls received Saturday at a nearby police station had warned that explosives were planted inside the stadium. More than sixty thousand spectators had had to be evacuated. There had been several other threats made recently, one of the newsmen said, in the IRA's campaign leading up to the UK general election.

Da walked downstairs as the newsman was talking. "The world's fecking mad," he said by way of greeting. I looked up at him; his hair was still mussed from sleep, and he had circles under his eyes.

I went to the kitchen and poured him a cup of tea. His hand shook as he took it from me, and I saw the flush of last night's whiskey on his face.

"Go on," he said. "Give us a nip, won't ya?"

I got the bottle from the cabinet and poured a splash into his cup. Enough to calm his shakes.

"Thanks a mill." He grinned at me a little guiltily. A look that made me feel uncomfortable and complicit.

Da's entrance always shocked me in how it changed the structure of our house. The walls seemed to shrink, the ceiling to descend around him. I felt claustrophobic, cramped. My body felt like it was attached to his by invisible threads, so that with every tiny movement—his jaw clenching or relaxing, the turn of his head, the thud of his steps—my own body was tugged into reacting.

It was the deepest kind of empathy, being afraid. When Da was drunk, we were all off-balance, unsteady on our feet. When he woke hungover, we were all sensitive to light and noise, wincing at nothing. It was how we knew when to duck or cower, when to go up to our rooms. We playacted his state of mind so we would know when to run.

"What are you doing up so early?" he asked.

"Nothing," I said. "Only I couldn't sleep."

"I heard voices."

"Sure it was only the TV."

"Go back to bed, then." His voice was gruff. "I've got to get ready for work."

I remembered how curious I'd been about his work as a child, begging him to take me to the customs station with him. He had once, and I'd perched on a stool he dragged into his cubicle for me. I was patient and quiet while he hummed over paperwork, his back slumped. I'd felt victorious, seeing a part of him that the rest of my family were strangers to. Holding his hand while he led me through the staffroom. But that was back before Ma sent Enda to fetch Da at the pub most nights. Back before the gin blossoms had bloomed along his nose.

He was telling me to leave. I turned and began to climb back up the staircase.

"It hardly matters now," he said, and I turned around.

"What does?" I asked.

"All that fighting. It'll be over any minute. They'll be talking peace before the New Year."

He grinned as he said it, showing three missing teeth. When he was twenty-two, a British dentist had removed them without anesthesia. Some sort of practical joke. Some sort of sadism. It didn't make him angry, his gaping mouth. It made him ashamed.

"You really think that?" I asked. "You think the RA'll give up without a united Ireland?"

On the television, in the newspapers, everyone was discussing the prospect of peace. Sinn Féin, under the leadership of swears-he'd-never-been-an-IRA-man Gerry Adams, was said to be in talks with the British and Irish governments. The IRA had declared ceasefires and then broken them, declared ceasefires and then broken them. The newspapers made it sound easy, like all we needed was the right frame of mind. But by arguing for peace, I knew, they were arguing for the status quo. For all their talk, we hadn't seen any changes. British officers still raided our neighbors' homes; young men still blew themselves up with car bombs. If we did not win this war, we would lose it.

"Ach get outta here," he said, gesturing for me to leave. "You sound like your bloody mother."

❖ ❖ ❖

Back in my room, Ma stood in the doorway. She looked like a specter in the half-light, her black dressing gown shapeless. Behind her, Ina's bed was empty.

"Was that Conor I heard?" Her voice cut in the early morning.

"Da's getting ready for work," I said. I passed her and moved into my room.

She followed me in and sat in the rocking chair that faced my bed. I hated that chair. The monotony of her movement in it. She could sit there for hours, moving back and forth. It made me seasick.

"Did you give him the bottles so?"

I looked at her.

"Aye, I gave him the bottles."

She smiled. "Good girl." The phrase had been gratifying when Conor used it; on her lips, it grated.

I got back into bed, pulling the covers up to my chin. We didn't need to be up for school for another hour, and I could do with a bit more sleep. For a moment, the squeaking of the chair was the only noise. I tried to close my eyes, but Ma kept rocking. I ground my teeth at each whine. I preferred Ma's fixation to Da's lethargy, but I would have preferred the quiet to either.

"I wish your da was man enough for it," she said. "I wish he'd at least let me be man enough."

It was the mantra of a wronged woman, but Ma had made her own bed. She'd been seventeen when she had Enda. The same age I was now. Always a wild one, Ma had worn a leather jacket over her school uniform, had gotten her knuckles rapped daily by the nuns. Back then, it had been even worse: Catholics were denied housing and jobs, subjected to violence, segregated. Unarmed citizens were shot dead en masse by British soldiers. Ma had wanted to be a fighter, had wanted to change things. She'd dreamed of running for office like Bernadette Devlin. But they did worse than rap you on the knuckles for being unmarried, pregnant, and a teenager. As far as I knew, she'd never even considered the alternative: going to England, undoing what had been done.

Ma had been lucky that my father wanted to marry her. It was the best thing that could have happened to her, even if he never let her fight, hardly let her out of his sight. She was pregnant too often to be a revolutionary anyway. Her potential had been snuffed out with her first child. Her possibility dwindled with each of our subsequent births. It was why it was me, and not her, who woke up at dawn to give Conor the bottles. But deep down, the fire still ruled her.

I couldn't sleep with her there. With the noise of the rocking chair and her vague pronouncements. I pulled the covers back down, got out of bed.

"I'm off to shower, then," I said, leaving her where she sat.

I could see her as a teenager, the bump of Enda pushing out the waistband of her knee-length skirt. She'd stayed in school as long as she could, counting down the days until she would leave class and never come back. I sometimes imagined her telling her own mother the news, how terrified she must have been. It was probably why nothing scared her anymore. Nothing could be worse than that original disappointment. She must have been frightened of the baby too, of the shape of her own body twisting in new ways. Of the part of her that would break when he was born. They each blamed each other. My father thinking my mother had trapped him. My mother thinking the same about him. They each felt stuck in different ways. So my father drank, and my mother raged.

I stopped at the window on my way to the bathroom. Outside, the sun was climbing in the sky, and the fields were illuminated with a hazy light. When we were wee, Enda used to take us out there, into the woods around the house. Twilight was the best time for fairy sightings, he said. We brought flashlights and jam jars to collect specimens. The tree branches were like arms in the darkness, and we did not know where to look, moving our eyes from the roots to the sky, afraid of what we might see if our gaze lingered too long, afraid of what we might miss if we did not keep looking. The forest was like an older brother, the way you wanted to know it and yet feared it all at once.

Sometimes, Enda would stop abruptly, and I would walk into him, my little ten-year-old body bumping up against him. He was large enough that I thought he was an adult, though he was only fifteen then. The crown of my head would hit the small of his back, the hollows where his kidneys lay. I would have been looking for tracks in the ground or at a worm, a snail, a leaf. He'd grab my head in the crook of his elbow, hammerlock me, making me laugh. Then he'd stop, still holding my head but gently now, and point ahead to a glimmer in the darkening sky or to some movement behind a tree. We would hold our breaths in fear, in awe. I think he might have really believed in it, some magical force out there. It was easy to, in the woods, when the night swallowed you and there were noises you could not name.

Everything would be different once he and Siobhán were married. The house would be hollower, the silences longer. Da's scowls would be concentrated only on Tad without Enda to share them. Siobhán was from Donegal, and he would be moving there, across the border. They would live in the South; we would stay in the North. The words were not literal. Looking at a map, you'd say Donegal was due west of Tyrone, not south. But he was moving to the so-called Free State, while we lived in so-called Northern Ireland, held tight in the grip of the United Kingdom, an assault passed off as an embrace. It was wicked, their assertion that our home was their territory, that we were their citizens.

With Enda gone, I would be the oldest in the house. Tad was a year younger, and Ina was fourteen. We didn't go into the woods much anymore. Tad played football with his friends. Ina and I went to the lough to swim, watched *Countdown* on Monday evenings, lip-synced to our favorite songs on VH1. And Enda lay in his room and dreamed, I supposed, of when he would be free of us.

❖   ❖   ❖

Ina was in the bathtub, her eyes closed as she lay with her head against the porcelain rim. Her nipples, puffed with adolescence, peeked out of the water like frogs' heads. Her cheeks were flushed with the heat of the bath, and her eyes still had the residue of sleep in their corners.

"Hi," I said quietly, not wanting to frighten her.

"Oh." She opened her eyes. "I'm sorry—I'll be out in a minute."

Girls at school complained about sharing bedrooms or bathrooms with their sisters, but I loved to be alone with Ina like this, when nudity was natural, when our bodies were present but not the point. We were like children again. The steam from the bath made the room smoky. I sat down on the toilet seat and waited for my turn. Ina had always preferred baths to showers. Seeing her now, I wanted to copy her, to sink down into the water she had risen from. To exchange my body for hers.

Ina had somehow turned out more beautiful than the rest of us siblings put together. It was like a taunt, like divine intervention. When I was twelve or thirteen, I'd asked Father Jim what the difference was between envy and jealousy. Envy, he said, was the second-worst deadly sin. It meant wanting to hurt someone in order to take what they had. Being jealous was only a possessiveness, wanting to protect something, or someone, from being taken from you. "Can you be both?" I'd asked. "Can you be afraid of losing someone but at the same time want to hurt them, to take what they have?" The Devil, Father Jim had said, has many talons. He can puncture the heart in more than one place.

"D'you know why Ma's acting funny like?" Ina asked after a minute. "Why'd she sleep in our room?"

"It's nothing," I said, shrugging. "They just had a fight. You know how they are."

"She wants us to go to Mass with her tomorrow. I don't know why we need to go two times in one week. Sure we were only just bloody there."

"But you'll go, won't you?" I asked.

Ina was rubbing a bar of soap over her chest, under her arms. "I don't think I can like."

"What do you mean?"

"I dunno if I believe in God, if I'm honest."

I covered my face with my hands. "Ina," I pleaded through my fingers. "Don't be talking nonsense like that. You'll get yourself in trouble."

"You know, lots of people don't believe in God," she said calmly. "George Bernard Shaw didn't, and we learned about him in school."

"What do you even mean, 'believe in God'? The Almighty's not up there worrying about whether or not Ina Kane believes in him. You've just got to go to Mass is all."

She shrugged, but I could tell by the way her mouth was set that I had done nothing to change her mind. I wondered if I should be afraid for her. But then I sighed. It was just Ina being Ina. She could never go to Hell. She was too pretty.

I went to the sink and opened the medicine cabinet. I studied Ma's makeup: old eyeliner pens and half-filled mascara bottles. I thought of the lipstick I'd seen in the magazine. *Vendetta*. I wanted the lipstick. I wanted to be someone new. I wanted to be like Ina, be with Ina. Somehow, she seemed older than I did, more self-assured. I wondered how she had gotten to be like that, while I still felt like a child sometimes.

"Ach it seems like a lot of worrying—"

Her words were cut off as she dunked her head underwater. She reemerged, hair dripping down her back.

"For no real reason like. All this hating each other because of which Mass we go to and what school and what sports teams we like. At the end of the day, what's the difference? We say the Eucharist is the body; they say it isn't. Who bloody cares?"

I watched her in the mirror as she spoke. She was detangling her hair with her fingers, focusing on a knot she'd found.

"Prods don't go to Mass," I said, my voice harder than I meant it to be. "And sure you know it's not about the bloody Eucharist." I turned back to face her, still shocked by what she'd said. "It's about them coming into our country and taking our language and our land and our houses and our jobs and our food and making us second-class citizens. It's about the fact that we're *Irish*, not British, and yet they still say we're living in the United fecking Kingdom. *United*, it's a bloody joke."

"Jaysus," Ina said, raising her hands. Her face looked pale, like I actually had frightened her. "I didn't know I was talking to Ma," she said. "Calm yourself; I was only thinking aloud."

She had sat up straighter in the bath, and I could tell that she suddenly felt strange being there, vulnerable and naked. A flush of guilt passed over me.

"Ach sorry," I said. "You caught me off guard's all." I rubbed a hand over my eyes. Was it giving Conor the bottles that had made me so edgy? That made me feel like it was my movement she was attacking? I turned back to the mirror.

"You're grand," she said, but I didn't believe her.

Behind me, I heard the sound of water splashing gently as Ina stood up in the bathtub. I didn't look at her, but I could see her shape out of the corner of my eye. The severity of her boxy shoulders.

"Your turn," she said. She'd wrapped a towel around herself. Her hair was wet and long down her back. She stood there, dripping onto the bath mat for a moment, looking at me.

❖ ❖ ❖

Ina hadn't been bluffing. The next day, she sat in front of the mirror doing her makeup, not even wearing a shirt over her light-pink training bra, while I sat on the bed, dressed head to toe in starched church clothes.

"Ina, you're to go," I told her. "Ma said so."

"I'm not going," she protested. "I've other things to be doing."

"Ina, you're to go," I repeated. "Don't make a fuss now."

Ma walked into our room then. She was wearing a red blazer and skirt suit. "Right, is that you set, Bríd?" she asked.

"I'm ready, aye, but Ina won't move." I nodded toward where my sister sat.

"Ach she's all right," Ma said, turning to leave. "Let's go on then; we'll be late."

I opened my mouth in disbelief. "She doesn't have to go?"

"Sure leave your sister alone, Bríd," she chided.

The sun was high in the sky, but the air was still fresh and crisp, not yet softened and lazy with summer. "We'll go to Saint Patrick's in Armagh," Ma told me as we got into the car.

"D'you not want to see Father Jim?"

"We'll go to Armagh."

In the driver's seat, she sat with her back straight. A woman who never slumped. I felt like I could feel the texture of her thoughts, their metallic smoothness. I knew the iron outline of her mind, but I could only guess at its substance. Why hadn't she insisted that Ina go? Ina needed church more than I did; I, at least, believed.

As she drove, I watched the fields and towns go by, Ma occasionally raising her hand when we passed a house whose family she knew. They couldn't see her; she just wanted to signal that she knew who they were, like a queen bestowing dignity with the slightest movement of her wrist. They were her friends from the parish hall, women she gossiped with over a cup of tea. One day, I thought, I would be one of those women, ushering my children to chapel on a Sunday. Playing bingo or swing dancing at the weekend. The banal a contrast to the horrific as marriage gossip was swapped with tales of car bombs and police raids.

At Saint Patrick's, we found a seat in the back, letting local worshippers take the front rows. I found it difficult to listen to the priest. The church was so large and grand, so different from our own. It felt luxurious and illicit. Its high white arches, its golden chandeliers. I kept thinking about Ina, how she was like this church—arresting, overdone. Why did she have to be so difficult? Why did my mother allow it? I felt uneasy as I remembered what Ina had said in the bath.

After Communion, we returned to our pew as the rest of the worshippers filed out. I wasn't sure what exactly Ma wanted. She lowered herself back onto her knees and, head down, began to pray again. Her eyes were screwed up tight so that she looked not like a godly woman in prayer but like a criminal facing her sentence.

"Bríd?" Ma was looking up at me, her knees still planted on the wooden plank. I had been staring out at the stained glass, thinking.

"Aye?"

"Would you not promise me something?"

At the back of my throat, I felt the softness of guilt or shame, like I had eaten too much sugar and was rotting with the sweetness.

"Sure, Ma," I said, knowing there was no other answer I could give my mother.

"Would you promise me you'll watch out for Ina?"

I was quiet for a moment. I did not know what she meant, asking that. Of course I would watch out for Ina; I always did. I heard again the clinking of the glass bottles—like the tap of cruet on chalice as the priest poured the wine—imagined the arc of a throw, like the line of a border.

Our eyes met. "Sure," I said. "I promise."

Chapter Two

The sky was whitewashed with smog, eclipsing the mountains. Smoke hung in the air like a shroud. Dust settled in a thin film on car windshields, on the front porch. Like a snowfall, except that it was seventy-five outside and sunny. When Mom hugged me goodbye that morning—standing in the doorway with a mug of tea, blue eyes straining in the sunlight—she'd stared out toward the horizon like she was sending me off to war. "Promise you'll come back?" she'd asked, just like she asked every time I left the house. "Promise," I'd told her. Her embrace around me was like a house I lived in.

In calculus class, there was a parabola drawn on the whiteboard. I imagined that it was a cask full of water, a limitless canteen. That it could drench all of California, end the drought. I had a practice AP test open on my desk, and I was working through the first free-response question, not listening to whatever our teacher was saying. Next to me, Mia was staring out the window, her gaze distant, as if she were looking out onto another world. I wondered what that world was like, the place she lived in behind her eyes. Her hair was unruly, down to her shoulders, and her T-shirt showed part of her collarbone. She caught me looking and smiled. I smiled back, feeling that familiar sense of teetering on the edge of something.

Our teacher had stopped talking, and I glanced to the front of the room. For a moment, I was worried he'd asked me a question that I hadn't heard, but he was only checking his watch.

"We're having an emergency drill shortly," he said, and our class groaned collectively. It was almost the end of the year. Wasn't it too late for emergency drills? I was looking forward to summer, when our lives would run in one long arc without emergencies interspliced. Without assemblies to discuss some new trauma in the news. Without fire drills and class debates. Just the mountains for us to walk through, breathing smoke from the wildfires.

The alarm sounded over the loudspeaker. Shrill and grating. Next to me, Mia put on her headphones to block the noise. We made eye contact and rolled our eyes in unison. At the front of the room, our teacher was trying to speak over the alarm. He waved for us to stay in our seats, but several students had already gotten to their feet, stretching. The alarm rang three times and then stopped, and my heart plummeted into my stomach. The number of rings told us what kind of emergency it was. One was a fire. Two was an earthquake. Three was an active shooter.

The room went half-dark as our teacher switched off the lights. The white sunlight slanting through the window met the shadows in a checkerboard pattern. I looked at Mia, felt the urge to put my body in front of hers, to cover her with myself like an embrace or a shield. Like a mother would a daughter, a man would a woman.

"Okay now, remain calm," our teacher said. "Go ahead and find your hiding spots." He pushed his chair up against the door and then added two desks, barricading us in.

Over the loudspeaker, the sound of shots, piercing and hot in my ears. I jumped, and Mia grabbed my hand, pulled me under the desks, up against the wall. She had been my friend for almost as long as I could remember, and the feeling of her hand in mine felt as familiar to me as the taste of my own mouth. But there was something new there, too, something in the way our fingers grasped at each other that I'd never noticed before.

We crouched under the desks, our faces close in the tight space. There was a slight hint of laughter around her eyes and mouth, like she found the situation funny. I felt my heart in my throat, felt myself swallowing it down like an apple. If this were real, I thought, this was when I would text my mother goodbye. She would not survive long without me, I knew. It was one reason why I had to stay alive.

It took five shoves for the shooter to knock down the hastily built barricade. Our teacher hadn't blocked the door handle, either because he'd been instructed not to for the sake of the drill or because he was terrible at self-defense.

"What the fuck kind of barricade is that?" I whispered to Mia under the desk.

"It's good to know we wouldn't last five minutes in real life," she whispered back.

Around us, other students were whispering, too, their bodies black shapes, twisted together under the desks. The initial fear they'd felt, caused by the screech of the alarm and the recording of gunshots, had subsided. Now they were teenagers again, hiding under desks to playact a scenario that would never happen, unable to believe anything the teacher told them or to take his instructions seriously. We'd had these drills our whole lives. After a while, they became jokes to my classmates. But they still frightened me, still gave me nightmares for days. Even if I could see the absurdity in them.

When the door was pushed open, shoving desks out of the way, the shooter stood in its frame, black balaclava masking his face. He looked unsure on his feet, glancing around the room like he was lost. I looked up at his eyes, brown with creases around them. It was Mr. Mark, the science teacher. He looked afraid.

The whispers stopped. There was a long pause. A strange moment as we oscillated between fantasy and reality. Between the nightmare and the truth. Then the lights turned back on, and we emerged from under the desks like shell-shocked trench men. Mr. Mark took off the balaclava and began to talk in a low voice to our math teacher, something about the barricade. Then he turned and left.

We returned to our seats, jostling each other, moving swiftly from gravity to hilarity, breaking into cascades of laughter. A boisterous, giddy mood that our teacher could not tame. I stared back up at the purple vein of the parabola on the whiteboard, feeling our bodies reacclimate to the fact that nothing was wrong. Under the table, I felt Mia kick my foot. I looked up at her.

"You'd think if we were as gifted and talented as they say we are, they wouldn't need to teach us how to hide under a desk." She was trying to make me laugh. She knew that these drills bothered me, climbed into my body and stayed with me. I grinned at her, letting her calm me down. There would be time to worry later.

"You'd think if we were gifted and talented, none of us would ever take an AR-15 to school," I said.

❖   ❖   ❖

We had Climate Club that afternoon, but Mia and I were the only ones who showed up. We had both joined last year, when the drought had been so bad that people had started talking about turning to the ocean for drinking water. Millions of trees had died across the state, and the governor had ordered 25 percent water restrictions. I set a 120-second timer on my phone every time I stepped into the shower and, walking around town, we passed lawn after lawn of dried yellow grass.

We sat in the empty classroom with our feet up on the desks. We were trying to measure the school's carbon footprint, though the endeavor felt somewhat useless. I kept replaying the sound of the barricade being knocked out of the way, kept remembering the feel of Mia's hand in mine, the way she smelled like peppermint Altoids and fresh grass.

"Do you want Froyo?" I asked finally.

We walked into town with our backpacks slung over our shoulders, our steps in unison like we were mirror images of one another.

The yogurt place was inside a shopping center, and I made sure I knew what I wanted before I stepped inside. I liked to hold my breath when I went into crowded, enclosed spaces, so that I never spent more time than was necessary pressed up against other people's bodies. It was those kinds of places where they came for you: white men in T-shirts and jeans, holding their guns like they'd been given no other choice. The random shooting spree, the aimless shower of bullets. No cause, no war. Just destruction.

"How's your mom?" Mia asked when we were back outside, eating our yogurts on a bench. Above us, a palm tree reached up toward the smoke-drenched sky. I swallowed the cough that was building in my throat. I'd had asthma since I was a child.

I shrugged. "She's okay," I said. "I don't know; she seems okay."

Mia nodded.

"Does that ever feel worse to you?" I asked. "When things are okay? It's like you're waiting for it to get bad again. You know it's coming."

"But you can't help being disappointed anyway?" Mia asked. "When it does come?"

"Exactly."

"Yeah," she said. "I know what you mean."

"How's Riley?" I asked. Riley was Mia's older brother, a sophomore in college.

She sighed. "I don't know," she said. "He invited us to a party this weekend."

"He can't be that bad if he's throwing parties." I thought about Riley, his self-effacing laugh, his worn baseball caps, his fingertips calloused from playing guitar. He had taught me how to swing a bat, back when I was intent on trying out for the softball team. And he'd taken me and Mia into town for ice cream even when we were annoying sixth graders, driven us to parties once he got his license. I wasn't particularly close with him, but I loved him as if he were my own brother, feeling, as I did, like I was a part of Mia.

"You'd think." Mia bit her lip. "He's so hard to predict. It's always up and down."

I sucked the last mouthful of yogurt off my spoon. It was cold and sweet, somehow nurturing. I could still feel the adrenaline in my body from the school drill, could still see eyes through the slits of a balaclava.

I knew what she meant about up and down. Lately, I'd felt like Mom was cresting the hill, preparing for the descent. When I left for school, she seemed more afraid than usual. The same way she used to get when I was in second or third grade, marching into the classroom in the middle of a lesson to tell my teacher there was an emergency with my great-aunt or the family dog. We would get home and I'd ask where my aunt was—eager to meet a woman I'd never even known existed—only to be told that that had been a lie. That she had just needed to see me, that she was afraid school wasn't safe. It hadn't been bad like that in a while. These days, it was mostly just Mom taking to bed.

Mia hadn't known what depression was when she first started talking to me about Riley. We'd been twelve or thirteen, up in her bedroom, lying on her twin bed. Her parents had told her Riley was sick, and she had imagined something physical, brought him Advil like the doting younger sister she was. But when she described his symptoms, I knew what it was. She was describing my mother. She was describing the reason I never invited her over to my house, the reason I never spent the night at hers.

It occurred to me, watching her now as she stood and stretched— empty yogurt cup in her hand, her T-shirt riding up at her waist—that the problem I kept running into was that I could not love in moderation. It was always all or nothing, just like Mom had taught me.

❖   ❖   ❖

When I got home that night, the kitchen was warm with the stove's heat. Mom's face glowed in lamplight: radiance and reddish-brown hair, pale-blue eyes and the secretive twist of her smile. A smile she only ever gave to me. People said we looked like sisters. We were only twenty years apart—close enough in age that we could have been. Mom had practically been a child herself when she had me.

She kissed my forehead hello, and I rolled up my sleeves to help her cook. Tomato sauce stirred in a pot, splattering her dress. RTÉ Radio streamed on her laptop, a nightly tradition. Nothing political, just the murmur of accented voices or the Gaelic-language station playing Justin Bieber because it was the middle of the night there and we were probably the only ones listening. I said this out loud, and she laughed and threw her head back, took a long sip of cold white wine. When she went to the bathroom, I took a swig from the bottle.

We had taken a cooking class together a few years back. We'd learned how to make real Italian sauces and pasta from scratch. Olive and rosemary focaccia, fresh out of the oven and so oily that it stained Mom's shirt. We'd talked about going to Italy, just the two of us, drawn the route we would take on an old atlas. We talked about what it would be like: thick pasta, black beaches, volcano on the horizon, the burnt-red Siena buildings, the stained glass of the cathedrals. We had gotten as far as the passport office: my unflattering headshot bound in a leather book and mailed to us. My old passport—toddler me squinting seriously at the camera—was mailed back to the passport agency. But we never ended up going. I didn't ask why; I knew money was often tight, that it was hard to get time off work. It didn't bother me. I liked the imagining, liked the two of us having the same dream.

Half the reason I had wanted to go to Italy was to be that much closer to Ireland. I'd thought there was a possibility—maybe even a likelihood—that crossing the Atlantic would create some kind of magnetic pull, that she would be called back home to that island. That I would get to see that country, too, the place where we came from. A happy place, I imagined, full of dancing and music.

In my phone, texts arrived, went unanswered. I wanted the night to stay like this: golden whispers, sweet smell of sizzling tomatoes.

"Where's Kaleb?" I asked as we sat down to eat.

"Conference in Berkeley," she said.

I nodded. For a moment, I considered talking to Mom about Mia, getting her advice. But it seemed too dangerous. Mom got jealous of Mia, the only other woman I loved. And I wanted things to stay soft between us tonight. I did not want to be at each other's throats, the way we sometimes were.

"Were you like me?" I asked instead, looking up at the face that both did and didn't look like my own. "When you were sixteen?"

She waved the question away, took another bite of pasta.

"Really," I said. "I want to know."

She waited until she finished chewing before saying, "You're much better than I was."

I rolled my eyes. "But what were you like?" I asked.

"You know how I feel," she said. "Nothing worth remembering in the past. My life started when you were born." It was a line I'd heard many times before.

With her right hand, she fiddled with her necklace, gold plating rubbed down till you could see the copper underneath. Her name spelled out in three letters: *Ina*.

❖   ❖   ❖

I slept in her room that night. The adrenaline hadn't fully left me after the emergency drill, and I kept expecting to hear the alarm again, to be asked to find a hiding spot. I put a chair in front of Mom's door, and she eyed it but didn't ask why.

I brushed my teeth with her toothbrush, a child's toothbrush, which she said was softer on her gums. Once, I'd borrowed Mia's toothbrush without asking, and Mia had been so grossed out that she'd thrown it away. You can't share toothbrushes, she'd told me. But Mom used mine whenever it was closer, like everything that was mine was hers too.

I watched myself in the mirror as I finished brushing. The three colors of my eyes. My mother's light blue in my left eye. Green and brown in the other. I didn't look like I was sixteen. I looked like I was still in middle school. Like a girl about to get her first period. But I felt like I was a hundred years old. Like my skin should be withered and weathered.

Mom gave me some of her melatonin, and we watched a movie together until I fell asleep, my head on her shoulder, waking up a few minutes later to find that I'd drooled on her arm, freckly in the moonlight against the white sheets. I wiped off the saliva, and she kissed my head good night.

That night, I dreamed of a man in a balaclava, white face wrapped in black fabric. He stood in a dried-up riverbed, holding a gun. It was a long black thing, like a snake, and he held it close like a lover. His eyes were two dark holes, in which I could not make out a single emotion or glint of light.

He pointed the gun, checked the sights, and fired. Water erupted out of the tip, a hard spray like what came out of a hose, the kind that would hurt if it hit you. He kept his finger on the trigger, and the gun kept firing, until long after I was sure it couldn't contain anything more. And the land around him drank and drank and drank.

Chapter Three

Then it was summer, warm and young, and Ina and I were one animal, four legs carrying us over the fields where we ran. We danced to the Spice Girls and Boyzone, spinning each other around in circles as we sang off-key. Down by the lough, we snuck beers and cigarettes, coughing into each other's faces when we inhaled too quickly. We went to the bowling alley with the arcade in back and played Pac-Man, our hands greasy from Tayto crisps from the vending machine. When Ina laughed, her head fell onto my shoulder, and I loved her then, my sister, in a way that held my whole body captive, a straitjacket embrace. Her being beautiful had nothing to do with it; I loved her when she was least beautiful. Her eyebrows grown wild and her face bare of makeup. She would look at me like a child, like the girl I had taught to walk, holding her wet hand as she tried to find her footing, again and again, until she could do it on her own.

Every Friday that summer, our parents went out. Something had softened between them, a temporary truce. Ma wore heels and a dress, pale blue or deep red. We watched her go out of the house on Da's arm. She pulled the fabric of her seat belt across her body, like a swimmer doing a slow-motion stroke. And then the engine started and off they went.

While they were out, we had the house to ourselves for two hours or so, and I heated up chips while Tad found whatever film was playing.

Enda came back from Woolworths, his face as soft as marshmallow, carrying a six-pack of Guinness and a six of Magners—my mother's drink. Tad and I ran to him like bees to a flower, hanging off him, telling him how we loved him, until he shook us off and told us to shut up and have a bottle. Laughing the whole time, happy like I'd never seen him. We would all pretend to chide Ina when she asked for a sip but then give in and get her a bottle too.

When the film got old, we played poker and gin rummy and blackjack, and Tad made us all listen to David Bowie on the record player, and then we would lie on the ground, the four of us, looking up at the ceiling like we were stargazing, a little bit drunk, with greasy mouths and hands, and we would talk about nothing and laugh, and I could feel Enda drifting away in those moments, thinking of other things, of other places, and of her, the woman he was to marry in a few weeks' time.

When our parents got home—the sudden surge of headlights through the darkness, the crunch of the chipping stones beneath the tires, the slam of car doors sounding like adventure—they were always in a good mood. My mother looked younger, eased, as if she had just put down a heavy bag. My father was pink-cheeked and delighted, and he reveled in our attention. We loved him like this, the oaky smell of him, as he told stories about their night. The shake in his hand minimal. His eyes unusually focused. Ma would accept a whiskey from him, and in church when they talked about holy days, it was this that I thought of.

❖　❖　❖

Without school, Ina and I had long days to ourselves. We got part-time jobs collecting glasses at a pub, and we spent our pocket money at the chemist's, buying lipsticks, sweets, perfumed soaps.

Our local Coalisland pub, the Falls, would never have hired us, inexperienced as we were. Instead, we went to work at Sláns, on the outskirts of town near Lough Neagh, biking the twenty minutes there before our shifts. Most of Sláns's patrons came from Coalisland, too, wanting, for various reasons, to get some distance from the center of things, the heat of the gazes on their backs, the chatter in the shops and houses. The Falls was the pub where the IRA men drank; Sláns was where the teenagers and the women drank. The boys biked down after football or came in to dry off after a swim in the lough. And the women came to drink without being gossiped about or to get space from their husbands who drank at the local. Women like Susie, who sat in the corner almost every night with a glass of cider, drinking until she was red in the face, shifty and apologetic. Susie's son had been interned for his involvement with the IRA. When he got home from prison, she'd barely recognized him. Now he stayed at home mostly and shouted out the window at passersby.

Inside the pub, there was table football and two television screens. Booths lined the walls, and the bar was a semicircle of polished wood. When there was an important match on, the place filled up with our schoolmates, and the regular women would sit in the corner watching them, the boys' bright exuberance a contrast to their prim jackets and pearl earrings. I loved the sounds of people talking, laughing, their fast chatter and familiar accents, the gulp of them sucking down their drinks, the music on in the background, alternating between Irish rebel songs and the Top 40. I loved to watch the barman pull pints, the smooth movement of his arm, like the careful steps of a waltz. He let me pour a Guinness once, instructing me on when to pull and when to pause, the angle of the glass. I watched the dark liquid fill the cup and imagined that the nozzle I was holding was tapping deep into the earth and pulling up something hidden below the tree roots, some dark sap or magma.

There was a lad called Harry working at Sláns that summer. He was from Derry, but he'd moved to Coalisland to live with his aunt and uncle after his mother died in a car crash. We knew this like we knew everything then, through word of mouth, and we took it like we took everything then, with a little sigh and a "God bless," and then we ogled Harry from behind our trays of food.

Harry was obscenely handsome. His face was designed so you could not resist your gaze wandering down from his eyes to his mouth. His lips were pink, slightly parted, wet and raw-looking. Together, Ina and I loved Harry. Loved him without wanting anything from him, so that our affection was something that existed more between the two of us than between us and him.

Sometimes, Harry felt our gazes and looked back at us. It made my stomach drop to my knees. I felt like I could see there, on his face, the fact of his mother's death. Like it was hidden in his cheeks when he grinned, like it was lurking just beyond his beauty.

One Thursday, on our break, Ina and I walked out to the lough. It was warm, and we took off our shoes and let the water move around our ankles like high grass.

"It's so boring here," Ina said as we stood in the water. "I want to live in America."

"Me too," I said. Though I had never thought of it before.

"We can get a house together," she said. "Maybe in California. And we'll walk out in the morning, and it will be warm, and the palm trees will be waving at us. We can go to Disneyland! And we'll go shopping every day, and we'll learn to roller-skate. I want pink roller skates. And we'll go to diners with strawberry milkshakes and cheeseburgers."

"They sell roller skates at Dunnes," I said. "You could ask for them for Christmas."

Ina rolled her eyes.

We walked back to the pub through the car park. She was singing something under her breath, some pop song. She had a terrible voice. It made me love her more. I looked up at the pub, thinking that she belonged somewhere else. Somewhere brilliant, somewhere beautiful.

Our town was a tight, warm place, almost entirely Catholic. An old coal-mining town, it was not a poor place, just a simple one. We were better off than most of our neighbors, who lived side by side in white-roofed houses or gray flats, and we felt lucky to have the space around our home:

the woods and the fields that were ours alone. The shops let us buy what we needed on credit when Ina or I left the house without enough cash, and our classmates' fathers would drive us home if we got caught in the rain. In the winter, you could always smell the smoke from someone's chimney, and in the summer, the pub doors would be open, and you could hear the music from someone's fiddle all down the road. Coalisland was closed as a fist to the outside—suspicious of strangers, gossipy about anyone who looked or dressed or spoke differently from us—and while to me that felt like protection, I could imagine it feeling like a prison too. Maybe that was why Ina was always looking over the horizon line, studying the backdrop of the music videos we watched on VH1, looking for palm trees and white beaches and skyscrapers. For cacti and exotic birds.

I stopped in front of a wall in the car park. It had a facade painted on it—a red door and curtained windows. From afar, the perspective tricked you into thinking that it was a real house. But as you got closer, you saw it was only paint. I studied it, like I always did when I passed, trying to find the point at which the illusion revealed itself.

"Come on," Ina said. "What are you staring at?"

We walked back upstairs to the pub, hearing laughter and voices. Tad was in the corner with a couple of friends. He always came in on Thursdays to watch the football and play pool. The boys with him were a blur of bright colors: blue jerseys, orange sweatshirts. Ina and I ducked into the back room and put our aprons on.

We were particularly giggly that day, high on the dream of our future. Ina kept whispering things to me like, "Ach they'd never order that in Los Angeles" or, "D'you think the bastard knows he's talking to two wee starlets?" We fell over ourselves, hysterical. And though that word has always been used as an insult, in our hysteria, we were beyond anything I have ever felt: transcendent, enamored.

The pub was nearly empty—it was almost closing time—and we waited tables together, poking each other with our pens and writing curses on our order pads.

"I suppose you girls'd be at that stage where everything is hilarious," Frank O'Connell said. Frank worked with our father at the customs station. A loud, boisterous man, he was in his fifties, mustached and pot-bellied, wearing a leather jacket with a striped shirt underneath. His daughter was Ina's year in school. He meant the remark kindly, I knew; he was excusing our misbehavior, or else he was trying to be funny.

I nodded. Ina nodded. We looked at each other and began to laugh again.

But as I walked away from the table, I had a sinking feeling, that of an oar dropped overboard. I had never thought to wonder whether this was a phase. Whether our playfulness would not last, our humor not prevail. It felt so right to laugh, to always be laughing, to find the same things funny and then to find the mundane funniest of all. But Frank's words echoed in my head, "that stage." Like this was a common condition, passed through by all teenagers, who came out the other side straight-faced.

As we walked home from the pub that night, Tad singing loudly in the dusking sky, I watched the birds settle along the phone lines, a few trailing off from the others, like the first seeds to escape a dandelion. Ina's face hued blue in twilight, Tad's lips still wet with ale. It was of Harry that I thought then, and of a boy in an orange sweatshirt. Their bright eyes lent a meaning to the darkening sky. I did not long to be with them at those moments, but the idea of them carved out a place inside me, so that I myself expanded into the night and felt alive. Tad was singing an Oasis song. Ina was skipping beside him, her plaits swinging out behind her like lassos. I walked between them, the perfect middle, the sweet spot, and felt the heat emanating from them as their bodies fought against the night air.

❖ ❖ ❖

"And then he said, 'Thanks, dahling, I'll have a pint of Guinness.'" Ina exaggerated the British accent.

"No," I corrected her. "He said, 'Pinta Guinness. I'll have a pinta Guinness.'"

We were behind the house, lying on our stomachs, sleeping bags spread on the grass. Enda had offered us an old tent, but we'd said no; we wanted to be out in the open air. Ina was wearing her matching pajama top and bottoms. She'd braided her hair so it would come out curly in the morning. Torches, positioned under our chins, lit up our faces so that we looked ghostly. Around us, I could hear the choir of crickets, robins, starlings. Animals shifting in the night, calling to each other.

"But he called me 'dahling'—you heard it!"

"Aye."

"He was so cute," Ina said for the hundredth time. "He looked like Nick Carter." Her eyes were wide, eyelashes illuminated by the eerie light from her torch.

"He was cuter than Nick Carter," I said, just to get a reaction from her.

Ina gasped, faking outrage. "Sure nobody is cuter than Nick Carter."

"Ach no thank you." I pretended to shiver. "He looks like a baby. Like a baby girl, he does."

"He looks like Princess Diana!" Ina squawked, and I laughed so hard that my stomach hurt. Ina rolled onto her back, laughing too, the torch falling to her side. I could see her body shaking with giggles as she stared up at the starlight. Her chest rising and falling, she could have been laughing or crying, and I thought for a moment that she looked like she was experiencing divine ecstasy, like there was a spirit moving through her.

❖　❖　❖

The week of Enda and Siobhán's wedding, tensions ran high in our house, a tap turned on too hot. There were visitors whenever I went downstairs, women sitting in the living room and talking in low tones over tea. A constant buzzing like bees on flowers, the gossip spreading from lipsticked mouth to lipsticked mouth. How Enda was leaving the North, leaving his mother. How heartbroken she must be. Ma watched over them, her face as blank as an actor's between scenes.

Instead of acting heartbroken, Ma fell into my father with an abandon I had never seen. In the evenings, as the dark seep of the sky bled down to the horizon, we watched them dance in the living room, clinging to each other like drowning men. They were a beautiful couple, young and magnetic; my mother wasn't yet forty.

We'd never met Siobhán. Enda had gone to work on a boat on the coast and come back engaged. He'd left as our brother and returned a stranger, a man who always seemed to be looking for the nearest ocean.

"Risky business," Da had said, "life of a seaman."

"Not as exciting as the customs station," Ma needled.

Enda had winced at their old bickering. But somehow, he seemed less afraid than he used to. He looked at our parents like he was trying to make them out across the ocean.

The evening before we left for Donegal, Enda went out with his friends, a final hurrah for his Tyrone crowd. His absence lent a premonition of what the house would be like without him, and, outside the windows, night snuck up like a black dog.

My parents were downstairs with company when Tad, Ina, and I wandered down, wondering when we were going to be fed. The time for dinner had come and gone, and nobody had yelled for us girls to set the table. In the living room, we found them, halfway through a bottle of Jameson, my father's friends smoking out the window, and Ma deep in conversation with one of them.

"Wee 'uns!" one of Da's friends cried, lunging for Ina like you'd reach to pick up a cat.

I caught her hand and pulled her back instinctively. He staggered a bit and righted himself. For a moment, we stood frozen, waiting for anger. But he fell into a laugh instead.

"You'll be wondering about dinner, will you?" my da said more than asked. Ina giggled. Tad looked at me. They were drunk. They were out of their heads. I looked over at Ma.

Something was wrong with her, and it occurred to me that her face was much too close to that of the man she was talking to. It wasn't that, though, that unnerved me. It was her look of utter fascination, the lip-bitten awe like she was being converted to a new religion.

I knew the man she was talking to, not by name but by sight. He was not one of Da's friends from work. He came from one town over, and I was dead sure he was in the IRA.

Da had followed my gaze.

"Aoife," Da growled. "It's dinnertime. Go on, get cooking."

She looked over at him, cool and hard as metal, and for a moment I was sure she would spit at him or slap him.

"Aye," she said instead, her head bowed the slightest bit. "I'll put together your supper now, Sean."

Only as she pushed past us to the kitchen, calling for Ina's and my help over her shoulder, did I notice the anger in her eyes, burning bright as a petrol bomb.

❖ ❖ ❖

The next morning, we piled into the car. Ina perched on my lap in the back seat, as jittery as a hummingbird with anticipation. Tad sat between Enda and me.

In the passenger seat, Da had his sunglasses over his eyes and the brim of his cap pulled down. He looked like he was feeling the night before, an ache I imagined like a bruise after a fight. Like the first day of bleeding. I knew he would not tolerate much from us in that state, much excitement or much noise. I felt bad for him; there were few things he would hate more than being in a car with all of us.

Ina'd brought seven cassettes for the three-hour drive. I could see them stuffed in the seat-back pocket: Oasis, Alanis Morissette, the Backstreet Boys, No Doubt. Ma insisted on talk radio instead, the newscasters a constant hum warning listeners about the threat of upcoming violence, the possibility of unrest at the Orange Order's parades that weekend. The event—named for Protestant King William of Orange's defeat of Catholic King James—was a procession of oppression, an in-your-face celebration of three hundred years of Protestants abusing Catholics. And every year, it was a site of violence, as Catholics protested the injustice. We all knew the story like the backs of our hands; it was why Enda's wedding would take place in Donegal and not Tyrone: to avoid the conflict that would, inevitably, arise.

Over Ina's shoulder, I could see the celebrity magazine she was flicking through. Something glossy, the smell of ink and perfume samples. A headline asked the *real* reason why Gwyneth Paltrow and Brad Pitt had called off their engagement. Ina turned to look at me with starry eyes.

"Do you think I could look like Gwyneth?" she asked, tilting her head to the side as if that might enhance the effect. Her hair, so much lighter than mine that she insisted on calling it blonde, was pinned half-up with barrettes. Her small mouth and nose looked perfect to me; I could not find a single flaw in them: a jagged line, a protrusion. Her pale skin was lighter than mine, too, giving her a somewhat ethereal look, like she was made of starlight. Even the thin, practically see-through hairs on her top lip seemed glamorous somehow.

"Sure," I said. "In your leather jacket, sure."

Beside us, Tad scoffed. "No fucking way," he said.

Ina punched him in the arm.

I looked at the magazine, at the photo of the actress on a night out. Her jacket velvety against the slick black of a Range Rover. She did look a bit like Ina, the round baby face, wide, innocent eyes. The way she stared at the camera, fascinated. She looked fresh-faced and real, the way Ina did, in baggy jeans and Kickers.

"Sure isn't that the saddest thing," Ina said, pointing to an article about the legacy of a rapper who had been shot in Los Angeles in March. "This fella was just driving down the street in America and bam!" She clapped her hands for maximum effect. "Poor man."

"Ach no it isn't," Tad said, craning to look at the magazine too. "Your man'll be a millionaire; who the fuck cares?" Tad loved looking at Ina's magazines, though he always swore he just liked taking the piss.

Ina glared at Tad.

"They're bloody mad," Ma said from the front. "Killing each other for no reason."

In the back seat, Enda caught my eye and started to laugh.

"Ach sure," Ma said over her shoulder to Enda, eyes still on the road. "But it's not the same, is it?"

But weren't they reading about us in America? The Irish killing each other again. It had been eighty years since the 1916 uprising, the rebellion against British occupation that had led, eventually, to freedom for most of the island. Eighty years and we still couldn't keep the peace. I stared out the window at the green hills we passed, at the Union Jacks flying from flagpoles in Protestant towns, at the occasional tricolor flag that Catholics raised each May in honor of the hunger strikers' deaths. Ma was right. It wasn't random, our violence. It was a war.

Next to Ina and me, Tad was playing with his Tamagotchi and Enda was watching curiously. Da had come back from the pub with it one day, like a prize he'd won playing cards. My da was always trying to make up for how he treated Tad and Enda. For the bruises he sometimes gave them when he drank too much.

"What's she like?" Tad asked, face looking down at the screen of the small toy.

"What?"

"Siobhán?" Tad asked. "What's she like?"

Enda smiled. "You'll like her," he said.

"Are you in love?" Tad asked, disgusted.

"Getting married, aren't I?"

Tad rolled his eyes.

"I never want to be in love," he said. "The single life's the life for me." As far as I knew, Tad had never so much as kissed a girl. Not that I had kissed anyone, either, but it was different for boys than it was for girls.

Enda hit Tad on the back of the head, not hard enough to hurt.

"Quiet back there," Da growled. His voice like car brakes whining, something awful and pained in it.

The first checkpoint we stopped at had a line fifteen cars deep. In the back, we groaned as loud as we could, the vibration so deep it felt like it would shake the windowpanes. I was so cramped in the back seat, Ina's weight cutting off blood flow to my legs. She was hunched over so her head wouldn't hit the ceiling, her hair in my face, smelling like lilacs and the sickly sweet shampoo she used.

"Quiet!" Da said again, banging his fist on the roof of the car. He was still hunched over in the front seat like he might be sleeping.

We stiffened.

"Ina!" I hissed, pushing her off me.

"What?"

"Checkpoint. You've gotta sit next to us."

"I won't fit!" Ina whined.

"You're not wearing a seat belt," I said. "You'll get in trouble."

"We can squeeze," Enda said, scooching as far as he could toward the car door.

"Tad—" He pulled my younger brother toward him. By shifting and shimmying, we just managed to fit, though Ina's left hip had to stay lifted at an angle. I was squeezed between Tad and Ina, the sides of our bodies as tight as paving stones laid out in a row.

With almost any movement now impossible, we sat and waited for it to be our turn with the Brits. I could see three of them up ahead, one in a green army jacket and peaked cap, the other two in camo fatigues and helmets. All three held submachine guns, the strange black shapes looking too thin, too geometrical to cause real damage. My heart climbed a little bit higher in my throat than usual, even though there was no reason to be afraid. Surely the worst they would do for having four kids in the back seat would be a fine. And they would not be able to see the memory of Conor on me, the ghost of the shopping bag handles in my hands that morning. But still, some small flame—of fear or desire—was alight inside me as we waited.

One of the men approached, asked Ma questions that she answered with a tight, pursed mouth. He went around to Da's side, questioned him. Da was obsequious and polite, his lips curled in an attempt to hide his gums. The man looked past him, into the back seat. A faint smirk twitching the sides of his mouth. I felt us all shrink from him the slightest bit, like a girl being called at as she walks down the street. The sense of invasion and hurt pride. Even Ma seemed smaller now, slightly cowed. The flame inside me caught the breeze and burned and burned.

❖   ❖   ❖

We arrived at Siobhán's house after nightfall. We'd showered and changed at the hotel. Ma was wearing black dressy trousers and a blouse the color of blood.

"We'll all be on our best behavior," Ma said when we'd parked in the driveway. She looked sideways at our father. "But we'll not compromise our values," she went on. "We're not ashamed of where we come from."

"I think the lady doth protest too much," Tad whispered into my ear as we got out of the car, and I elbowed him in the ribs. On holidays, I'd noticed, he tried to blend his accent into a southern one, something resembling starchy Dublin or drawling Cork. He was just as ashamed as Da was, as Enda was.

I looked at Ina, stretching as she climbed out of the car. I could see the bright red of one of her bra straps. No doubt she'd positioned it perfectly to peek out from the V-neck of her jumper. She wasn't ashamed of where we were from, just oblivious to it. For all Ina cared, we may as well have been from Mars.

I was the only one who was proud of where we came from. The only one who shouldered the heavy burden of Ma's pride. But I was not equal to her. I would wake up early to give Conor the bottles, but I was not taking any oaths. If anything, the way she tried to reel me in repelled me slightly. Her own unfulfilled dreams grafted onto me. But still, I couldn't forget the feeling of it. Conor's lips twisting into a grin as I came out with two big bags that morning. I'd stuffed an old bedsheet in one of them, thinking they could use the fabric.

"There've been great women, y'know," he said.

"I know," I said.

We'd stood there for a minute, his eyes on me like we were two fighters entering the ring. All day the words had been in my head, "great women," "great women," "great women." I wanted to know what that would look like, what that would feel like. What would a great woman dress like? Who would she be? Someone like Ma, but happy.

I felt Ma shift beside me when we rang the doorbell. She looked over at Enda with a blank expression. I knew she was angry with him. Her father had gone when she was young. She was not a woman who could be easily put behind; she was not suited to being left.

"D'you think it'll go all right?" Enda asked in my ear. I hadn't realized he'd come up beside me.

"It'll be grand," I told him. "Don't worry." I reached for his hand and squeezed it. He shook me off like he always did, but he gave me a nod that I knew meant, *Thank you.*

When Siobhán opened the door, Enda smiled, revealing crooked teeth. His mouth a sloping, half-formed thing, twisting to the left. He bowed his head slightly, like he'd been looking at something too bright, like he was embarrassed. Then he looked back up at her, unable to stop himself.

She was a small woman with a body like a surfboard and a face like the side of a cliff, sharp edges of rock, jagged and beautiful. She smiled at us in a way that made me feel Enda had prepared her to greet a pack of wild animals. I hadn't expected to feel jealous at the sight of her, but I did. I felt both jealous of his eyes on her and of their collective escape, wishing I was both or either of them. The double prongs of that feeling.

Siobhán's parents, Davin and Kate, came up behind her, wearing nervous smiles and starched clothes: tan pants, shapeless skirt, dowdy blouse. Kate's legs were covered in peach tights, several shades too dark for her own pale skin. I saw her stare at my mother, standing there in clothes so beautiful, you wanted to touch them.

Ma put them at ease, taking Kate's hands in her own.

"What a beautiful family you are," she said, looking straight into Kate's eyes. "And what a beautiful home. I can't tell you how excited we all are to be here."

"Oh, yes, well, we're very happy to have you so we are." Kate blushed, tripping over her words like she'd forgotten her lines. "You're very welcome to Donegal."

"Enda is a fine young man," Davin was saying to my da, clapping a hand on Enda's back.

I saw my father's eyes dart to the place where Davin's hand lay. Then he smiled.

"We're glad he didn't give you any trouble," he said.

"A born seaman!" Davin cried.

"We've no idea where he gets that from," Ma said, her voice the sound of tinkling flutes. "His father and I can hardly swim."

They all laughed a little too loud.

"Well come in now, will you?" Kate said, holding out her arm. "Don't be standing in the doorway catching cold." It was summer. Ina and I looked at each other.

❖   ❖   ❖

"Do you watch *Eurovision*?" Ina asked, leaning across the table to Siobhán. We were sitting down to dinner, some mess of meat and sauce.

"Course I do!" Siobhán exclaimed.

"Marc was robbed!" Ina squealed, almost knocking over her glass of Coke in her excitement as she leaned even farther across the table.

"Aye, he was, though." Siobhán seemed almost as eager as Ina. "And in his own country, sure."

"I swear it was rigged," Ina said. "I mean, it'd've been a bad look for the UK losing like that, don't ya think?"

"Aye, it would've been. Sure, I believe it. And it was a great song too."

"Did you think Marc was cute?" Ina whispered, darting a look at Enda.

Siobhán laughed, looking at Enda too. "Aye he's very cute."

Ina was delighted.

"So who were people going for up by you?" Siobhán asked. "The UK or Ireland?"

I froze. Ina and I looked at each other. Even Ina knew this was not a question to be asked.

"We were going for our own country," I said.

Siobhán blushed, and I felt immediately guilty for my clipped tone, the implied rebuke. Why couldn't I be more like my sister? I looked down the table at my parents, hoping for some distraction.

"He won't have to worry walking down the street down here," Siobhán's father was saying to Ma. "I mean, there'll be the odd scrape now and again, but nothing like youse have up north. So long as you keep your head down, you'll be grand."

Ina was quiet now too. Tad and Enda looked down at their plates. None of us kids looked at Ma, though all our attention was focused there.

"Must be nice," Ma said. "Getting to keep your head down."

Enda swore under his breath.

"Aye, well I hear you've quite the weekend going on," Davin went on, oblivious. "Orange Order's parade, is it?"

It was what they had been talking about on the news. "Tensions are high," they had said over and over, like tensions were weather—temperature or humidity—something that could be measured. But we were not there this weekend. Tonight, at least, we did not need to live there.

"I read that Protestants parade at ten times the rate of Catholics," I said, hoping to change the subject. Trying to make my tone sound like Ina's, the happy-go-lucky way she talked about television and celebrities.

"Ach Prods parade at everything, sure," Siobhán's mother said.

The tension broke, and we all laughed. A sharp, serrated sound, slouching toward frantic.

"Aye, it'll be a weekend," my mother said in a tone that made me shiver. She alone had not laughed. I glanced at Enda. It was supposed to be his weekend.

"When it's your turn," Ma said to me, "you can have my dress."

We were in her hotel room. Da was down at the pub.

"If that's what you want," she continued.

"Your dress?"

"To get married."

I wanted to ask: *Do you wish you hadn't?* I wanted to know why. Maybe she saw the question in my eyes.

"I'm glad I had you," she said. It was, I supposed, enough.

The day of the wedding, riots broke out all over the North. Just as Davin and my mother had guessed. Just as the newscaster had predicted. Thousands of plastic bullets were fired. Vehicles were stolen and destroyed. Hundreds of bottle bombs thrown through glass windows, into barracks and armored cars. Streets were evacuated, and an IRA man in South Belfast opened fire with an AK-47. In the towns around where we lived, loyalist halls were burned to the ground.

I thought of Conor, back home. How it might be our bottles he was throwing. Glass I'd put to my own lips, stuffed with a torn-off piece of my old bedsheet. The things I'd kissed and lain in, soaked with petrol, lit on fire. How there were pieces of me back home, burning, breaking glass, destroying.

Even over in Donegal, with all the excitement of the wedding, we still felt it. The deafening shriek of a bullet just missing you. I'd missed the violence, sure, but I also *missed* it, in some absurd and morbid way. A homesickness that I didn't voice to anyone. We went about the wedding like normal, but I felt the whole time like I was carrying something inside myself. Like I was a car the IRA had stolen, explosives tied to my soft belly. A vehicle of destruction, to be set off at any moment. It was like when Ma had first given me the bottles for Conor, turning me into something dangerous. Passive myself, I'd been shaped by others until I became potent, frightening, with the potential for disaster. I could smell the fire from across the border, and I could not help wanting to get closer to it. Wanting to be warmed by the flame. While we were getting ready, and later at the reception, I kept sneaking off to the pub next door, not for a drink but for the television. Grainy footage of men in black balaclavas, their eyes sharp as knife blades through the openings in the fabric. I could imagine how they were sweating, the heat of the wool on their necks and behind their ears, their bodies as hot as coals as they leaped from shadows into the chaos. Whenever I could sneak away, I went to watch them greedily; it was better than beer, drinking in what had happened.

❖　❖　❖

Ina did my makeup for me. We slithered into our dresses like we were fitting into new skins. Violet and scoop-necked, the dresses cut a straight line just below our collarbones and then fell to the floor in a waterfall of fabric. Ina looked like Venus emerging from the Mediterranean Sea, still clothed in the violet froth of the water. I looked like a ghost wearing purple, with my dark hair and slightly sallow face, the freckles across my skin making me look dirty, earthly compared to my celestial sister. My nose jutted out, my cheekbones were too pronounced, the harshness of my face made me look sinister, angry. The dress somehow made this worse, made it look like I didn't know this about myself, like I was trying to be someone I was not. I missed my baggy jeans and Cranberries T-shirt.

The wedding was organ music and the ubiquitous, sinister vows. The white taffeta of Siobhán's dress and Enda's hair slicked back. His nervous tick of jiggling his right leg and the way the leg of his suit trousers rose and fell on his ankle as he did so. My mother's rarest, smallest, truest smile. Bouquets of flowers and whispers and us filing out of the church.

Ina and I had been looking forward to this reception for months, practicing our dancing, perfecting the hairstyle we were both wearing: dozens of small plaits pinned up in the back. In the reception room, we slipped off our high heels and ran like children around the men and women, around stouts poured into thick glasses and deviled eggs held in fingers, teetering on the edge of the dance floor until the first dances finished, the music started in earnest, and it was our time.

We'd lost our self-consciousness with our strappy heels. The Spice Girls were playing on the speakers, and we jumped up and down, shrieking. It felt like being at the center of a small, beautiful world. It felt like we were the hot magma of the core. It felt like this moment would one day be historical or like it was ahistorical—important, essential, and yet held above that muddy mass of events. We had stepped out of the house of our lives to find another, better world. As we slow danced together, Sinéad O'Connor sang about the world outside your mother's garden. And it felt that way too. Like we had found the place beyond Ma's grasp, found the wilderness that had not been planted.

If only we could have stayed there. Spinning on the dance floor, a slow, contained circle like the hand of a clock, ticking us forward in time.

Chapter Four

2016, Los Angeles County

The sun was high and bright, and, in the distance, I could see snow on the mountains. Mia and I biked up the winding trails of Mount Baldy, past the school and the houses hidden in the valleys and up farther, to where the road split and there was a boulder we could sit on, overlooking the town. We raced each other as we rode, calves burning with the effort, panting and laughing. The best part would be when we turned around, sailing back down the mountain at peak speed, no longer needing to pedal, flying next to each other, our hair whipping back like horses' manes.

We found the boulder and dropped our bikes to the ground. Below us lay the town, the haze of Los Angeles in the distance, and the smog that covered the horizon. Mia reached into her backpack and took out a bag of Fritos. She always had a snack with her: a cheese stick, an apple, a bag of chips. It made her seem younger. She tore open the Fritos, and we dug our hands into the bag together, our fingers tangling as we grabbed for the chips. We looked out at the horizon in silence, both of us thinking.

"Can you see your house from here?" Mia asked after a minute.

I shook my head. "I don't think so. Can you see yours?"

Mia pointed into the distance. I had no idea where her finger was aiming.

"I think that might be it," she said. "The blue house next to it, that's Mrs. Fischer's, isn't it?"

I tried to find where she was looking but couldn't.

"Here." She moved my head to where hers had been. "See the spire?" she asked. I nodded. "Okay, down from there. You see the street? Follow it to the end of the block and then—" Her breath was hot on my ear.

"I see it," I said. I wasn't sure if it was her house, though. A little white smudge in the distance. It was hard to imagine her and Riley and their parents living there. Their big smiles and dinner parties. Riley writing songs on his guitar. Mia dancing to make him laugh.

"I think I'd like to live up here," Mia said.

"What, in the mountains?"

"Yeah. My kids could go to the school we passed."

"Where would you get groceries?"

"I'd have to bike into town, I guess."

"You'd be in such good shape."

"My thighs would be insane. And my calves." We both looked down at her legs in the bike shorts she was wearing. They were already strong from the soccer she played six months out of the year. Of course she would be happy up here; Mia loved the outdoors. She was so different from me. I liked the people of the world: the residents at the homeless shelter where Mom worked, the scientists I read biographies about. She liked the shape of cacti and the bewitching light of a harvest moon. Last month, she'd dragged me up this mountain so we could lie on our backs and watch a meteor shower. I had been so intent on watching her, the side of her face lit up by the starlight, that the meteor shower had been half-over by the time I realized it had started.

"I think it would be nice," she said. "To be away from everyone. I think life would be simpler up here."

"There's no reception," I offered, and she laughed.

"Well, you'd have to come too," she said. "Otherwise I'd be bored out of my mind. You'd have to live next door to me."

"Have you ever heard of Giant's Causeway?" I asked.

She shook her head.

"It's this place in Northern Ireland, near where my mom grew up." I did not know if that were true. I pulled out my phone, opened Instagram, found a picture to show her. A square slice of a place, like a glimpse through a window. The rocks cut in hexagons, like stairs up to some kind of heaven.

I had discovered Giant's Causeway in my elementary school encyclopedia. Soft pages under my small fingers. We had done some project, drawing lines on a map to indicate where our families were from. One red thread running from California to Ireland, like a thin river of blood. "What's Ireland like?" the teachers had asked. "Where did your mom grow up?" I hadn't had the answers, so I'd looked the place up, searched the pages for something that felt right.

"It's beautiful," Mia said now, handing back the phone. "Picturesque."

"I want to go there," I said. "I want to see it for myself."

"It's like the opposite of here," Mia said, gesturing around us at the mountains that never got enough rain.

As we rode back down the mountain, I watched Mia's hair streak behind her.

"Hurry up!" she shouted back to me, and I released my hand brakes, let the bike soar down the steep slope until I was beside her. When I looked at her, she was grinning, her face bright and warm in the afternoon sunlight. The palm trees and firs glowed on the side of the road, like they were putting on a show for us. The warm haze making everything feel enchanted.

❖ ❖ ❖

Mom dragged me to an evening Mass that Saturday. I sat on the stiff pew with a straight back and thought about Hell as a metaphor for the climate crisis. Mom crossed herself rigorously. I tried to glare hard enough at her that she would feel it. Afterward, I texted Mia: we better be going out tonight. She texted back almost immediately: Riley's party. Thank God, I thought. I needed to wash off the holy water, to feel normal and human again. I had gone to Sunday school growing up, had learned to say grace before we ate. But I hated the suffocating purity of church: the onerous confessions, the worship of a dead man, the strictures against all I was. And while I loved my mom more than anyone in the world, sometimes I wanted to strangle her. Her embraces were like rubber bands around my skin, digging in too tight.

"Are you going out?" Mom asked when I came downstairs after dinner. I could feel her words grasping at me, trying to hold on.

"Yeah." I walked toward the door, reaching for my jean jacket, hoping I could get it on quickly.

She stood up from where she had been sitting on the couch.

"Bernie," she said. "You're wearing that?"

"Duh."

We both looked at my reflection in the mirror above the coatrack.

"At least put a bra on," she said.

"Why?"

"Sure I can see your nipples, Bernie."

"What's wrong with that?" I asked. "Are they hurting you?" I turned toward her. We both looked down at my small breasts, the triangles of my nipples visible through my tank top. I imagined that they were fatal missiles.

"And what if you see Father Michael?" she asked.

"Mom, if Father Michael is at Riley's party, we'll have much bigger problems than my nipples."

"Bernie, are you having sex?" she asked suddenly, her eyes narrowing. It was one of her irrational fears, those monsters that lurked under the surface of her mind. For some reason, the thought of me having sex terrified her.

"Christ, Mom!"

"Lord's name—"

"Do I ask you about your and Kaleb's sex life?" I demanded. Kaleb and Mom had been together for four years, and while he and Mom had agreed that he should keep his apartment—a one bedroom several blocks away—he slept over a lot.

"Bernie, don't be obnoxious." She was getting angry now. "We're both adults."

"I'm basically an adult."

"You are not. You're too young for that sort of thing."

I glared at her. "Can I go now?"

"You know my mother had to drop out of school when she got pregnant," she said for the millionth time. "I'm not saying you should wait until marriage or anything, but I think Father Michael has a point when he says that to use your body unintentionally is to abuse it. If you have sex this young, you'll regret it."

I didn't say anything.

"Please, Bernie, just wait. You can never get those years back. And there will be plenty of time when your brain is fully formed. Because you know—"

"The brain is not fully formed until twenty-five." I chanted the words with her.

"Exactly," she said.

I didn't know why she cared so much about what I put in my body. I had no illusions about sex. I thought of it as a physical thing. All this *using your body to please Jesus* shit felt weirdly kinky, as if Father Michael and my mother were climbing into bed with me.

"I am not having sex," I said, which was true. "But you do know there are ways of *not* being pregnant, right?" If she was going to be difficult, I would be difficult too.

She looked at me with concerned eyes.

"Like birth control?" She said the words carefully.

"Or, like, abortion?" I saw her brace herself. I knew how the word needled her. It was like a weapon.

"That's the kind of thing," she said slowly, "that you'll regret for the rest of your life."

We stared at each other across the room, like boxers in a ring.

"What was your mother's name?" I asked suddenly, like I could surprise her into telling me. I'd never met my grandmother. Never even seen a photo. It was a constant tension between us, an underwater current. It was the place we always ended up whenever we fought.

"Margaret," she said without hesitation. The last time I asked, it had been Rose.

I stood there, staring at her, holding my ground. She knew that I knew she was lying. She wasn't even trying to convince me.

"I'm going out," I said. There was only a little twinge, in the corner of my heart, the southwest part; I hated leaving in the middle of a fight. I hated leaving her. I turned around so I wouldn't have to see her face.

"Bernie?" she called after me.

I was almost at the door.

"Promise you'll come back?"

"I promise," I said. Then I hesitated, turned back around. "I'm sorry." I gestured toward the air to mean what had just happened. Already I felt the flush of guilt creeping up my neck. "Are you sure you'll be all right?" I asked.

"Of course," she said, like that was a silly question to ask. Like she had never not been all right.

❖ ❖ ❖

I could remember the first time I asked my mother about our past. We were standing in my kindergarten classroom, and I was spinning in circles, excited to have my mother and my teacher all to myself, to be the last one in the classroom, free of the other kids who thought I was a show-off, who I thought were dull. There had been a family-tree project in class, one I'd been miserably unable to complete. It had made me cry; I did not like being behind on any assignment.

"What's my grandmother's name?"

Mom stared at me. Eyes like windows looking out on a wall.

"Mom?" I stopped spinning. "What's my grandmother's name?"

"You don't have any grandmothers," she said.

Ms. Watson made a funny noise. I looked at my mother, confused.

"But Ms. Watson says everyone does. That it's . . . *scientifically impossible* not to."

"We don't have any other family," my mom said to Ms. Watson. "It's just me and Bernie." She turned to me. "Right, Duck?"

I nodded slowly. Ms. Watson turned around to retrieve my lunch box from my cubbyhole.

"Ina," Ms. Watson said quietly as she handed it to Mom. "You really should consider alternative options for Bernie. Somewhere she won't be as . . . out of place. Somewhere that can nurture her academically *and* socially. She's way ahead of grade level, but she needs other kinds of support too."

Mom's smile brightened again. She leaned down and kissed the top of my head.

"My brilliant Bernadette," she said.

The teacher frowned. My mother had missed the point.

"The tantrums at drop-off," Ms. Watson went on, "it's not exactly normal at this age. I mean, a few times would be all right, but every day is a bit much. And she's inconsolable for a long time after you leave. That's what really worries me." She was trying to speak quietly, but I could still hear her. "She doesn't make an effort with the other children either. She'll sit in the corner all day rather than play with them." It was true; I was suspicious of the other children.

My mother was still smiling at me, even as Ms. Watson continued about the tantrums. She was, I realized, proud of me. She was glad I couldn't stand to be left; she was glad I cried for her.

"We're very close," she told Ms. Watson. "We're very, very close."

It was the excuse we had used all my life.

Ms. Watson said nothing. Then she nodded, briefly, and turned back into the smiling teacher I knew so well.

"I'll see you tomorrow, Bernie," she said in her usual singsong voice, and Mom and I left the classroom. Mom's hand around my own was tight as a brace.

She must have been listening, though, because I did change schools after that year. I got a scholarship to a private school, where I had "special attention" to focus on my "social challenges." I skipped a grade to be with older kids. I was still bored, though, and I was still unfriendly. My peers seemed to be a different species from me, with their brothers and sisters and aunts and uncles, with their apathetic faces turned blank as they stared at the whiteboard. The exception was Mia, who I liked from the moment I met her in fourth grade; she seemed just as strange as I was, just as nervous about the world around her.

It wasn't higher grade levels that I'd needed back then. It was the raised veins of a grandmother's hands. It was the jigsaw puzzle of the larger world, pieced together to form an explanation. It was my mother to stay with me always and nothing to ever change. Not the climate, not the world, not her, and not me.

❖   ❖   ❖

"How was it leaving?" Mia asked as we walked to the party.

I shrugged.

"Did she cry?"

"No, that was just one time. She's been better."

Mia didn't say anything.

"Really," I said. "We're just very close."

We were almost at Riley's off-campus apartment.

"I don't think it's healthy," Mia said softly. "I don't like how it changes you. She makes you sad and faraway and—"

I grabbed her hand quickly and squeezed. I didn't know what I meant by that squeeze, whether I was admitting she was right or asking her to drop it. But the fact that she cared made me want to grab hold of her and not let go. Mia moved her hand away, fixed her hair. I wondered if tonight was the night I would talk to her, the night when I would say what I had been wanting to say.

"I had to go to church today," I said as we turned onto Riley's lawn. "I'm going to need three or four drinks to recover."

There were already people standing on the brown grass, holding bottles of beer and talking loudly. Mia laughed, pushing her hair behind her ears again as we approached the small crowd.

"How do I look?" she asked, turning to me in the moonlight.

"Great," I said. Her shirt was low cut; her shorts showed most of her thighs. They looked like beaches, stretches of gold sand, the night air lapping against them like water. "The college boys are going to be all over you."

She laughed again, giddily, and I felt something move in my stomach. The worry lines on her forehead had disappeared.

"I hope so," she said.

❖　❖　❖

Riley's apartment was small and thin, like a doll's house. Outside, furniture had been arranged into a makeshift living room, and that's where we sat, on some moldy floral couch that must have belonged to someone's grandmother. Mia said she'd be right back and went in search of her brother. I watched her disappear into the house with anxious eyes.

A boy a few years older than me sat down on the couch. He was white, with a narrow face like a waning moon, high cheekbones, and a sharp jaw. Handsome, I thought, if that was your type. The kind of guy Mia would point out to me on the street.

"I fucking hate these kinds of parties," he said. And I laughed, despite myself.

"Do you want a beer?" he asked.

"Sure," I said.

I followed him into the house, which was cramped with bodies and hazy with marijuana smoke. He took two beers out of the fridge, and I looked around for Mia or Riley but saw neither of them.

"I'm Avery," he said over the sound of the music.

"Bernie." I was still looking around. "You're in school with Riley?"

"Yeah. I do engineering. I have a big summer project coming up, actually. Hospital ventilators."

I felt something catch in my chest.

"Wow," I said. "I was hooked up to a ventilator. When I was born."

Every year on my birthday, Mom retold my birth story dramatically, endowing it with biblical significance. Early birth. Hospital ventilators. My father had been gone by then, deployed to the country he would die in. She didn't like to talk about him, wouldn't even say his name. Every time I asked, she seemed to sink into a well of sadness so deep that I had no choice but to stop asking questions, to pull her out. His name was not listed on my birth certificate; I had checked.

"Really?" he asked. "That's wild."

"Yeah, I was super premature. They didn't know if I would make it."

"Jeez," he said. "Your parents must have been scared shitless."

I fidgeted with the buttons on my jacket, not knowing what to say, whether to correct him. Had my father been scared? Had he known? Had my mother called him international? Or had I arrived after he was already gone?

"Do you think it's immoral to buy a candy bar?" I asked instead.

He frowned at the swerve in conversation. It was a thought experiment I'd read in a Peter Singer essay that Mom's boyfriend, Kaleb, had given me.

"Okay, so you're walking to a party through a park," I said. "You're wearing a tux you bought for a hundred dollars."

"A hundred dollars?"

"I don't know. How much do tuxes cost?"

"Try a thousand."

"Okay, a thousand dollars. As you're walking through the park, you see a boy drowning in a lake. There are several people standing around the lake, looking at the boy, but nobody is going to help him. You have a choice: wade through the lake, ruining your thousand-dollar tux, and save the boy or keep walking. What do you do?"

"Save the boy."

"Of course. Now, a mosquito net costs one dollar and is the most effective per-dollar way to save a life. When you buy a Mars bar or, like, a beer"—I raised the Bud Light in my hand to demonstrate—"you're choosing to spend your dollar on the tux instead of on the boy. You're walking past the lake."

"Okay," he said. "Meaning what?"

"Meaning we're all essentially murderers."

"Are you really in high school?" he asked.

Here it was, I thought, the thing Mom had warned me about.

"Yeah," I said. I took a long sip of the cold beer.

He leaned in close to me. He smelled like beer and weed and potato chips. Up close, I could see the tiny pricks of stubble protruding from around his mouth. His breath was hot and humid on my face.

"Can I kiss you?" he asked, and I felt his grasping mouth attach itself to me, like he was trying to pull something out of me, a hand reaching into water to retrieve a sunken object.

I pulled away.

"I actually need to go," I said, spotting Mia as she emerged from one of the bedrooms. She looked a little shaken.

I saw the moment when she noticed me, saw her frown as her eyes went to Avery. I felt proud, flattered to have a college boy interested in me.

"Can I have your number, then?" he asked. His face was still too close to mine.

"Sure," I said, distracted, and typed it into his phone.

❖   ❖   ❖

"What happened?"

Mia and I were sitting on the grass half a block from Riley's house. She had grabbed my hand and tugged until I followed her out of the house and onto the street.

"He's just being a dick," she said. She was picking at the skin around her fingers. She worried them until they bled. I had seen Riley in one of his moods before, kicking furniture and snapping at anyone who tried to comfort him, self-pitying and aggressive. It was not a side of him I liked to think about.

"I'm sorry," I said. I put my arm around her, and she leaned into me. I felt a quivering feeling in my chest.

We lay back on the grass, both of us looking up at the stars. The smell of her heady and strong next to me. Some of her hair falling onto my right shoulder. The temperature of the air was almost exactly room temperature, neither hot nor cold. It felt like we were lying in a place of complete neutrality. My arm was still around her, under her head.

"Who was that guy?" she asked after a minute.

"Some friend of Riley's," I said. "Avery."

"Ew," Mia said, and I laughed. I knew she had been jealous, though, of him liking me. Of me, for one moment, not needing her. I tried to imagine what it would be like to tell her that I liked him. I tried to imagine actually liking him. Maybe I could, with effort. But it felt ridiculous to force myself when my other feelings were so easy.

We were quiet for a long minute. I remembered last summer when we would sunbathe in her backyard. Dressed in bikinis, lounging on Adirondack chairs, and drinking lemonade. Her legs in my lap as we talked about nothing. Her skin hot against my own and the sun making me feel like the moment would last forever. I thought about her emerging from Riley's bedroom, her face pale and her eyes scared. Me standing with Avery, acting like I cared at all what he had to say. I wanted to stop pretending. I wanted to be seen for who I really was, how I really felt. And I wanted to fix her, to make her feel better. I wanted her to know that she would be okay, that I would always be here, that I could be enough.

"I want to tell you something," I said. Mia turned to look at me, and our eyes met. Our faces turned toward each other.

"Bernie—" she said, like she was going to try to stop me. Around us, I could hear crickets singing.

"I think I'm in love with you," I said before she could cut me off. The words were so easy to say, I knew they must be true.

Mia stared at me for a long moment. Then she sat up.

"I should go," she said. "I'm sorry." She stood. She did look sorry. For a second, I thought she was going to say something else, but then she walked away.

❖   ❖   ❖

In the hall, I shed my shoes. Mom was watching the world news, like she did most nights, eyes glazed over unless they happened to mention her country. She spent hours watching just for one little glimpse of home.

I came and sat next to her on the couch, and she turned to look at me, put her arm around me. I felt like if I looked her in the eye or opened my mouth, I would start to cry and not stop crying. I tried to tell myself that it was only the beer I had drunk that had made me say what I'd said. I would explain it to Mia in the morning; I would tell her I hadn't meant it the way she had heard it. But I knew that neither of us would believe me.

"What happened, Duck?" Mom asked.

I didn't say anything. I laid my head against her shoulder. She sniffed me, smelling, I was sure, the stench of weed and the beer on my breath. She said nothing. With her left hand, she played with the loose strands of my hair.

"You should've stayed," she said. "It's better when you're here."

I nodded against her, my cheek on her warm shoulder. I could feel the straps of her tank top and bra. I could smell her, warm and woody. My head was swimming with everything that had happened. I felt my phone vibrate and looked down, only to see a text from Avery asking how the rest of my night had been. I put my phone in my pocket.

"I'm always going to be here for you," she said. "The rest of the world won't be."

She didn't know it, but she was lying. Only the second part of that was true.

❖   ❖   ❖

I cried into my pillow that night. Hot shame like a sunburn all over my body. I sobbed silently, my chest heaving as I gasped for breath. When I finally was too exhausted to cry anymore, I just lay there, feeling the emptiness of my own body.

In the middle of the night, my phone vibrated noisily on the night-stand. I reached over to grab it, squinted at the screen. It was Mia. I felt my heart squirm in my chest. My hand shook as I accepted the call.

"Mia?"

Her breathing was hard on the other end of the phone, ragged.

"It's Riley," she said, her voice high and twisted. A chill passed over me at the sound of her brother's name.

"He's in the hospital," Mia said. "He tried to kill himself."

Chapter Five

1997, County Tyrone

The sun sank lower in the sky. The long days of summer exhausted themselves. The IRA called a ceasefire, and peace talks were renewed. We went back to school. And Ina and I were no longer one beast, separated only by skin. Now, she had a boyfriend.

Peter was from school, and he rang her after dinner most nights. She would run up to our room, squealing, and my father would yell at her to be quiet, but we all knew he didn't really mind. All the forgiveness he was capable of, he spent on her. It was how most people were with her, but the contrast to Da's other relationships was unmissable. It was a sign of Ina's power that she could draw even him in, that she could pacify a man as rough as our father. I stayed out of our room until long after Ina was finished talking to Peter, not wanting to see her sitting on her bed with the cordless phone tucked under one ear while she painted her nails, her happy sighs so loud, I thought they must be exaggerated.

Peter was not in the IRA, but he held himself like a soldier. Stiff-backed and proud, he was always rolling out his neck, as if it was too much to hold up his own head. He called her "E," as if he were perpetually misspelling her name. Each time he said it, I thought of choir at school, the reedy sound of teenage girls singing the scale on "E." I had always wished my name was simpler, more like hers. The kind of name a pop star might have, the kind of name you could find on a mug at a petrol station.

It had been Ina and me. Now it was Ina and Peter. And so I tended to my fury, that I might have a partner. I watched his close-cropped thick hair and I dreamed of it falling out overnight, leaving him bald. I watched her wrap her arms around his middle, and I imagined his breath being squeezed out of him, her arms tightening fatally.

"What are his flaws?" I asked Ina one night after he had gone home.

"What?" She was painting her nails a bright orange.

"Everyone has them," I said.

"Well, Peter doesn't," she said.

My body burned.

❖   ❖   ❖

She began to miss classes. She had to go see *L.A. Confidential* at the cinema with Peter, to "prepare for her future." She was always running off after school, and I was left staring after her, picking up the scarf she'd left behind. Wrapping it around my own neck as I walked home alone. She and Peter went out with his friends, half of whom were Protestants: boys who went to the Royal School and talked in snooty accents. They tried trendy restaurants in Protestant neighborhoods. She stopped going to Mass entirely, said she was protesting the conflict. I thought she was really protesting getting up early on Sunday.

"She doesn't understand," I told Ma one day. She was cooking, and I was sitting on the kitchen table, drinking a Fanta and eating a packet of Taytos. The salty oil of the chips mixing with the sugary fizz of the drink.

"Doesn't understand what?" Ma asked distractedly. She was counting something off on her hand.

"Everything!" I said. "The whole conflict. It's like she doesn't care."

"Maybe she doesn't," Ma said.

"That doesn't bother you?"

She shrugged. "Themselves don't even care anymore." She gestured to the radio to mean the IRA.

That autumn, a Catholic man's body had been found in a dumping ground for animal carcasses. He'd been beaten to death, doused in petrol, and burned. Then, just last week, Loyalist paramilitaries had planted four bombs in Dundalk, over the border in the free state. The IRA had done nothing about either incident. For the first time I could remember, they were honoring their ceasefire. I'd watched Ma's jaw churn as she listened to the radio. "What are those men doing with themselves?" she'd asked no one in particular. "Who's going to defend us now?"

"Do you still care?" I asked her now.

She looked at me long and hard, like she was trying to find out what I was made of.

"Are we still dying?" she asked finally.

I felt the fire inside me, the old anger that was my inheritance.

She turned away from me, back to the recipe she was studying.

"Don't be jealous of Ina," she said without looking up.

"I'm not—"

She cut me off. "Ach I see you look at her," she said.

I was quiet. I hadn't known it was so obvious.

"You're different girls. You'll never have the same things at the same time."

She walked over to the table I was sitting on and picked up a rolling pin.

I was frowning at her. If we did not have the same things, it was at least in part because she treated us so differently. It was because she treated Ina like a daughter and me like an accomplice. She minded and scolded Ina, whereas she expected me to carry out her assignments, to do the dirty work she couldn't.

She paused to look at me, pushed back my hair. "But you have your belief, Bríd. Don't forget that."

Was that true? I wondered. Had I ever had my own belief? Or had I just followed my mother, let her lead the way? Hadn't my opinions about the conflict, my interest in Conor, been inherited, learned?

"So some people get to be beautiful and happy and have boyfriends and go to parties and other people get *belief*?"

"You got the bigger prize," Ma said. "You'll see."

I rolled my eyes. It felt enormously unfair that Ma had chosen me to give Conor the bottles, to have these conversations with her, and had let Ina be. But, at the same time, some deep-down part of me glowed at having been chosen. At having been the special one for once, if only in this way.

"Try to love her." Ma was back at the counter, rolling out dough. She was not a natural cook, and her movements in the kitchen—rolling, stirring, deboning—always had the look of fighting. "Don't let the jealousy hold you. It'll destroy you both."

❖   ❖   ❖

But I couldn't help it. One afternoon—as I helped Ina pick flowers for the vase in the dining room—I brought it up gently. I told myself I was doing what I had promised my mother: I was looking out for Ina. But I knew deep down that I wanted to break her, to change her.

The truth was that Ina was unafraid, and I envied that quality in her more than I envied her beauty or her charisma or her boyfriend. I wanted to make her afraid, to open her eyes to the seizing mass of threats I saw around me every day. Bomb scares. Shootings. Raids. But subtler things too. The way everyone was always watching one another, evaluating one another, identifying one another. Judging who was Catholic or Protestant by the set of their shoulders, the shape of their nose, the color of their shirt.

"Ina, I know you're not interested in the conflict," I started. "I know you'd rather it weren't happening." She glanced up at me, and I hurried on. "And I understand that! You don't have to be involved. But you've got to remember that you're a Catholic, and that means something. And these days especially, you've got to be careful like. You can hang out with your Prod friends and all. Just—don't forget who you are."

Ina was quiet.

"D'you remember Bobby?" I asked.

"Which Bobby?"

"Flannigan," I said. "Mick's son."

Ina shrugged. Of course she remembered Bobby. All the town had talked about last December was Bobby Flannigan. He and his girlfriend had been shot dead by a British soldier for speeding on a deserted road. He'd been murdered for driving too fast in his own da's car. She'd been murdered for riding shotgun. The whole town had burned with anger, and the IRA had paid tribute to Bobby at his funeral. Now his ma, Cliona, drank at Sláns almost every night.

"I'm just saying," I went on. "If you forget for one minute who you are, how people look at you—it's dangerous. You have to keep your guard up."

"I love a violet," Ina said, pulling a bluish-purple flower from the ground. "This is my new favorite color." She tucked the stem behind her ear.

"Ina, did you not hear what I said to you?"

"Aye, I did." She sighed, the sigh of an exasperated teenage girl on the TV. "This whole conflict . . . it's just not who I am, d'you know? It's not in my nature." I stared at her. Where did she ever get those ideas? Enda and Tad and I had never decided who it was we were. We had been told who to be, and we had become it. "I don't really *identify* with any of it or whatever."

"What do you mean, '*identify*'?" My tone had steel in it. She could say she didn't believe in God all she wanted; she was still one of us. It wasn't a question of choice.

"Anyway, it's almost over," she said. "There'll be the peace treaty soon enough. And sure there's a ceasefire already, isn't there? Even Ma said the RA will honor it this time."

"People are still being killed," I told her.

She looked at me with sad eyes and said nothing.

I watched her as we finished with the flowers. The thin folds of her ears like the hollows of caves on the coast. The pink flush at the rim of her skin, the rim that held the violet. I wanted to reach out and touch the stem, to feel how it was at peace with her. I pulled my own violet up from the ground, but it would not stay behind my ear, kept falling to the earth, and finally I stepped on it with the heel of my boot, grinding it into the grass so that the sweet scent rose into the air.

I felt then that I was not a real girl. I was an imposter, plucking my eyebrows to look like them. My hair never smelled sweet when I got out of the shower. I did not know to think about my legs, to wonder at their length or smoothness, to clear them of hair each morning. My mind was not used to female pathways of thought. But when I saw Ina like this, her red jumper riding up at her waist, her jeans low on her hips, I wanted to be made real, feminized. I would have ground a thousand flowers into the earth if the smell would stay on me, the dusty scent of girlhood.

❖　❖　❖

When we were small, we'd spent a week or so up in Belfast taking care of my nana, Ma's mother, before she died. It was early July, and it was just Ma and the wee ones who had gone up. Just Tad, Ina, and me. I was no older than seven.

We'd heard the shouts and smelled the smoke through the open window during the Eleventh Night celebrations. Walking carefully, Ma had taken Tad and me to see what all the noise was. We'd left Ina asleep in the bed that she, Tad, and I were sharing.

From around the corner of a drab Belfast building, the three of us spied the giant bonfire. It loomed taller than the surrounding buildings. The smoke wafted toward us, sending Tad into a fit of coughing. The burning was spectacular, and it was horrible. I felt my whole wee body tingle with it. The fear, the excitement. I came alive with that nighttime vision. I wanted to know everything, see everything. I wanted the whole world to be as fascinating as that pillar of fire, that glowing icon.

"Do youse see what's at the top there?" Ma asked when Tad's breath had evened out. The wind had carried the smoke in a different direction.

We looked. I saw the tricolor flag we hung in our living room and something white—a doll? It would be visible for only a moment; the flames were lapping higher and higher. Soon the flag and the figurine would be burning with the rest.

"What is it?" I whispered. I was squinting into the distance at it.

"It's the Pope," Ma said. And I heard something in her voice I'd never heard before. "They're Protestants, burning the Pope because they hate him, and they hate us."

I did not ask what a Protestant was or who we were. I knew that was a question you weren't supposed to ask. The us and them, that was set in stone. So we must have known why, must have known where the division lay. Even if I couldn't put it into words.

"Fecking taigs!"

The voice, more than the words, made me jump. The three of us turned, Ma instinctively moving in front of Tad and me, her arms lifted off her sides as if she were about to take flight. Three men were walking by us, laughing, their faces—red and unshaven—stretched in grins as they soaked up Ma's discomfort. They each carried a bottle, and the glass objects hung in their hands like weapons.

One of them stopped in front of us and spit on the ground. A wet, slurping noise and a yellow-green swirl of saliva and mucus. Then he laughed and kept walking. I felt afraid. I felt embarrassed. I was not sure why.

Ma kept her eyes on the footpath as they passed, but she kept looking up in little glances to check their progress. I watched the shape of their backs, hunched slightly like animals. The strong smell of the fire had mixed with something dangerous: the smell of copper or blood. When they were gone, Ma took Tad and me by the hands and marched us back to Nana's.

"What did that man say?" Tad asked.

"What does it mean?" I asked.

She told us to be quiet. We were never, she said, to tell our father what had happened. She made us cross ourselves and swear to it.

All that night, I heard Ma turning over in her bed, unable to sleep. I stared at the ceiling and saw the burning of the bonfire, felt the jolt behind my navel at the sound of the man's voice. The fear and awe, the awe and fear. In bed next to me, Ina's eyes were still and closed, her breaths even. She never even knew we'd left. That was the difference between us: Ina had gotten to sleep through violence, had been able to believe in peace.

❖   ❖   ❖

On her fifteenth birthday, Ina wore a short-sleeved yellow dress that fell to her ankles. She got to choose the music on the record player, and we listened to George Michael for more than two hours. Alone in the center of the living room, she closed her eyes and spun, and her skirt bloomed into a wheel, a flower, a sun.

For her birthday, Ma gave her a gold necklace with the three letters of her name spelled out in cursive. She'd had it made at a shop in town. I bought Ina an eye-shadow palette. She had taken to wearing a full face of makeup, cakey on her young skin. She also wore tampons, much to our ma's chagrin. "You have to be careful what you put in your body," Ma told us ominously. It was the same thing she said when we ate fish and chips two nights in a row. I felt it was a threat, but I knew neither what she was threatening nor how to avoid it.

I didn't know how to use tampons. I watched Ina on the toilet, removing one, inserting one. The awkward act of self-penetration, the way the cotton dragged on dry skin and made her wince, how she screwed up her face, searching for the place inside her where it should settle.

"How do you do it?" I asked from the doorway.

She released the thing inside herself, checked the string, and then looked up at me. There was a little watery blood on her thumb and pointer finger.

"It's like it doesn't fit, it doesn't fit, it doesn't fit, and then something opens, and it swallows it up."

We both burst out laughing.

I'd had only the faintest idea of what menstruation was when I got my first period. I sat on the toilet at school and tried to remember what my mother taught me, what she'd said to do with all the blood.

"Do Protestants get them?" I asked when I found the courage to go to my head of year's office. She handed me a giant sanitary pad with a sad smile, like I'd suffered a personal misfortune.

"Yes, love," she told me. "They're not so different like."

That night, at home, I told my mother that I needed to buy a pack of sanitary pads.

"Oh," she said. "It came already?"

I felt like a baby with the pad the nurse had given me between my legs. Like a toddler in a nappy. My face was hot, and I wished I had never been born a woman.

"All right. I'll buy you some," Ma said. "I thought you had a little longer."

I bowed my head. "I didn't want it," I said.

"You can avoid it by exercise," she said. "Or by eating less. Lots of women in the movement don't get theirs."

At the time, I believed her. But later, it began to seem unlikely that my mother kept track of the menstrual cycles of foot soldiers. It was what she wished were true. That she could've been a fighter. That she could've stopped bleeding, getting pregnant, bleeding.

❖ ❖ ❖

It was 5:00 p.m. in December. We were on winter break. Ina and I were up in our room.

"Eimear is having people over tonight," I said. "It should be class. Her parents are in London for the holiday."

"Mm-hmm," Ina hummed, only half listening. She was curling her eyelashes with a clamp that I'd never been able to figure out myself.

"Would you want to go, then?" I asked. I felt nervous, though I wasn't quite sure why. She was just my little sister, but she had been spending so much time with Peter—so little time with me—that I felt like I was a burden on her, her big sister begging her to hang out.

"Go where?" she asked, one eye already darkened with mascara.

"Good to know you're listening." I rolled my eyes. "To Eimear's party like."

Her smile had a twist of pity in it. My chest tightened with anger.

"Peter and I are going into Armagh," she said. "Ach I'm sorry, Bríd, but I promised him."

I tried to shrug like I didn't care. I was sitting on my bed, picking at the nail polish Ina had painted on my nails a few weeks ago.

"Will you tell Ma, though?" she asked. "That I'm going to Eimear's?" She was rushing to get done with her makeup.

"Now?" I asked. "Sure it won't start until nine at least."

"Aye, just tell her. She won't know the difference. Just say you're meeting me there like."

I'd managed to remove all the nail polish on my first finger. I shrugged.

"What the hell are you doing in Armagh anyway?" I asked. "Going to Boots?" My face felt hot. "There's no TK Maxx there; you'd be better off going to Craigavon." My tone was icier than I'd meant it to be, the slip of frost on the stones by the lough. It hadn't snowed once this winter, and I felt sickly sad for the days when Ina and I would run out in bare feet at the first flurry. When we'd lay in a half inch of snow to make angels like we'd seen in American films.

"Ach we're not going shopping, Bríd." She shook her head at me. "There's a new dance club's opened up."

I tried to scoff, but it came out more like a grunt of pain. I stood up and went to my dresser, riffling through my shirts. I'd have to find something to wear to Eimear's if I was going to go. If I was going to be Ina's cover.

"What kind of club?" I asked.

"Ummm, like dancing, music, y'know?" She looked at me like I was from a different planet. "A *dance* club like."

"A dance club *for who*?" I clarified, reminding myself of the father in a Hollywood film. *Will there be drinking? Will there be boys?* Except this worry was very, very different.

"For anyone," Ina said easily.

"For anyone," I repeated.

She turned to look at me, her face fully done up now. She was holding the curling iron in her right hand.

"Ach it's almost the new century, Bríd. Things aren't just *for Catholics* or *for Protestants* anymore. They're for everybody."

"It's dangerous, Ina."

She rolled her eyes, turned back to the mirror, and wrapped the first strand of hair around the curling iron. She was not bothered by what I thought.

"I'll tell Ma," I said impulsively. It was a threat I never made. She caught my eye in the mirror.

"You're in foul form," she remarked. "Is this all 'cause you want me to come to Eimear's with you? Is it 'cause you're jealous of Peter?"

"I'm not *jealous* of your boyfriend." My voice was raised without my meaning it to be. "I just don't think you should be messing about like this."

"Ach give a rest, Bríd," she snapped. "For fuck's sake. You're a bit pathetic, y'know?"

I turned on my heel and stomped over to the door. "Suit yourself," I said. "If you want to shake your arse for every Prod in the bloody county, that's fine by me." My heart was hammering in my chest.

She grabbed her makeup bag off the desk and threw it at me. It missed and hit the wall behind my head. The contents went flying— lipsticks and mascara bottles, eyeliners and foundation blotters—and landed on the ground like the shards of a broken bottle.

I slammed the door.

❖   ❖   ❖

Tad was sitting at the kitchen counter, listening to his Walkman.

"Do you want to go to Eimear's with me?" I asked. My chest was still heaving with anger.

"What?" He lowered the headphones. I could hear the beat of a rap song evaporating into the air.

"Eimear Gallagher," I said. "She's having something on."

My face felt flushed. I wanted to go back up there and apologize to Ina, but that would be to admit defeat. And she would still go with him.

"Sure," Tad said. "What time?"

"I dunno," I said. "We can head over at nine or so." I paused. "Ina's going earlier," I said.

I didn't know why I'd said it, why I was helping her, even now.

"Sure," Tad said again, pulling his headphones back over his ears.

I should have had a friend to invite—a girl who would get dressed with me and do my hair—but my closest, my only, friend had always been Ina. Ina and Ma and Tad and Enda, when he lived here. But I would get points with Eimear and her friends for bringing Tad. They would giggle when he walked in and whisper about how cute they thought he was, and I would laugh and roll my eyes. Tad would help me pick out a dress anyway. He was used to doing stuff like that for me and Ina.

Ina ran downstairs a few minutes later, wearing jeans and a hoodie, her hair all curled out.

"I'm off to Eimear's," she told my mother, who was doing the dishes, sliding a rag over the blade of a bread knife.

"The Gallagher girl?" Ma asked.

"Aye." Ina leaned over to kiss her cheek. "Bríd'll be meeting us there in a few hours like. I'm going first 'cause I'm giving Eimear a makeover."

Ma cut her eyes at me for confirmation. I looked away.

"When'll you be home?" Ma asked.

"Dunno," she said. "After dinner sure."

I pursed my lips. Ina's eyes darted to me and then away again, satisfied that I would say nothing. In the driveway, I heard the crunch of tires and saw Peter's car. A red MINI that I despised. Ma looked up at it with suspicion.

"Peter's just giving me a lift," Ina explained quickly.

Again, Ma's eyes on me, asking for a confirmation. I tried to keep my face neutral, neither confirming nor denying Ina's story.

"All right," Ma said. "Be safe. Home by eleven."

"Sure," Ina said. And then she was darting to the door, a blur of soft hair and sweet-smelling perfume.

"Have fun with Eimear, Ina!" I called to her, my voice jagged and stony, sarcastic and cruel.

She didn't look back at me once.

❖   ❖   ❖

The clock ticked later, and we did not go to Eimear's. Every time Tad asked, I put him off. I didn't want to go without Ina. I didn't want to watch Tad get swallowed by a group of giggling girls. I didn't want to have to wonder if Ina would get home before me and blow her own cover or if I was supposed to wait for her at Eimear's so we could arrive back at the same time.

Ma came down at nine to ask why I was still home, and I said I had a headache. She gave me a long, hard look, and I knew she thought I was just jealous, that I couldn't stand to go and sit beside my sister and watch her be fawned over. It made me furious that she thought that of me. That she didn't know that I was the good one, and Ina was rotten.

"Ina's there, aye?" she asked me.

"Aye," I said. "She's there."

At half ten, Da was on the sofa watching football, and Tad and I were at the table, playing gin rummy and each drinking a bottle of Smithwick's, the smell reminding me of Da's hugs.

"Three threes," Tad said, laying down his hand. I groaned.

The doorbell sounded. It was a lovely chime that nobody ever rang. Everyone we knew walked right in. It was too late for visitors anyway. Da went to get it.

It was Conor O'Malley, bike propped up against the steps. In the light pouring out of the house, he looked strangely beautiful. His hair wild, his forehead creased. He was shifting from leg to leg.

"Mr. Kane," he said.

My father scowled.

"I'm sorry to bother you, sir," Conor said, "but I think you should come down to Armagh." He looked back into the room as he said it, nodding at me and Tad, who had stood up to better see him. He made no sign that he knew me any better than he knew Tad or my father. I wanted to go to him but stopped myself.

Da still didn't speak.

"There's been a bomb, sir," he said. "Theirs. Not ours." I thought I could hear something in the back of his voice, a tremor of excitement.

"Nothing to bloody do with me," Da said.

Conor was still shifting from leg to leg. Back and forth. Back and forth.

"Gerry's down there, sir, Gerry from the pub. He said you should come. They're identifying the bodies, sir. There are some injured." Da and Conor both drank at the Falls in town.

Da looked back at Tad and me. For a moment, the three of us stared at each other: a terrified man and two children. I thought of the men and women Da worked with. Surely it was one of them.

"Tell your ma, Bríd," Da said. And then he was leading Conor to his car. I waited for Conor to glance back at me, to give me a reassuring smile, but he didn't.

Tad and I looked at each other.

"Mrs. McClintock lives alone," I said. "If she got hurt, they might call him down."

"Ach, I hope they're all right," Tad said, closing the door that my father had left open. "Whoever it is."

"I'll go tell Ma."

Tad went to the kitchen and put the kettle on, his actions slow and dreamy, automatic. I didn't move toward the stairs.

"Go on, then," he said, "when you're after it, you'll feel better." He didn't offer to go in my stead.

I went up the stairs slowly, hearing each creak in the wood as I had a thousand times before. Ma's door was closed. Through it, I could hear her singing one of the old songs her father had taught her. I opened the door.

"Brigid." She smiled. She was going through her dresser, sorting her clothes into two piles. "Have a seat, love." She was in one of her good moods. I couldn't bear to spoil it, to drag her back to the woman she usually was. Against my better instincts, I came into the room, closing the door behind me, and sat down on Da's side of the bed.

The elevated floor was Ma's kingdom. Downstairs, Da reigned. But up here belonged to her. Sometimes, as I walked outside, listening to my Walkman, I saw her standing in the window watching me.

"How are you, Ma?" I asked. The bed was extremely comfortable, and I felt a sudden urge to close my eyes and sleep.

"Aye, how are you?" she said without answering my question. Then she put one of the piles of clothes onto the armchair and climbed in beside me.

I watched her for a moment. She was still so young, so beautiful. There were actresses I knew of who were her age. Actresses who were still unmarried and childless. I thought again of her as a teenager, pregnant with Enda, terrified and alone except for the looming shape of my father, older than she was by several years. A man who had become her only option.

"I was thinking," she said. "When do you think Enda will be back to visit so? Surely he's missing Tyrone by now."

I was quiet for a moment.

"Ma, there's been a bomb in Armagh." I tried to say it casually, but I could hear the nerves in my voice; she must have been able to too.

"Where?" she asked.

"I'm not sure. Conor came for Da. He said he ought to go down." She looked away from me and then stood up.

"Is Ina still at Eimear's?" she asked.

❖ ❖ ❖

Downstairs, Tad was watching the news.

"Has Da rung?" I asked. He shook his head. I stood beside him to watch the report. The Loyalist Volunteer Force had already claimed responsibility. The bomb had targeted an IRA man's residence, the newscaster was saying, but had injured civilians in a nearby establishment. They cut to live footage of the lamplit street. It was smoky, hard to make out on the screen. "One is presumed dead," the newscaster said.

Tad and I crossed ourselves. I felt like I was spinning. Waves beneath a boat, a stormy sea. I would be thrown overboard. Why hadn't I stopped her, blocked the door? Why hadn't I told my mother?

"We'd better get Ina home," I said, but I was stalling. The longer we waited, I knew, the longer the possibility would exist that Ina was safe somewhere. That she had listened to me.

"I'll call Eimear's," I told Tad and went upstairs.

Ina's diary was on top of her dresser. I found the address book easily and scanned the names she'd written in her loopy handwriting until I saw Peter McKenna. There was the telephone number and the address, next to a dozen hearts. I'd guessed that she'd gone to Peter's house first. Maybe she had even stayed there, never gone into Armagh after all. I felt something fluttering in my chest. I wanted Ina back now, wanted her lying in her single bed looking up at the ceiling while her headphones played A-ha at a deafening volume.

I said a quick prayer, and I dialed Peter's number. I thought I could smell her perfume faintly as I clutched the receiver to my mouth. On the third ring, a woman picked up. "Hullo?" Her voice sounded urgent.

"Mrs. McKenna?"

"Aye." I could hear someone in the other room.

"This is Bríd Kane here. I was wondering if Ina's round your place? Only we're after hearing about this bomb in Armagh and we'd like her home so."

The voice in the other room had gotten louder. I heard the phone rustle, and then Mrs. McKenna yelled, "Paul, it's Ina Kane's sister on the line!" She uncovered the mouthpiece. "Ina's not here, love. She and Peter went out, and now we've only just seen the news—God save us—and we haven't heard a word."

"Where'd they go, Mrs. McKenna?" I asked, knowing the answer and wishing I didn't. Wishing Ina had never told me.

"Sure they're only at a friend's house, I think. Someone round your way. Is the name Gallagher?"

So she didn't know either. I bit down hard on my lip.

"All right. Thank you, Mrs. McKenna. Youse be safe now."

"Aye, same to you. God bless."

"God bless."

I hung up the phone. My head felt hot, as if I were hanging upside down and all the blood had rushed to it.

I walked back downstairs, off-balance and unsteady, feeling Tad's eyes on me.

"What happened?" he asked.

"I couldn't get through," I lied.

We stared at each other, and I knew he could read something on my face.

For some reason, I kept trying to remember what Ina had been wearing while she did her makeup. She'd worn a jumper and jeans out of the house, but she and her friends were always wearing baggy clothes to get by their parents. As soon as they got to the main road, they'd pull off the cardigans to reveal tight, cropped shirts and switch out their trainers for the high-heeled boots they kept in their handbags. I wondered if Ina had changed on the ride into Armagh, telling Peter not to look as she swapped one shirt for another, as she took off her jeans and swapped them for a short skirt. Would we be able to recognize her if we saw her on the TV? Would she look shameful, exposed? The kind of woman Ma would judge on the street and Tad would snigger at? I felt my heart pounding. It was ridiculous to think of these things.

There was a knock at the door. Through the window, I could see Father Jim standing on the welcome mat. I hadn't heard his car approach.

Tad and I looked at each other. Neither of us moved. Father Jim could see us through the glass of the unshuttered windows, and yet we would not walk toward him to let him in. We could not.

There was a noise on the stairs. "Tad?" Ma asked. "Tad, isn't that Father at the door?"

"Ma—" I said and then stopped. There was no way to go on. To tell her that Ina had not gone where she said she was going.

"I'll get it," she said. And she walked to the door.

I could hardly hear Father Jim's greeting over the pounding of my heart, could hardly hear what came next. My mother's gasp reached my ears as if it were being carried by the weakest of transistor radios. I saw, without reaction, as Father Jim helped her to the sofa, her body sagging limp like a doll's. Tad had moved into the living room. He was crying without making any noise.

Ma was shaking her head too quickly. I was worried she would hurt her neck. She was hiccupping or sobbing or laughing—it was hard to tell which. "No," she said. "No, no, no."

Father Jim went to the drinks cabinet and poured us each a dash of whiskey. When he gave me mine, I realized that I was crying too. The ringing in my ears was so loud that I couldn't hear my own ragged breathing, but when I looked down at the glass, I saw my chest rising and falling like a horseback rider moving at high speed.

Ma was silent now, her body shaking as if she were being shocked by an electric current. Nobody spoke for a long time. I finished my whiskey and wiped my mouth. Slowly, the ringing in my ears was subsiding. Slowly, I was starting to understand what was next. The truth began to fall into place, and when I finally had the courage to look up at my mother, I knew we were both thinking the same thing.

I had promised I would look after Ina.

Chapter Six

The night of Mia's phone call, Mom stayed awake with me until three or four in the morning, holding me as I recounted what Mia had said. She had gone back to the party after she left me, a bad feeling in the pit of her stomach. There were still people there, drinking and smoking, but she'd found Riley unconscious in the bathroom next to a bottle of gin and an empty orange pill bottle. She'd called me from the hospital waiting room, while he was having his stomach pumped.

All night, I cried for Mia, for Riley, for me. It seemed as if my life would now exist in two halves: before and after that phone call, before and after that moment on the grass. It was clear to me, even then, that things between Mia and me would never be the same.

The next day, Mom brought me soup in bed, like I was sick, and hot water with honey and lemon, sickly sweet and acidic in the back of my throat. I called Mia and was sent to voice mail. Instead, I typed out a text saying I was sorry, asking how she was. All Mia texted back was Thanks. I cried again for a long time, until my cheeks were sore from the salt and my body felt exhausted, like I'd just swum a long distance. Mom and I went out to the garden, briefly, and then I climbed back in bed and took a nap.

When I woke up the next morning—two days after Riley's suicide attempt—it was with a familiar dread that took a moment to crystalize into a memory. Mom had her back to me. I texted Mia again—how's Riley doing?—and got out of bed.

"Mom," I said after I'd brushed my teeth, gotten dressed. "You've got to get up for work."

She didn't reply.

I went over to her side of the bed. She was awake, eyes open and staring at the wall. That dead-end look I knew so well. Panic welled up in me.

"Mom," I tried again, my voice less steady than I wanted it to be. "You need to go to the shelter. They'll be waiting for you."

"I don't feel well," she said. She didn't look well.

I did not have the energy to be calm and kind and soft-spoken like I usually was. I felt like I was about to spin out of control: cry or scream, throw a tantrum like I used to do when she left me at school all alone.

I pulled the covers off her. Underneath them, her body looked small and frail. She was clutching her gold necklace, the one with her name on it. The one she always tugged on when she was going under.

"I'm cold," she said, suddenly angry. "Give me the blanket back."

I dropped the blanket, turned on my heels, and left the room. My eyes stung.

"Bernie?" she called down the hallway.

I stopped, took a deep breath. "Yeah?"

"Promise you'll come back."

I closed my eyes. "I promise," I said, with an effort.

❖   ❖   ❖

Mom's dark periods used to come every five or six months, though lately they had been less frequent. I thought of them like hibernations, like deep-water diving from which she emerged a little quieter each time. Sometimes, they were triggered by something: a mass shooting in the news, a difficult encounter at work. But sometimes I could not work out their origin. These were the ones that scared me the most: the ones that had no logic to them.

The thing about depressed people is that they never remember their depressions. When they wake up, it's all about them. *They're* feeling better. *They* had a bad month. They forget to say: *Thank you for taking care of me, daughter.* They forget to say: *I owe you.* They forget to say: *You took care of me like I took care of you, so I will no longer treat you like a child.*

And you forget too. So that the next time it comes around, it hits you with the same force. The same fear. The same anger. The same grief.

This time, I really needed her. And she was gone.

❖   ❖   ❖

I couldn't face school, so I went to the shelter instead. I told Mom's colleagues she was sick, and then, because I had nothing else to do, I stayed.

I'd been volunteering at the shelter since I was young. Mom used to bring me to work when she couldn't find childcare, sit me on a stool with a coloring book or my homework. Later, I came because I wanted to, because I knew the people who lived and worked there: they were the closest thing I had to an extended family. How many Thanksgivings had I spent doling out store-bought turkey and Mom's homemade mashed potatoes? Sitting down to eat with new and familiar faces, drinking a soda, helping myself to Entenmann's for dessert. While Mia was with her aunts and uncles, grandparents and cousins, I had been here.

That day's snack at the shelter was Popsicles. It was a hot day at the end of April, and I stood in the middle of the shelter, a large, nearly empty, church-like room, holding a bucket filled with ice, out of which the Popsicle sticks stuck like the quills of a porcupine. The bucket was cold and heavy, and it was slowly numbing my hands as I held it.

JoJo, one of the staffers, walked by me. She was taking her time carrying a dustpan and broom across the hall. She smiled sympathetically at me when she caught my eye, and I gave a forced smile in return. I did not want JoJo's sympathy. I wanted to know if Mia was okay. How Riley was feeling. I wanted to know when Mom would be better, wanted to fast-forward to that time. I wanted to know what it was about her life that she couldn't live with.

My hands were losing feeling fast. I put the bucket down, closed and opened my fists a few times, and then picked it back up. Nobody seemed to want a Popsicle. Most of the residents were outside anyway, soaking up the last bit of sunshine. Playing dice, smoking, reading. My favorite shelter resident, the Mississippi Man, was nowhere to be found. I kept looking around for him—long, narrow frame, pale skin, hands like a musician's—my eyes darting over the large, mostly empty hall. The air was soft and warm; all the doors were open. It would have been nice to see him now, to stand with him. It would have been like aloe vera on a sunburn, to have a moment with him between moments with Mom.

The Mississippi Man had arrived two months ago. He had bright eyes and all his teeth. He couldn't have been older than twenty-five. As I served him corn bread the first night he came, he told me that he was just passing through, just needed a place to sleep. The way residents felt a need to justify themselves, to apologize, to explain. He had been a race car driver and had given it up, he said. He had taught himself computers. He was going to Fresno.

"Don't listen to him," Mom said after he moved down the line to the baked beans. "He's got liar's eyes."

But the next time I visited, I played tic-tac-toe with him. He had not gone to Fresno after all. He told me about breeding horses and about his years in the army. He told me about driving up to Tennessee one night and jumping the fence at Graceland. How the guards had laid into him until he was spitting blood.

"He's a liar," my mother told me again on the way home. "None of those stories are real."

"I like hearing them," I said. The Mississippi Man was lying, but he wasn't lying to me. He was telling stories without asking for anything in exchange. He was not my mother, burying the past. Saying that she loved me and then leaving me all alone. He shared things with me, however small, however embellished; it was something she'd never done. The fact that she had warned me away from him made me want to be near to him even more.

I glanced over at the shelter TV, where a reality show was playing. The episode was about women who didn't realize they were pregnant until they went into labor and gave birth. It's called a cryptic pregnancy, the television doctor said, when the fetus doesn't show up in blood or urine tests and the typical side effects of a pregnancy are absent: no weight gain, no morning sickness, no baby kicking in the uterus.

I shifted the bucket so I was holding it in the crooks of my elbows, giving my hands a chance to regain feeling. I wondered if Mia had gotten my text, decided not to respond. If she was angry with me for what I'd said that night or just preoccupied. If she regretted how close we'd been.

Complications with cryptic pregnancies are common, the woman on the TV continued. There is no prenatal care for the fetus or mother, and there is no emotional preparation on the part of the mother or parents. One day, they are living mundane nine-to-five lives, coming home to a bottle of wine in front of the television, falling asleep to *Bob's Burgers*. And the next day they are taking home an infant to a house where there is no crib, no formula, no diapers, no baby name. The children born from cryptic pregnancies are often victims of child abuse. The silent fetus becomes a child quieted by neglect.

In the back of my mind, I saw Riley. I remembered his eyes, dark and shadowy, rings of exhaustion around them so that they looked bruised. His face covered in freckles. His hair, the same dark brown as Mia's, falling past his ears. I thought of him as a baby, how he must have looked, and how he must look now, having had his stomach pumped. Sitting scared in a hospital bed, wondering how he got it so wrong.

I gave up and put the ice bucket down. There was no point in my doing a job that a table could easily do. Especially if the Mississippi Man wasn't here to notice me, to watch me with those gray eyes.

I walked over to where JoJo was pretending to sweep the floor, her eyes glued to the screen.

"I'm going to head out," I said.

"Okay," JoJo said, giving me that smile again. "I hope Ina feels better."

I knew she was just trying to be nice, but I wanted to rip my mother's name out of her mouth. I wanted it to be a secret, a word only I knew.

"It's only the flu," I said. "She'll be back soon."

❖ ❖ ❖

The Mississippi Man was out back, leaning against a brick wall. Sticking to the shadows like the undead. I almost walked by him without noticing. I was still thinking about cryptic pregnancies, about Mia.

"I was looking for you," I said when I saw him. I stopped walking, looking down at the ground and then back up at him.

The Mississippi Man raised one eyebrow. "I'm always here."

His face was cast in shadow. His eyes hooded. Even his voice was worn, full of history.

"Shouldn't you be at school?" he asked.

"Yeah," I said.

"Why aren't you?"

"My mother won't get out of bed."

I knew I shouldn't say this to him of all people. But who else could I tell?

He made a noise in the back of his throat, like this was not surprising. There was probably nothing on earth that could surprise him.

"I don't know why," I said. I was looking at him, hoping for an answer. Surely he would understand, know what to do.

"It's happened before?" he asked. His gaze was intent and yet unfocused. I was pretty sure he was high.

"Not in a while, though."

"Genetics," he said. "Always is."

I didn't say anything.

"Your grandparents have it?" he asked.

I shrugged.

"Aunts and uncles?"

It felt like being at the doctor's office, that embarrassing unveiling of fears and secrets. Strange habits and aches. Teeth growing at odd angles and ingrown hairs. And the dreaded question they always asked me: Family history? To which I had to say, I don't know, I don't know, I don't know.

"*I* don't have it," I said.

He gave a short laugh, though I wasn't sure what was funny.

"You must have gotten your dad's genes."

"Maybe." I thought of my father in a country whose language he did not speak, the sun hot on the back of his neck and his gun heavy as a child in his arms. I had no way of knowing what I'd inherited from him; my mother claimed to have burned every photo of him in her grief.

The Mississippi Man fiddled with a pack of cigarettes, pulled one out, lit up. I heard his intake of breath, the release. I wished he would offer me one. I could have used a cigarette just then.

"Or maybe it's coming for you," he said, twirling the ash of the cigarette in the air so that wisps of smoke floated toward me. "Sometimes you don't know till later. Something to look forward to." He laughed.

I didn't care about that: what would happen to me later. Climate crisis or depression. I knew it would end badly, one way or another. All I cared about was now.

"I think something happened to her," I said. "I think something caused it."

He blew out another exhale of smoke, hazy in the already-dusty air. Sand flying under car wheels, forest fires in the distance.

"Everyone always wants to believe that," he said. "That there's something in the past that can be resolved. A switch can be flipped, and everything will be better."

"You don't know her," I said a little too sharply. "I just, I mean—she says things sometimes. It makes me think there was something. Before I was born."

He shrugged. "Sure," he said. "It happens. PTSD."

"She wasn't in battle," I scoffed.

"It's not just that." He took another drag. "All sorts of things cause it." He didn't give any examples.

"The thing you need to know," he went on after a minute, "is that she's at war for you. In her own mind—she's at war trying to get free from it."

I thought of how her body had turned in on itself when I pulled the bedsheet off her. Her fingers wrapped around her necklace. Her blue eyes full of fear.

"What's your real name?" I asked. "I always think of you as the man from Mississippi."

He looked at me like he was trying to decide if I deserved to know it.

"Damon," he said, finally, and the word felt like a little gift he had handed me. Something as fragile as a baby bird, cupped in the palm of my hand.

❖   ❖   ❖

I biked home, the wind on my face, coasting downhill, standing up on the pedals, feeling the spin of the chain beneath me. I thought about cryptic pregnancies. The absurdity of discovering that you were no longer one person but two. People must laugh at the mother afterward. They must ask how you could have thought things were normal, how you had failed to notice the weight of it, the heaviness on your chest.

You probably asked yourself the same question. Somewhere, in the back of your mind, did you know? Did you know what you were carrying?

The air outside smelled like honeysuckle, jasmine. I thought about moths crowding around the plants to drink their nectar, like my classmates around a keg as soon as the sun set. It was a twenty-minute bike ride home, a ride I had done hundreds of times. Twenty minutes of feeling like I was flying until I was back inside the house, my wings pinned under a sheet of glass like a butterfly in a lepidopterist's lab.

I was four blocks away when I knew something was wrong. A wooziness came over me like drunkenness or dehydration. I'd been thinking about Riley, how he must have looked when Mia found him, lying there, sweaty and unconscious, slumped over the rim of the bathtub, white bile on his lips. In the distance, I heard a siren. And then, suddenly, I could see her in his place, her hair hanging in her face, her eyes with that stony nowhere look they sometimes got. Gin, pills, more gin. I had to get home before it was too late. I biked as fast as I could, my feet pounding on the pedals, my heart crawling up my chest like it was trying to escape my body. My skin hot and sweaty, the feeling of insects crawling on me.

I threw my bike on the porch, fumbled with the key in the lock. The whole time I could see it, the hundreds of ways she could do it. And I hadn't told her I loved her when I left. Why had I gone in the first place? I should have stayed by her bedside, attendant. "She's at war for you," he'd said.

The door burst open, and I left it standing there, gaping like a mouth, as I ran upstairs to her room. The thunderstorm of my feet on the stairs, my breaths ragged in my chest now. I threw open the door to her room.

And she was fine. Lying in bed with her iPad. She looked up at me. "How was school?" she asked.

Chapter Seven

1997, County Tyrone

After, I kept walking into things around the house. The sofa in the living room, the rocking chair up in my bedroom, the banister of the staircase. Things that had been in the same place since before I was born, and yet I kept not knowing them, being surprised by their existence. I wanted to call out to her, my vocal cords straining to yell her name and then stopping, like the shudder of a suppressed cough. Like a sob. I thought of her always; her face was everywhere. Her laugh ringing in my ears. I buried my face in her pillow to smell her.

Da told us, the night after we heard the news, that he had known as soon as he saw Conor on the doormat. He had looked at that son of a bitch and wanted to ignore the doorbell. He had known it would be about his Ina. Bastard, I thought when he said it, lying bastard.

If anyone had known instinctively, it would have been me. I would have leaned down to pick a flower or clear a plate from the table, and I would have felt it hit me, the loss, like going over a waterfall in a canoe. But there had only been my breaths, coming as normal, and my heart, beating its regular rhythm while Ina's thudded—fear, adrenaline, pain—and then stopped.

❖   ❖   ❖

Ma went to see the body and came back with the violence of it written across her face. We each went up to our separate rooms and wondered if we could live with what had happened. My room was Ina's room. It was half-empty. I wondered if I would die from the pain in my chest, the throbbing in my head. Surely no human being could withstand this: the loss on top of the guilt, like bodies stacked on bodies. There was no avoiding what I knew: this had been my fault.

In the corner of our bedroom, by the door, I found the cap from one of her lipsticks, cracked from when it had landed on the floor. The edge flecked red with the color that had once lived inside it. She had thrown it at me the last time we spoke.

We had a closed-coffin wake, a closed-coffin funeral. My forehead bounced on the wooden box, up and down with my sobs as my body shook on top of hers. I wished that I, like her, was asleep, unknowing. We had been sisters, and now I was alone.

I imagined her dancing as it happened, spinning in a circle on the dark floor, her plaits flying out to the side, just like the skirt of her dress in blossom.

❖   ❖   ❖

After the funeral, Enda and Siobhán came back to the house and helped to set up tea and coffee for the mourners. Enda was acting strange, kept talking about Ina as if she wasn't his little sister. As if they weren't the oldest and the youngest, two sides of the same coin. "I'm sorry for your loss," he told Ma. Ma looked like she was going to slap him, but she only turned her back and walked away.

Peter came too. I had not seen him at the chapel, but now here he was, eyes wide. He had a burn on his left hand, and I couldn't look at any other part of him. He came up to me to say he was sorry, came up to all of us. His eyes were red-rimmed and bloodshot, and his "sorry" seemed to acknowledge that it might be him, more than any paramilitary group, whom we blamed.

I wanted to feel angry with him as he stood in front of me, but I just stared. I thought I could see the reflection of what had happened in his eyes, the images he was forced to watch again and again. He was the only one who knew how it had been; the only one who could tell me if she had still been angry with me, if she had been scared, if she'd been dancing when the bomb hit or in the bathroom fixing her makeup, if he had been holding her when she died. All I knew from Da was that she had been wearing a yellow dress. I knew which one it was, though it had been too burned for us to keep.

I found Tad sitting on the front steps, having a smoke.

"The fuck is up with Enda?" I asked. He offered me a drag, and I took one. I had a bruise on my forehead where it had come in contact with the coffin. My voice was hoarse from crying. The rush of the nicotine made the world spin for a minute, and then I felt steadier.

"The fuck is ever up with Enda."

We both looked out over the grass. It was misty. The line of trees that blocked the road from sight looked ominous and wild.

"What are we going to do?" I asked. I imagined I could see her there, still young, still running.

"What do you mean?" Tad looked at me.

"They killed her," I said. "We have to do something."

"Like what? Ride in on our white horses?"

My leg was bouncing up and down without my meaning it to. I felt like I could have run a hundred miles without stopping; there was an urgent, furious energy inside me.

"Don't you feel like you need to do something?" I asked. "Don't you feel like if you don't, you'll, like—die?"

"There's nothing to do, Bríd," he said. "She's gone."

I shook my head. I refused to believe that, refused to even hear the words.

We sat there for a long time in silence. I knew that things would never be the same between Tad and me. He was not Ina, but I loved him. My little brother.

❖   ❖   ❖

My grief was a migraine. I didn't sleep or eat. I could tell that when my parents looked at me, all they saw was Ina's absence. They could hardly stand to speak to me, to meet my eye. Even Tad wouldn't come inside the bedroom I had shared with her. He went back to school and played football, coming home long after the sun had set if he came home at all. If I passed him in the hallway, he'd walk away quickly, like he had seen a stranger in a deserted alley. Like he had seen a ghost.

Da had time off for bereavement, but he went into the office anyway. He came home late, creeping into the house like a burglar and sleeping on the couch next to a bottle. In the morning, he took whiskey in his tea, and his hand shook badly enough that he spilled amber liquid on his white shirts. He reeked of onions and of alcohol and I almost never saw him in the same room as my mother.

The house no longer functioned. We never sat down to dinner. Milk went off in the fridge and laundry piled up, undone. We wore dirty clothes for days in a row. I only saw my parents speak to each other twice, and both times their whispered conversations ended in a full-blown argument. The second time, my mother threw a plate. It hit the wall and shattered on the floor.

They were arguing about what had happened that night, about how they had let Ina go so easily. Nobody asked me if I'd known the truth, and that somehow made it worse. I wanted to be asked. I wanted to tell them. Instead, I went up to my room and kicked my bedpost again and again, remembering the lie I'd told, remembering letting her leave, remembering how cruel I'd been. Again and again, the things I'd said came back to me; I was desperate to block out the memory. It was like everything between us—the laughter, the makeovers, the late nights we'd spent under the covers gossiping, the mornings on the school bus, the dancing in our bedroom—had been boiled down to one sentence: "If you want to shake your arse for every Prod in the bloody county, that's fine by me."

❖   ❖   ❖

When Ina had been dead two weeks, I opened her dresser and looked through her drawers. I held up her dresses to the light, felt the fabric of them. I pretended it was how it used to be: us trying on each other's clothes, me staring at her enviously, her telling me what I looked best in. In her bottom drawer, I found an old shirt, one she hadn't worn in years. It was baby blue and cropped, with buttons down the front. On Ina, the top had always looked simultaneously childlike and obscene; the buttons seemed flimsy, as if they might fall open at any moment. I tried it on and studied myself in the mirror; I looked so good that it took my own breath away. For the first time in my life, I fancied myself prettier than Ina had been.

I knocked with my elbow on Ma's door, pushing it open when she said to come in. I was carrying a tray with a few slices of soda bread and a cup of tea—no milk, how she liked it. Seeing her, I felt the tears rise. I wanted to be beside her more than I'd ever wanted anything. Wanted the heat of her body holding me at night. It had always been my bed she came to when she fought with Da. Why wouldn't she come to me now?

As I walked over to place the tray on the side of the bed she was not occupying, she narrowed her eyes at me.

"What's that shirt you've got on?" she demanded.

"It's just an old top." I could feel my face going red.

"Let me see it."

I tried to keep my back to her as I walked to the door. But when I reached for the handle, she grabbed my wrist. Her fingers were cold and long and firm. They felt scaly.

I remembered being a wee girl again, feeling the threat of her fingers on me. Back then, that had been worse than Da's displeasure. She had been a pioneer of rage. It had come so beautifully, so naturally to her; she was a woman on fire.

I was six years old. We'd been playing Easter Rising. Tad, Enda, and I. Running around with wooden swords for guns, proclaiming Ireland's freedom from England. And Ma had stopped us for twenty minutes to lecture about the history, sat us down on the couch to give us the long version. The Irish Republican Brotherhood seizing buildings across Dublin, an armed insurrection against the British. The women's paramilitary group Cumann na mBan, standing tall beside the men to proclaim Ireland a free country. The sixteen men who were executed and the mass grave they were buried in so that their tombstones would not become sites of worship. On and on she went when all we'd wanted was to play.

"Why don't you join them, then?" I'd asked her, Enda kicking me under the coffee table. "If you love the IRA so much, why don't you join them?"

I was small enough that both my wrists fit in one of her fists. She squeezed too tight. I cried out. When she looked me in the eyes, she did not seem like my mother anymore.

"We all do our part, Brigid." Her eyes sparkled, stars on water. "Not everyone's a soldier, but we all do our part. I gave birth to you three, aye?" She looked from one of us to the other. "You're going to make me proud, aren't you?"

We nodded. She had a ruler in her right hand. I hadn't seen her reach for it. Five strikes across my palm. I had no calluses there, and it hurt.

Now she yanked me toward her. I stumbled, resisting. She was stronger because of her anger. Or I was weaker because of my guilt. I stood in front of her, looking down at the floor, seeing, as I did so, the delicate buttons that ran vertical up my chest.

"That's Ina's shirt."

"She gave it to me," I protested. I was feverish with the lie, with the shame.

"Take it off." She made a wild gesture, pushing herself up from a seated position so that she was kneeling on the bed. Our eyes were level. She grabbed the collar of the shirt and pulled. Buttons fell onto the floor like tears. There were tiny clinks as they landed on the wood. I felt the cold air hit my chest where I had been exposed. Ma pulled the shirt, now torn, off me. I was limp.

I stood there in my bra, which Ma had bought for me when I turned thirteen. It was peach-colored and too small for me now. My right nipple poked out of its shell, embarrassing and fatty. I felt the tears moving down my face. It had been years since my mother had seen me undressed like this.

Ma was holding the fabric of Ina's ruined shirt. She was staring at my exposed body, my old ratty bra.

"Go cover up," she said, and she turned away from me, putting the baby-blue fabric on the bed beside her.

❖   ❖   ❖

January came and went, and I did not go back to school. I would not take my exams. I would not graduate or go on to university. A dropout, like my mother. My voice got hoarse from going unused; there was no one around to talk to.

On the radio, they said peace was guaranteed now. Only a few months and it would all be over. Forty years of fighting. Eighty years since the 1916 uprising. And it would all fizzle out, our land signed away in a conference room. Politicians smiling as we became equal citizens of an empire we did not belong to. We would never get to sew our stitches; we would never be united. And Ina was dead.

The IRA had split in two; a new splinter group had formed. The old IRA's plans lay shattered like broken bottles on the ground. Their cowardice, clear now, made me wonder why we'd always been so terrified of them. In the end, they were only a messy group of men arguing over things that hardly mattered. Men Da had bowed his head for and pretended not to see. Men Ma had trained her eyes on like a lustful girl. The new IRA, the "Real" IRA, I knew nothing about.

In the kitchen, Ma stared out the window. There were two lines down her face where her skin showed through her foundation. I could see the little freckles that she hid, the lightest brown, a coating of sugar. I put my arms around her. I was taller than she was, and when I clasped my hands on top of her ribs, I could feel the wire of her bra on my thumbs. I put my chin on her shoulder, but the weight seemed too much for her, and I lifted my head again, held the weight myself.

Lately, I was the one to wake Ma most mornings. If I did not come wake her, she would sleep till three or four in the afternoon. She might sleep forever. I despised the job, hated seeing her face move from the surrender of sleep through the hardening, hated watching her remember more and more as each second passed. I watched her lose a daughter in the span of thirty seconds. Watched her hear the news again, watched the shock hit, watched Ina die, again. Then she would shoo me away, and the next time I'd see her, she'd be wearing a full face of makeup, a thin layer of disguise, and her mouth would be set straight as a pencil. It was the same thing for me. Every morning, Ina died. Every night, while I slept, we were together again, laughing or fighting, picking flowers, talking in the bathroom while she soaked in the bath, her eyes closed like she was sleeping.

Standing there in the kitchen, Ma's body felt untethered, like it was moving out of my grasp even as I held it there. Then she struggled free of my embrace. She had not given in to me even once, the way she used to when I hugged her, when I held her.

"I'm going to kill your father," she said. The words were low. They sat at the back of her throat and, from behind her, I could feel their vibrations. "I'm going to kill all them who think the fight is over."

I knew then that the house had been split forever, a scar growing over what had once been whole. I knew that it was up to me to make it right.

Chapter Eight

2016, Los Angeles County

Once, when I was ten or so, Mom shut off all the lights in the house, saying that a strange car was parked outside. "Should we ring the police?" she'd asked me, her eyes wild.

I was sitting on the sofa with my hands under my thighs. It was December, and our house didn't have heat. Mom hadn't believed it would get cold enough in California for us to need it. The rent had been cheap here, worth the few weeks when we had to wear extra sweaters and take hot bath after hot bath to stay warm.

"I think it's okay, Mom," I said. I was old enough to know that this was not right. That it was unlikely that the forest-green Jeep belonged to anyone other than a tourist or a backpacker who didn't know he had parked on private property. But I was not old enough to parse out what was real and what was not. I did not tell my classmates what my mother was like, but I stopped bringing the few friends I had over after school. I went to their houses instead. And I studied their mothers' mouths, how they turned upward in bright, cheery smiles, how there seemed to be no threat of danger, no clinging love, no fear.

There were things Mom said and did that I could not decipher, things I did not know if I should hold on to or discard. She told me not to trust police officers, to give them a false name if they asked for one.

On crowded train platforms, she couldn't catch her breath. And once, on the highway, she had cried so hard that I had leaned over to hold the wheel steady, my hand small against the huge leather ring. I carried these memories around with me like the ephemera the kids in my class collected: baseball cards, Lego sets. My mother's lessons.

❖　❖　❖

"Do you need anything?" Kaleb was in the kitchen, putting a pot of chicken soup in the fridge. It had been five days since Mom had taken to bed.

He'd made the soup from scratch, and I was grateful. I could feed myself, of course, but there had been many nights of scrambled eggs for dinner in my life, and I was relieved to have someone looking out for me when Mom couldn't.

"For her to stop this," I said.

Kaleb sighed.

"She wants to stop it too," he said. "But I know that doesn't make it any easier for you." He looked at me for a minute, but I avoided his gaze, fiddling with the dishes in the sink. I was worried he would say something about Riley, and I would start crying. What had happened with Riley and what was happening with my mother had morphed into one oily darkness. They were the same problem: the fact that, on some level, neither of them wanted to be alive. The fact that I was not enough to change her mind.

"Is Mia all right?" Kaleb asked instead.

I shrugged. "I don't know how she would be." The truth was I did not know how she was.

"I'll go up," Kaleb said, nodding toward the stairs, my mother's bedroom. "See if I can talk her into a shower."

I nodded, and he squeezed my hand before leaving the room.

In the years when it had been just Mom and me, before she met Kaleb, we had been a self-sustaining ecosystem. If I had a fever, Mom would bring me two translucent blue pills in the palm of her hand. She would lay a hand on my forehead, wiping away the sweat seeping out of me, and then she'd prop up my neck so I could drink ice water, the coldness burning my lips and throat. If Mom couldn't get out of bed, I would make her a cup of tea and bring her two thin wafer cookies. The offering would sit on her bedside table as I did my homework and watched over her. I counted the hours she lay in bed. I kept sharp objects away from her because the internet told me to. I faked a cough to stir her sympathy. I went to school and came home and went to school and came home and then, suddenly, she would be better. For a while, I believed this was how all mothers and daughters were. How I, too, would be as a mother.

We had our good times too: cookies for Christmas, half the dough eaten before it made it into the oven. Long walks on the beach in winter, when we were the only people there, her telling me that the salt air on our faces was like Ireland and me closing my eyes to imagine that other place. Books in bed together on a Sunday morning, her drinking coffee, me cocoa or hot tea. The warmth of her next to me, duvet piled around us like a fort.

When I was twelve, she'd met Kaleb. Late-night phone conversations, long email exchanges. They debated the academic papers he sent off to journals; she disagreed with his premises, his prescriptions for achieving justice. Soon, he was over all the time, and we three became a precarious unit. Still, there was something off about the whole thing. I could see it, every now and again; it came in waves, in cycles like the moon. She pulled him in. She pushed him away.

Kaleb was adopted, so he was good about kind of adopting me. When he was six months old, his white adoptive parents went to Ethiopia and took him home. They always said they "just knew" the moment they saw him, but Kaleb never understood what it was they knew. It ate away at him, growing up in the richest, whitest part of San Francisco, dark-skinned, with only one Black friend. He was depressed. Real depressed. Sleep all the time, no appetite depressed. Mom depressed. He wasn't Ethiopian, really, but he wasn't quite American either. He was an immigrant who didn't remember his home country. He was the child of two sets of parents who made him feel alien. Like me, he knew there was a past running to catch up with him, a wolf pack of genetics and forgotten memories nipping at his ankles. Like me, he knew there were things he didn't know.

It took him a long time to find himself. It took a community of people who looked like him, who cared enough to ask his story. And when he did find himself, it was in Southern California, three blocks away from our house on Alley 19, with a job teaching in the Africana Studies and Philosophy departments at the college that Riley went to, a token from AA reminding him that he was six years sober, and an affinity group he'd created for transracial adoptees. "The work and the love of Black people saved me," he'd said to me once.

Mom had taught me to keep all my love for her, but I could not help loving Kaleb. He was sturdy and kind and had been, since I was a child, good to me. I did not have to hide the sharp objects once Kaleb came into the picture. He brought her to a doctor; she started the yellow pills. He was a deeply moral man. Like my mother, he was always thinking about ethics, about who was suffering and how we could help, about how to resist injustice, about modes of revolution. She worked at the shelter; he wrote essays about morality. They were a good pair. Kaleb had made me laugh the first day I met him, though I was not the kind of child to laugh easily or willingly. Now he made me lunch when he was at our house, and we sat in comfortable silence, and he was interested in whatever I was doing at school, and he was funny when he told stories about his students. He wore wire-frame glasses. He gave me essays to read. And he let Mom and me have our space, our silences, our love.

❖   ❖   ❖

I went out back, into the garden. The sun was too bright in my eyes; it felt dishonest, too cheery. Mom had planted seeds a few weeks ago, and some of them had sprouted. I knelt down to study the dirt, wet soil seeping through the knees of my jeans. Absentmindedly, I twisted my finger around a weed, the way Mom twirled her hair around her fingers. Then I uprooted it.

If my life were a patch of soil—wet and dark and growing strangely—the past was what had been buried, planted underground: a body coffined or a seed watered and prayed for. The past had sprouted into me, into my mother as I knew her, into our life together. I did not know what the seed was, but I knew the texture of it, could feel it rolling between my fingers. It was made up of the days and nights that fogged the back of my brain. The backgrounds of my childhood photographs. Motel rooms that looked out at parking lots. Flatlands passing out the car window. Mom's legs cracked and itchy from dryness, her skin flaking against the inside of her corduroys. Day-care centers and kindergartens where I was dropped off and then retrieved like a package. The faces of children I met and then never saw again. One town and then another. This was the soil I'd been planted in. And somewhere in there was the shape of a man, the contours of his face resembling my own. Somewhere in there was the truth about my mother.

I got up, wiped the dirt off my knees. Back inside, I logged on to Mom's iPad, which I'd taken from her room when she was asleep. I usually checked her devices when she was low, just to see what the screen could tell me about her mind. Her iPad had twelve tabs open. I always told her to close her tabs so it would run faster. She never listened.

As I clicked to close them, I saw that it was the same news story, again and again. "England to vote in so-called 'Brexit' Referendum." "England contemplates withdrawal from the EU." "Britain's exit from the EU could bring a hard border back to Ireland." "How Brexit could renew violence in Ireland." There were articles from news sites I recognized but also threads on Reddit and other forums. She had gotten deep into the threads, reading comments filled with acronyms I did not know, following tense discussions I could not quite understand.

Lots of jargon that was alien to me: unionist, loyalist, Ulster, free state, republican.

My heart pounded. What was she doing looking at all of this? Why had she been worried about the wider world while I was having the worst week of my life? I checked the time stamp on her browsing history. It was from the morning I'd gone to the shelter to hand out Popsicles. She'd been wasting her time on Reddit while I was skipping school to go to her job, while I was lying to cover up for her, while I was terrified that—

I couldn't think it.

I heard the shower turn on in my mother's room and looked up. Kaleb had come back into the kitchen.

"She's up," he said.

"Thanks," I said, closing the iPad. "You're a miracle worker." I felt distracted, angry, hurt.

"Dinner tonight?" I asked as he pulled on his sneakers. We often ate together when Mom was low. I could be quiet around Kaleb in a way that was difficult with most people. Tonight, especially, I did not want to be alone.

"I wish I could," he said. "I'm meeting with a student."

For dinner? I wanted to ask but didn't. It was not my business—he was not my father—but still I felt the anger that had been living in me lately. Wasn't anyone going to look out for me? Didn't anyone realize what I was going through?

❖   ❖   ❖

Mom came out of her bedroom a little while after Kaleb left. She had a haggard, grayish look about her. Her hair was wet and down to her shoulders. I was standing there with the iPad. I was done taking care of her. I had been thinking about what to say.

"Where are you from?" I asked as soon as she came into the room. "In Ireland."

She looked at me like I'd pointed a gun at her. "The North," she said. She sounded exhausted, but she had been sleeping all day.

"Northern Ireland?" I asked.

"The North," she said again.

"What's the name of the town?"

"Doesn't matter," she said. "I don't live there anymore." She sat down on the couch, reached for the TV remote. I came around the side of the couch to face her.

"Why were you looking at all this stuff about Ireland?" I asked, waving the iPad. "What does Ireland matter?"

She just stared at me, like she didn't understand the question.

"I looked at your browser history," I prompted. "You were searching all this stuff about European politics while I was at the shelter lying to everyone about how you had the flu!"

She was quiet.

"Mom." I took a deep breath. "We have to get you to the doctor. Maybe it's your meds. Sometimes you just need to switch prescriptions; I read about—"

"Bernie," she interrupted. "This has nothing to do with you." She still looked hazy, but the usual sharpness of her gaze was coming back. In some twisted way, I thought, fighting with me was good for her.

I opened my mouth in shock. "Your depression has nothing to do with me?" I scoffed. "Sorry, but that's just not fucking true. Who calls in sick for you? Who makes you tea? Who brings you your pills? If you're not going to talk to your doctor, you at least need to talk to me!"

She looked battered. "One day you'll understand."

"I understand now!"

"You're still a child," she said.

"I'm sixteen!" I yelled. "My best friend's brother tried to kill himself! I think I'd fucking understand."

"You're still a girl," she said. She was trying to keep her voice steady.

"You always say that! You always say I'm too young to know anything. I'm too young to have sex; I'm too young to drive. But guess what? All my friends have sex and drink and do everything else you're afraid of!" I yelled. "I'm not as young as you think I am."

"Bernie!" Something in her voice made me freeze, something jagged and mean. "I don't care what your friends do. I raised my daughter better."

I scoffed. "I raised myself," I said. "While you couldn't get out of bed."

I turned and walked to the door.

"Where are you going?" she asked.

I said nothing.

"Bernie."

"It has nothing to do with you." I repeated her words, my voice hard as gravel in my throat.

"You're not to go out," she said.

I reached the door and slammed it behind me. I heard her call my name, but I ignored it. I would not promise to come back. She'd never promised me.

❖ ❖ ❖

On the street, I stopped, suddenly wondering where I was going. Mia was probably at the hospital, and she didn't want to see me anyway. The thought made it difficult to breathe, like I was submerged in freezing water, my heart constricting in my chest. The shock of being without her was not something I could have anticipated; it was like I had lost an eye, the world strange and lopsided under my gaze. I tried to think about where else to go; I couldn't keep showing up at the shelter. Even Kaleb was busy tonight.

The sun was just setting, the late stretch of a spring evening. Around me, I could feel the light dimming like I was on a dance floor. The idea came to me easily, as if my mother had suggested it herself; in some ways, she had. "Don't have sex," she'd said again and again. "I should go," Mia had said. I pulled out my phone and texted Avery.

I watched my feet as they led me to the campuses, walking without any signal from my brain, without needing to ask the way. Like I was a wind-up toy, like I was remote-controlled. Like there was only ever one place I was going. My hands shook at the thought of what had just happened, what would happen next. I could act like a normal teenage girl, I told myself. I could pretend I was one of them: boy crazy and stupid, just like Mia.

The hallway buzzed with fluorescent lighting, making the whole space seem off-kilter, electrically charged. The walls were made of that bumpy material that looks like a skin rash. Avery let me in to his little single room. Chance the Rapper was singing through a small speaker, a slow song that I liked. Avery had lit a Febreze-brand candle in some strange attempt to be romantic. Beneath the "fresh laundry" scent, I could smell something like wet socks and bong water. Still, I appreciated the gesture, the fact that he had tried anything at all. I imagined telling Mia about this.

I sat down on the twin bed. There was nowhere else to sit. In my pocket, my phone buzzed with a text from my mom. **Bernadette**, it said. I snorted, amused and annoyed simultaneously. It was just like her to send a text in which the only meaning was implied.

Yeah? I texted back. There was no reply, and I put my phone back in my pocket. My heart was beating too fast. I wanted to go somewhere I could not come back from. I wanted to break my mother's heart. I wanted her to know how it felt, this loss, this loneliness.

"I've been thinking about the boy in the lake," Avery said.

I nodded, though it took me a moment to remember the thought experiment.

"It's a matter of sunk cost," he said. "You've already bought the tux, so you've already spent the money. It's different than buying a mosquito net for someone. When you buy a mosquito net, you're not reallocating money you already spent; you're spending new money. It's a different decision process."

"But does that change the morality of it?" I asked.

"It changes the economic framework," he said.

"Do you have anything to drink?" I asked, standing up and then sitting back down.

Avery grinned. He opened his closet and retrieved a bottle of room-temperature white wine. As he poured the California Pinot Grigio into two plastic cups, I looked around the room. It was a desolate place, with blue-checkered sheets on his twin mattress; one sad, thin pillow; and a bookshelf of textbooks looming above the foot of his bed. On his desk was a prescription bottle of Adderall, an assortment of abused writing utensils, and some crumpled pieces of paper. I thought about his summer project, the new design for hospital ventilators. I thought about it as I accepted the wine from him, as he sat down on his bed close to me. He helps people breathe, I told myself. He helps people breathe.

Avery and I talked for another hour, and everything he said seemed to have a double meaning, a secret motive. The pinched look of his face that I had taken to be sadness began to seem more like hunger. I kept reminding myself that he did good things, that he cared about Peter Singer and the boy in the lake. I thought of myself as a baby, attached to a tube that was breathing for me. It was people like Avery who had kept me alive. I wanted him to shut up so we could get this done. I wanted it to be over. I wanted it to be after, wanted to be marked by what we'd done. Severed from her, standing at a distance.

When we finished the white wine, Avery began to kiss me sloppily with a prodding tongue. I kissed him back; besides my anger, I was curious. It was like reading an essay, wondering where the next jump would take you, following some man into the forays of academia. This was what women were supposed to do, I told myself. And some part of me still believed it. Some tiny, shivering thing inside me still wondered if my mother would love me more this way. If I would feel like I belonged.

I slid off my underwear and looked at Avery's face. Long, sallow, with dark eyes. His forehead creased in concentration, like he was back at the lab, working on the ventilators. I kept waiting for him to say something, to pull out a square of foil, to unroll it, to protect me. But he didn't offer anything as he dug his fingers into me. The sensation was interesting, different from when I'd done it myself.

I opened my mouth to say that he needed to wear a condom because I was not on any contraception, because I had been to every health class my school ever offered and had asked lots of questions so I knew what to expect, because I had an IQ that was so high that my mother wouldn't tell me the exact number—she said I'd never listen to a word she said if I knew—so I was certainly not going to end up *sixteen and pregnant*, but then I stopped.

I'd felt it for a moment. What she must have felt when she was low. It didn't matter, I suddenly thought. None of it mattered. Why should I worry about what would happen to me? I had no family. Mia seemed like she was a hundred miles away. The world was teetering on the edge of apocalypse. I needed something that was mine: my own surprise, my own life, my own secret. I leaned my head back, and I closed my eyes.

Mia and I had spent hours talking about sex. Who was having it and with whom, what base each couple had gotten to, and how the girls said it felt. I found it all vaguely disorienting, performative and strange, but Mia was obsessed, desperate to know when it would happen to her. I knew how she imagined it: outside, a camping trip under the stars. Or else candles, a small vase of daisies. No music, no alcohol: she wanted to pay attention. I knew what she wanted so well, I could have planned the night myself.

It hurt when he entered me. I bit down on my hand. So this was it, the end of my childhood. It felt dirty enough, that was sure. I looked up at the ceiling and imagined I was seeing the night sky. I remembered the nights I had lain with my mother, when neither of us could find sleep. And now here I was, walking away from her, closing the front door in her face.

I tried to remember something sacred from my childhood, to distract myself. Mom and me at the Museum of Natural History in Santa Barbara, when we were new to Southern California—palm trees, temperate heat, flowering bushes, wind off waves. The wet, heavy heat of the butterfly pavilion.

"Look." Mom had pointed at my shoulder. I craned my neck. A monarch butterfly was perched there. Then she pointed at my stomach. A bright-yellow butterfly was clutching the fabric of my shirt. It was paler than an egg yolk, more defined than the sun.

The third butterfly landed on my hand. Overwhelmed now, I shook my fist up and down to dislodge it, but it didn't move. This one was black and red; there was something menacing about it.

I blew on it; nothing happened. I shook my fist more violently. Still nothing. By then, I had begun to cry. I needed control over my own body, needed it to be mine and mine alone. For the first time, I realized it was possible for that control to be taken away.

Avery's hips were moving more frenetically. The noises he was making sounded like snorting laughter.

"Get them off," I'd said to my mom, hysterical now. "Mom, get them off me."

Who would have expected that something as innocent as a butterfly could cause such panic? I learned that day never to underestimate a creature in its own habitat; half its power comes from its surroundings. And I learned, too, that sometimes your only two options are to bear something or destroy it.

She swatted at my shoulder. I craned my neck and saw her push it off. It fell straight into flying and moved away from us. The one on my shirt was more difficult. She grasped it in the palm of her hand, and when she let go, I thought I saw a broken wing.

I wasn't sad when she crushed the third butterfly, but it startled me into silence. She was quick to drag its body off me, but it left behind a piece of color, soft and beautiful, like a tattoo on the back of my hand. Three stripes of red on a black background. Mom picked me up and carried me out of the pavilion, muttering, "Bastards," as we passed a sign cataloging the species.

The air outside was cool after the heat of that insect womb. We left the museum and went to the beach. Mom watched as I stood shin-deep in the gray-blue mass of the ocean, the slate slush of the sea. The waves dragging at me, cold water sucking like a greedy mouth. Mom was afraid of the ocean and did not go in. She watched me from behind the thin line where the white surf puckered on the sand.

When I walked away from the water, pulling against the swallow of the waves, Mom picked me up. Her skin was hot on mine, like the greenhouse had been. Her head blocked the wind off the ocean. I was warm in the shelter of her body, in the cedar smell of her. I was comforted knowing what she would do for me.

As Avery finally neared the end and groaned like an 18-wheeler braking, I saw the slight curl of my mother's mouth, caught between anger and dismay. I saw her lake-in-winter eyes and remembered her hand on my shoulder, her crisp-apple voice: "Please, Bernie, just wait."

I stood and pulled on my underwear. I felt sore. I felt like I needed to pee. Avery's cum was leaking out of me. It soaked the crotch of my black briefs. I had Calculus at 8:00 a.m. the next morning.

"That was fun," Avery said.

I nodded and pulled on my jeans. My face burned from where his stubble had irritated it. The pain wasn't that bad, but the fact of it made me want to cry.

"I've gotta get back home." I gave him a weak smile. For the first time that night, my lack of real enthusiasm seemed to register for him, and he gave me a searching look, probably wondering if he was inadequate. He looked at me, saw past me.

"See ya," I said when he still hadn't responded. I looked at the two now-empty Solo cups, surely reeking of the sweet wine just as my breath did, just as his had. For a moment, I experienced an odd urge—coming not from any part of myself but from a decade and a half of indoctrination or from my oppressed female ancestors—to throw out the cups for him. But I shook my head and left his room. He called out, "Bye, Bernie," as I closed the door. "See you!"

I felt strange on my feet, unsteady, walking a little more bowlegged than usual. The ground seemed to roll under me without my meaning it to. The air smelled sweet. It was less sticky than it had been. The grass was dead on the quad, curling like tiny yellow snakes. The campuses had taken a pledge not to use excess water until the drought ended. As I walked, I let myself cry. Half for the dry grass and the drought and half for me.

At home, the house was quiet. The lights were out. I dried my eyes, my cheeks. Kaleb's car wasn't in the driveway, so he must have been staying at his place. Smart man, given the mood she was in. I unlocked the front door, shed my shoes in the hall, and tiptoed into the kitchen. The kettle glowed and hummed as I switched it on and waited for it to boil. It was what my mother would have done at this juncture: made me a cup of tea. However much she would have overreacted in the morning, she was good in a crisis. Great in a crisis.

My anger was ebbing. I felt muddled: sore and tired and alone. I wished there was someone I could tell. I thought of Mia, Mom. Both absent in their own ways.

As I walked to my room, I looked in at her. She was asleep. Or, at least, her back was turned to me. I watched her rib cage until I was sure she was breathing.

For a moment, I thought about waking her, climbing into her bed, under the duvet she always slept with, even though it was almost summer. I thought of telling her what I'd done, to ease the burden of my guilt.

But then I remembered her voice: "You're too young to understand." I imagined her fingers scrolling hungrily through stories about an island she'd left almost twenty years ago. I remembered asking for my grandmother's name and hearing her blatant lies: "Margaret." "Rose." The heavy bucket of ice and the absolute dread I'd felt at being alone. My terror as I biked home to her, sure she was dead, and all the while her lying in bed, refusing to get up. I had done what I needed to do. Now we both had our secrets.

Chapter Nine

1998, County Tyrone

The flat was above the dry cleaners. Standing on the second floor, I could smell the clothes, fresh with a hint of sweetness like hay. I could hear the machines, their circular movement. The clothes turning around their dials like the second hand of a clock. What was dirty, made clean. I had come to see Conor.

I stood on his doormat, the way he'd stood on ours, moving my weight back and forth, back and forth. I still thought it was heroic, his having come for Da that day. He knew Da hated him, yet he'd seen Ina as one of his own. Had seen anyone who went to our church on Sunday as his own.

The door opened to reveal Conor's face, his nose's long shadow, the plumpness of his lips.

He was wearing jeans, baggy on his hips, and I was acutely aware of how much I'd grown up since I'd last seen him, how much older I was now. I thought of the Monday mornings I had handed him bags of empty bottles. How I'd had to avert my eyes from his gaze. Now I looked straight at him.

"I want to do something," I told him. "I want—" But I couldn't say what I wanted. It didn't matter. We both knew.

He looked at me for a long moment. Up and down my body, jeans and a jumper. Underneath, my heart pounded. His eyes were hungry. Then he stepped back and held open the door.

Inside, Conor made a pot of coffee.

"I always thought you'd come around," he said. "A woman like your ma."

I bowed my head, half a nod.

"Will I be any use?" I asked. "At this point?"

"Sure," he said. "There's still time before they sign the treaty, and there aren't many of us left now. We need all the help we can get."

The words felt heavy on me, like chain mail. Violence like a dress you donned.

"You were right to come to us," I said. "When she—it meant a lot."

"God rest her," he said.

We were both quiet for a minute. He sipped his coffee, and I did the same. The drink made my heart pound. The grit of the taste was urgent as fire. I put down my mug.

"Will I introduce you?" he asked.

Again, he looked me up and down. I didn't think he was waiting for an answer from me. I was pretty sure he was making up his own mind. For a moment, I wondered whether he wouldn't ask something of me. Some sort of sacrifice, a proof that I was not as innocent as I looked or that I could do what I was told. But then he merely shrugged.

"Tomorrow evening," he said. "I'll give you the address."

❖   ❖   ❖

There was a woman behind it, this separation from the old guard. Like the women of Cumann na mBan, who had seized buildings in Dublin during the 1916 uprising. Like the women in the seventies who had led IRA cells, who had gone on hunger strike. The women who seduced soldiers for information or brought them to deserted roads and shot them.

Like the women before her, this woman had conceived and given birth to the new movement, the latest IRA splinter group. She had watched her brother die on hunger strike the year I turned one. For her, as for me, there would never be peace.

"Who are you?" a man had asked the first time her group had set up a checkpoint.

"I'm the *real* IRA," she'd said. And so she had replaced the old one, the one that had given up fighting. The one that was ready to sign the treaty. The Real IRA would not settle for peace until Ireland was reunited. Where the last group had compromised, this one promised it never would. The history of the Irish Republican Army was this: one splinter group after another, a constant ceding to the younger, angrier generation. A consistent remodeling by its members so that from year to year, it became a new shape, a different monster.

I went to the address Conor gave me. Underneath my jeans, I wore a pair of Ina's underwear and matching bra. Made for a fifteen-year-old, they were too small on my thick body. I felt the edges of the underwear dig into my upper thighs, cut the tender sides of my pelvis. The bra would leave marks on me by the time I removed it at night, a long band around the center of me, and two knots where the straps dug in the worst. But it did not matter; I could feel her on my skin as I rang the doorbell and was led inside.

The woman had hair as dark as matted blood. She wore a black turtleneck and a blazer. I could see the bones of her face, like the stone famine cottages we'd visited on a school trip. Her cheeks as hollow as those enclosures, like she, too, was famished. Like she had inherited our ancestors' hunger.

"It wasn't really a famine," I remembered my mother telling me when I was wee. "They starved us. They wanted us to die out so they could have this island for themselves."

The woman opened her mouth to speak—her voice the husky hum of a car engine—and I felt my heart rise in my chest.

When I got home that night, Ma was standing in the kitchen in her dressing coat, with my dinner on the hot plate, her smile like an archer drawing a bow. I knew, I'd always known, that war was a woman's thing.

Tad was smoking, leaning against the elm tree near the driveway. The tree that had figured in so many of our childhood games. He didn't look at me as I approached.

"Are you avoiding me?" I asked.

He laughed. "I heard you talked to Conor. He's, like, what, your boyfriend now?"

"Are you jealous?" More scathing than I'd meant it to be.

"Ah go fuck yourself," he said.

"Just say it," I said. "Just get it over with."

"She'd have been ashamed of you."

The words landed on my chest hard, even though I had expected them.

"She can't be, though, can she?" I asked. "They made fucking sure of that."

He stubbed out his cigarette and kicked the butt into the grass. Ma would yell at him about it later. I watched him walk into the fields and then disappear into the line of trees at the edge of the meadow. I remembered the line of the border, walking the path of it more than a year ago.

Conor found me alone at the Falls one night.

I was sitting at the bar, avoiding eye contact with the regulars. I knew what they all saw when they looked at me: Ina beside me, as she had been in life.

Conor sat on the stool next to mine, ordered a glass of whiskey.

"Taking after your father, I see," he said.

112

I jerked my head up to look at him. I could tell by the way he'd said "father" what he thought of my da.

"He used to sit right there," Conor went on, nodding to a stool in the corner, just out of view of the door.

I'd never thought to imagine what went on in this pub. I knew it was where the IRA men drank; everyone knew that. I also knew it was where my father drank, had even been in here to drag him out a few times. But I had never given much thought to the men's bodies milling around here, the way the space would begin to feel cramped as they drank, the glances passed back and forth like balls in a sports game. The rally, the volley, the low rumble of their voices climbing higher as they swallowed down the hours. Ma had told me that up until the seventies, women could be denied entry into pubs in Ireland; they could be refused beer if they ordered alcohol without a male chaperone. It was considered improper for them to drink in public. So women had had to do their drinking at home or else in a snug, the screened-off room hidden in the back of the pub for that purpose. Tight corners where they could sit and remain unseen, talking in low tones while the men outside roared.

"I'm not taking after anyone," I said. "I'm just sitting here thinking."

I looked out at the bar, the men in booths and the armies of empty pint glasses on their tables. I wondered if the woman came here to drink. I hadn't heard anything since that first meeting, when we had all sworn loyalty, secrecy. I did not know what to keep secret: there was nothing that I knew.

"You're angry," Conor said. It was not a question.

The words made my whole body tense. I wanted to scoff at him, acid words rising in my throat. The fury that washed over me surprised me; I hadn't thought I was angry, but now I could feel it leaping inside me, surging like a current through a wire.

I said nothing. I swallowed down my drink. My hand was shaking, and I saw Conor notice it.

"I'll talk to her," he said. And for a second, I thought he meant Ina or my mother. Either of the women who were at the center of my rage, my despair. Then I realized that he meant the woman. I didn't say anything. I didn't want to agree to something I might regret later; I wanted him to make the decision for me so I could remain passive like I always had before. My mother putting the bottles in my hand and sending me to the door.

❖   ❖   ❖

In February, Conor said they had a job for me. He found me at the shop, waited for me outside. He didn't say anything until we had left the main street, the grocery bags heavy on my wrists.

"What is it?" I asked.

"A drive," he said.

"What'll I be driving?"

He looked at me hard. "Do you really want to know?" he asked.

I thought about it for a long minute. How I was doing this for Ina and how much she had hated this war. How it had come for her all the same. How Ma was burning with her anger and how the house was splintered and scarred. How Ina had always wanted to leave and never got the chance to. How Ma had always wanted to fight.

"No," I said. "I don't."

Finally, I had something to do. To shake off the headache that clung to me like cobwebs. To drown out the noise of my guilt and grief. I had tried to pray. There was no solace in anything except for this: my own act of violence. My own attempt to reunite us.

❖   ❖   ❖

I picked the car up in Ardglass from a man called Eoin. We met in a car park on the water, and while I waited for him in Da's car, I rolled down the window so I could breathe in the salty air. It was the smell of home, like the feel of my mother's hands. I thought of standing on the shore at low tide, how the sea receded out so far that you could walk for half an hour on the sand bed and not reach the water. Passing seaweed and seashells, imagining you were at the bottom of the ocean, underneath the Irish Sea. How alone you were out there, too far for anyone to shout to. Alone with the calling of gulls, the slow ripple of water. The smell of fish and birds and air so fresh it stung your face, salty and briny against your skin. The sky enormous, stretching everywhere. And the ground like the surface of the moon.

Eoin pulled up beside me—a redhead with gray eyes—and gave me a quick nod, as if afraid that locking eyes might turn him into the weaker sex.

"You a good driver?"

We switched cars, like girls switching clothes.

It was an old black BMW with Republic of Ireland plates. When I pressed the accelerator, I could smell the engine, and on steep inclines, the car chugged like a child downing a glass of milk or my father taking the first long sip of his Guinness. The feeling in my chest was hot and thick, raw milk straight from the udder, a sweltering desire. The brown leather wheel was sticky under my hands. My mother was at the salon, getting her hair done. I thought of the heat they would apply, the way they would turn her hair around the brush, weaving curls into her as easily as children draw the hair on stick figures.

It is a two-and-a-half-hour drive from Ardglass to Donegal. More with the border checkpoints. I forced myself to drive slowly, but my foot was trigger-happy on the accelerator, my hand lustful on the gear stick. The air smelled like frost and mulch and pine. And the white line on the road was like the border Ma had shown us, the line that existed only on a map.

As I drove, I thought of my mother. I thought of my brothers. But mostly, I thought of Ina. Her name was in my head, always. On the tip of my tongue, lodged in the back of my throat: Ina, Ina, Ina. Her bright face, her cheeks so pink and flushed. Her glee whenever Ma went into Omagh to shop, how she would walk with her face pressed up against the shop windows even when, four doors down, a brick had been thrown through one. She had bought ribbons to tie in her hair, dark-green ribbons, like a pine tree, like a real republican. I thought of that old Eliot line: "breeding Lilacs out of the dead land, mixing Memory and desire." A stanza we'd memorized in school, a poem not written for me. I could not see the wilderness: the thin tree branches gilded with ice, the sunset casting the road in a golden haze. I could only see Ina. Her face the yellow of the sunlight, her head thrown back in laughter or in pain.

When the sun was gone and the sky was drained of any last traces of light, I pulled over on the side of the road. Outside the claustrophobia of the car, I breathed in the fresh night air, like black velvet in my lungs. I looked at the boot, closed tight like a fist. For a moment, I imagined opening it, seeing whatever was inside, the thing I was transporting, the true meaning of this drive. I stretched out my hand and then dropped it. I did not dare open it, did not dare look at what I was doing. They had told me to drive this car, so I would drive it. I got back in.

Enda had taught himself to drive in Ma's car. On dark nights, he'd take wee Ina, Tad, and me out on his practice rounds. To make us scream, he used to turn off the headlights so that we sang over the swoops and hills of Tyrone in the dead of darkness, unseeing and unseen. With the lights off, we saw the difference our presence made in the world. How empty our absence was. Now I drove with headlights on, eyes on the road, taking no chances.

I listened to the radio, in and out of stations, BBC to RTÉ, the buzz of the accents changing as it went local to international, Irish to British. The news from Northern Ireland announced to the UK as if it were the moon. I thought of the triangle of my bladder and how it was rounded below my stomach. The hollowness of my stomach and how it was concave atop my bladder. The hunger at the back of my throat that felt almost like nausea. The stiffness of my upper back and the tension in my hands from gripping the steering wheel so tight. I did not think about what was in the boot.

At the border checkpoint, a soldier loomed in my headlights, waved for me to slow the car. The same submachine gun that they all held, the same camouflaged fatigues. They were all the same: identical twins, mirror images, doppelgängers. It made them seem inhuman, like they were parts of a machine. Behind him, there was a table, papers scattered. It struck me how makeshift the checkpoint was, nothing like the passport booths I'd seen in films. Nothing like it would be to cross into a real country.

For an insane, suspended second, my foot hovered above the clutch, and I wondered whether I should accelerate into him, charge through the checkpoint, leaving his torn body behind me. For all I knew, it had been he who set the bomb that killed Ina. Didn't all the Brits moonlight as paramilitaries? And if it wasn't him, it was some friend of his, someone he laughed with down at his local.

But I was not in charge of these decisions. Someone else had chosen the best course of action, and it was my job to follow the road she'd given me. I slowed to a halt, my heart beating in my chest like feet dancing something fast and manic. Like the sound of Ina's and my trainers as we ran down the roads in summer, racing to some predetermined end.

"Evening." The soldier had bent to look in the driver's side. His face was blurred through dusty glass, and I rolled down the window to get a better look at him. A man a little older than Enda. His face all jaw, jowls like tennis balls, and the whites of his eyes the color of stained teeth.

"Good evening." I kept my voice steady, none of my country lilt, none of the edge that the Kane women all spoke with. "Long night, is it?"

I tried to look at him the way Ina used to look at men. The way she would have looked at this one, even as he rested his hand on his gun like a pervert on the back of a bus. That daring, full look she'd give, like she was ready for any- and everything. I tried to look at him like I knew how to help him with a long night.

"Seen worse, sure enough."

He didn't seem worried about me: a teenager alone in a car edging on midnight. He didn't seem about to ask me to step out, to open the boot. But he didn't seem like he was about to let me go either.

"Would you be visiting your boyfriend?"

I was wearing Ina's dress, soft and silky against my chest and thighs. He was not looking at my face or at my breasts but at the space between my jaw and the neckline of my dress, at the hollow of my throat.

"I'm visiting my sister," I told him. "It's been a while since I've seen her, and, well. We just got the call that she's had a baby."

I let the thought fill me with exhilaration, so that I smiled a real, full smile. Ina's smile. How lovely it was going to be to see her baby, I thought. How beautiful she would be.

"Well, isn't that lovely." The soldier's gaze had broken away from my throat. He looked out into the night ahead of me, as if he could see the child from this far off. "And where did you say she lived now?"

"Donegal." The word was like the thing I was doing: beautiful and rugged and free. It tasted like salt and fire and lipstick on my lips. Another thrill ran through me as I said it, and I smiled at my soldier. I wanted to lean out of the car and kiss him, and then I wanted to take the gun from his holster and shoot him in the head.

❖ ❖ ❖

When I delivered the car, I had trouble stepping out of the driver's seat. I felt like I was welded to the machine, my partner, my shell, my encasement. I had not thought of my having to part with it. Had imagined myself driving it always, down some forbidden road, to some unwitting end. Finally, I stepped out into the night air, running my hand along the roof of the car's body, like you might rub the flank of a mare.

Two men approached, eyeing the shape of me in my dress. I recognized Aidan; he was second-in-command to the woman. They grunted their thanks and climbed into the vehicle that had felt like mine. It felt like they were climbing inside my body. They drove the car a few houses down, pulling into another driveway and onto the grass behind the house.

I'd known not to expect an explanation; I didn't want one. But still, I felt their grunts as punches on my already fragile body. They seemed to exude violence, their eyes dead and angry. I shivered in the short-sleeve dress I had worn. Where was she now, the woman who was running this? What had she given me to do?

❖　❖　❖

When I got back to Tyrone the next day, I was not glad to see my mother, her hair still perfect from the salon, her smile showing all her teeth. I felt ill, fluish, submarine. Like I had slept outside in the skimpy dress I was wearing and caught a February chill.

"Well done, Bríd," Ma said, her hand on my shoulder like the lead on a dog. I could feel her pushing me under, deeper and deeper into the mess she had always wanted for me.

I went upstairs to my room, and for two days, I tossed and turned under my bedsheets, fighting a fever.

I woke on the third day, still submerged under the water of my dream state, and did not immediately remember the darkness of the drive, the feeling of the car moving under me like a living thing, the closed lid of the boot, sleek and black and shining in the moonlight. When I did finally remember, it was with the saltwater wave of absolute despair that I had felt only one other time in my life. I should have known—church had taught me—after the pleasure comes the guilt.

"They've been ringing for you," Ma said when I came downstairs for a cup of tea.

"Send them up," I said.

It was Conor who came that afternoon. I sat up in my bed, and he sat on the foot of Ina's bed, and I did not know if he was thinking about the parts of him touching the last remaining parts of her, but I was.

"Are you ill?" he asked.

"It's nothing," I said.

"You did good," he said. "A man wouldn't have been able to do what you did, getting by the checkpoint."

I nodded, remembering Ina's dress, pale pink and silky. The way I had cocked my head at the soldier and spoken in my best radio accent for him. My cheeks still stinging from where I had slapped them to induce color.

I didn't say anything. I was afraid he was going to tell me what I had really done. I was afraid he was going to ask me to do more. I was afraid that, if he did, I would say yes. I would climb higher and higher until I fell. My leg bounced uncontrollably on the bed frame.

"Well, you'll be wanted when you're better," he said. "We've got another job."

"Sure," I said. "Soon as I'm better." I stilled my leg and began to drum my fingers against the bedspread instead, the patter soft as rain on a roof. I felt that to be still in my body at that moment would have killed me.

Conor nodded and stood. He kept looking at me for one long moment. I had never noticed how calculating his gaze was. He reminded me of a vulture, circling its prey.

"I'll be seeing you," he said, but it sounded like a question.

And then he was gone.

I got up out of bed and looked out the window, out to where Ina and I used to race each other in the summers. My heart matched the rhythm my fingers had made, the soft patter of rain.

The news came five days later, like that was the incubation period for this certain kind of virus. I was at Sláns, the pub where we used to work, drinking tea, talking to Harry behind the bar.

Sometimes, when I'd come into the pub during the summer when we worked there, I could tell that Ina had recently left. A hair tie she'd left behind, the smell of violets, a mess in the sink anyone else would have been fired for. Now it did not smell like Ina at all. It smelled like fish chowder and ale.

Two men were sitting at a table behind me—I could just see them out of the corner of my eye—their voices barely audible, like a radio station coming in and out of range.

"'Course it was them," one said. "Since when have they been careful so?"

"But women and children?" the other asked. "When they've called a ceasefire? When they say the agreement will be signed any moment?"

"Sure they only call ceasefires so they can end them. It's always peace talks and never any peace."

"It'll have been tourists. Anyone'd know not to stay there."

The man on the right was eating shepherd's pie. Some of the potato was stuck in his beard, filling in the crevices between his whiskers.

"Anyone but politicians," he said. "That place is chock-full of them."

"Did something happen?" I asked Harry. He was wiping down the bar top.

"Something's always happening," he said.

"Down in Armagh?"

"Over in Donegal, on the border. A botched explosion on the coast."

I should have been used to the feeling of shock by then, the world falling out from under me. I wasn't.

"Dead?" I asked. The word came out in a rasp.

"Two or three injured. One lady was pregnant, they're saying."

"Was it an accident?"

"Aren't they all?" Harry asked. "Those feckers never can shoot straight."

The bar swam before me. Guilt and fear rose, persistent as a corpse floating to the surface of a river. They were talking about me. They were talking about what I'd done.

I took Da's car out to Donegal, saying I was going to visit Enda. As I drove, I tried not to remember the other car, following a similar route. Tried to banish the darkness with the daylight. On the coast, I felt the air off the sea. Cold and thick with salt, it stuck to my skin, sunk into my clothing, covering me in its impurity. I wondered which house Enda lived in, how close he was to the ocean. It felt strange to be his sister, to share blood with someone who was now a stranger.

The hotel was on the water. A pretty, old building, with flowers in the front garden that were untouched by the destruction. As I rounded the corner, my heart pounded in my chest, heaving like the sea in a storm; I waited to see what I had done.

The grass in the back was covered with dust and brick, sandcastles of ruin. Several doors were blown off, and a room on the second floor—the room I was sure would have been the best one, facing the sea, with big french windows—had had its facade ripped off. I could see the bed still lying there, submissive, the canopy twisting in the wind, the linens aflutter. The bathroom door was wrenched open, barely holding on to its frame. I thought of the skeletons in biology class, their goofy nudity, bizarre grins. The rooms on either side of it were ruined too.

There was blue tape wound around the scene like stitches sewing up a wound. In places, the tape sagged, too worn to hold itself taut. I was not the only person who had stopped to look, but I must have been the only person who had driven to see it. I walked back to my car and put my head on the steering wheel. Then I drove to the hospital and looked up at the windows, boxes of small light for the people inside.

There was a stack of newspapers in the entryway, and I picked one up. On the front of the local paper was a picture of her. The other people who'd been injured had been released from hospital already; only she remained in critical condition. She looked a bit like me, dark hair to her shoulders, light eyes. A plain, simple face, with small features. She was from Warsaw, Poland. Why had she come here? Who visits a war zone on vacation? I thought about the baby squirming inside her stomach, shell-shocked by the strength of the explosion. Thought of it being born, already scarred and angry, coming into the world like a veteran returning from war.

Had it been me who'd done that? I couldn't know. My contribution had been lost, a thread in the tapestry of chaos. It could have been a test, that drive across the border. The boot could have been empty, the group just seeing what I was made of. Or it could have been full. It could have been this.

I thought of Ina, her yellow dress, the sun of her spin. I thought of the hollow hotel, like a dollhouse, cracked open for the world to see. I thought of this woman with her belly swollen, child inside. I imagined the facade of her stomach ripped off, the child laid bare. I wondered if they would survive.

❖   ❖   ❖

I drove to the address my parents had given me, Enda's house. A small thing, about as big as two rooms in the house we'd grown up in. The table was neat and set when Siobhán let me in. She smiled wide to see me, and I noticed again her flat chest and soft hair and the apron she had wrapped around her body.

Enda sat at the table. He looked tired but happy too. Like it was a relief to finally show his exhaustion. I felt I shouldn't look at his face, felt that something private and naked was revealed there. The wall lifted off a bedroom.

We sat at the table and had tea. I ate two scones, and Siobhán stood to get me another. I hadn't realized how hungry I was.

"How are they at home?" Enda asked.

I didn't say anything. The pastry in my mouth had turned to glue, and I tried to swallow it down with my tea, now cold.

"Bríd," he said, and I looked up at him.

"Fine," I said.

"If I were you," he said, "I'd get out of there. Far enough away so you forget what it tastes like in that house."

"What does it taste like?" I laughed.

His smile was like a cut across his face. "I don't know. Steel, I'd say. Like the barrel of a gun in your fucking mouth."

I did not let myself cry as I drove home. To pity myself at that moment seemed a worse violence than the one I had just witnessed. The one I might have caused. But I felt a hot and heavy grief engulf me. It wasn't the pregnant woman I felt sorry for. It was the Ina I remembered now, the one who had despised all of this. Who had looked at me with frightened eyes when I talked about the conflict. Who had only ever wanted peace: a world of nonsectarian dance clubs and Sunday mornings without Mass.

If I'd been able to talk to her now, to tell her what I'd done, would she forgive me? Or was she looking down on me from the sky, shaking her head, turning away? Like that night when she'd run out the door, not looking at me as she left.

My hand was shaking as I parked the car, turned off the engine. I felt the two black roads stretch out in front of me. I could choose to go deeper, or I could choose to walk away. I could not do what I wanted: I could not turn around, go back in time, and change what I had done.

Upstairs, I went to my mother's room, knocked, entered.

She was sitting on her bed with her back to the door. She motioned for me to come brush her hair. I sat behind her, my thighs against hers. There were no knots in her hair. There was nothing to detangle. I ran the brush through it anyway. My hands had stopped trembling, my adrenaline calming me, readying me for a fight in which I might need steady fists.

"Did you hear about Donegal?" I asked.

She was quiet.

"A pregnant woman, Ma," I said. "She's in hospital."

"Sure she'll be all right."

We were quiet.

"It could have been me," I said. "I've no idea."

I had a hand on her bare shoulder. Her skin felt hot, feverish. It was like she was burning up from the inside.

"It's not your job to have ideas," she said. "It's your job to punish them."

She began to tremble. At first, I thought she was crying, but when I looked at her face in the mirror before us, I could see it was anger, her bottomless rage at what had been done to Ina. She was like a blur of red and yellow in front of me, hot as fire and ready to kill. I remembered then that she had seen the body.

"I've done my part," I said. "I got revenge."

She scoffed. "You think that's enough? You think that's all she's worth? You've only gotten started, Bríd."

I could see it now: she was insatiable. We could have burned a hundred cities to the ground; it wouldn't have been enough. Ina was worth a hundred pregnant women, a hundred unborn children. And it was my job to make the trade. It was my job to try to satisfy the loss. In the end, it came down to this: she could not stand what had happened. I could not make it right. I would have to fight and fight. I would have to lose myself, kill myself. And still she would not be satisfied. I knew I couldn't do it.

"Ma," I said. "I think I need to go."

I hadn't known I would say it until the words were out, but once I did, I knew it was the truth. I had to leave all of this: her grief, her rage, her shaky hand gripping my shoulder as she tried to direct me. I was already halfway gone. The other road would only take me deeper, darker. It would only turn me into her: pinched, hungry eyes; broken heart; anger throbbing through her like a pulse. I did not want to be my mother.

"Don't be silly, girl." She said it quickly, like she'd known what I was going to say.

There was a pause.

"Why should you get to go," she asked, "when she can't?"

A black stone between my stomach and my ribs. The weight of Ina holding me down, holding me there. How much I'd envied her when she was alive. How much I'd loved and hated her. How beautiful she'd been. Ma had turned around; the brush was clinging to her hair.

"And how is that my fault?" I could feel the stretch of my vocal cords. A pained pitch they weren't used to, something close to a yell.

She opened her mouth and spoke. Five words like a warm hand pushing me over a cliff. Like a knife between my breasts.

And I didn't think about what I was doing; I just did what I'd been wanting to. I slapped her hard across the face. My hand a whip on her soft cheek. The noise like a plate cracking down the middle.

I left her room. It had taken only ten minutes.

Down the hall, I packed a suitcase full of Ina's clothes. The remains of her makeup, powder foundation so worn down that a hole gaped in the center. Her Walkman. Her hair ties. Her jewelry I stuffed into a sock and packed next to her underwear, but her gold necklace, the one with her name on it, I clasped around my neck, and her passport—as well as my own—I took with me. Only once did I have to stop, standing over my suitcase, to take huge, gasping breaths, struggling for air in the still room. But I could feel Ina beside me, whispering in my ear, telling me to go.

The next morning, before the sun rose, I took the bus to Dublin Airport. I did not say goodbye to Tad or to my father. I did not say goodbye to my mother. And the whole drive, I thought about the last thing my mother had said to me, the five words it had taken to sever us.

"Did you know," Ina once said, "that you can never really touch another person? There are always air molecules between your skin and their skin, between you and them."

Chapter Ten

2016, Los Angeles County

The week that Riley came home from rehab, I woke with a now-familiar nausea spreading the length of my body. I puked in the bathroom, knees coming down hard on the tiled floor in my haste. I ran the shower so Mom and Kaleb wouldn't hear my retching, and then I got in, rinsed my hair and face, steadied myself with a hand on the shower wall. My braids, wet down my back, felt like two snakes. I had felt unwell for a while now: a dark fear that felt like a lingering hangover. All bright lights, loud noises, and a churning in my stomach.

I stared at my reflection in the bathroom mirror. My baby face. Eyebrows too serious for a teenager. I thought I could see the spread of Mom's smile, a ghost on my lips. There was something else on my face, too, something possessed. My hologram-thin skin, the greenish tint. Was it my father I was seeing, his features peeking through?

I felt like something was creeping up on me, some monster lurking out of sight, waiting to pounce. A sense of foreboding that reminded me of the active-shooter drills at school. The shadows in the dark classroom. The hot, cramped spaces under the desks.

When I was younger and knew a drill was coming up, I used to beg my mom to let me skip school. I'd hide under the sink in my bathroom, clutching the metal pipe. She would come into the room with me, shut the door, and sit beside me. It felt like we spent hours in there, her singing or talking, doing anything she could think of to calm me down. My mouth trying to form words, mute from fear and anger. Sometimes, after, she would take me to the shelter with her, and I would help her pass out the snacks and make the beds. It made us both feel better, being there. Like we were part of something larger than our strange dyad, like there was something to fall back on when we were both afraid. But other times, when I hid under the sink, my cheeks wet with tears, Mom would insist I go to school, that cloudy, faraway look in her eyes that I knew meant she was somewhere else. She said it was important that I be prepared, that those drills might one day save my life.

"This is a bad country," she would tell me. "It's better to know that now. You have to learn to protect yourself." It was very different from the messages my classmates got at home: calm assurances that nothing bad would ever happen to them.

But Mom was right. Last December, there had been a mass shooting and attempted bombing in San Bernardino, less than half an hour away from us. Homegrown terrorism, it had been called. Fourteen killed, over twenty injured, at a Christmas party. I wondered how many active-shooter drills the victims had done, if being prepared had helped them in the end.

"You normally don't see a woman involved," I'd said, watching the news a few nights after the shooting. The suspects, a husband and wife, had been killed in a shoot-out with the police.

"Sure you do," Mom had said.

"Like when?" I asked.

"Sure you do," Mom said again. I'd rolled my eyes.

Standing in the bathroom now, thinking I might throw up again, I felt like I was back in one of those shooter drills. Like I was at that Christmas party, beginning to feel uneasy, hearing bangs and asking that most American question: Fireworks or gunfire? I felt like I was hiding under my desk, seeing my science teacher open the door. His face covered, his eyes terrifying and terrified. I both recognized and did not recognize him. I both feared what was happening to me and refused to see it. I flushed the toilet, left the bathroom.

Days passed, and the nausea did not subside. I started skipping breakfast, waking shaky and nauseous in the afternoon. I threw up halfway through my comparative government AP, running out of the room in the middle of a section. Mia still wasn't at school, but she had begun to text me back more frequently. I spent hours on my texts back to her, making sure to word them correctly, to be caring without being pushy, to be kind without seeming too intimate. We didn't mention what had happened between us. She sent me short messages, updates, a funny picture. But it felt like we were miles away from each other, like she was a soldier sending letters home from war.

Mom wanted to take me to the doctor. Though I'd managed to hide the worst of my illness from her, she'd noticed my decrease in appetite, my shakiness, my exhaustion. I told her I was just nervous about Riley and Mia, about senior year next year, about the SAT. I was getting good at hiding things from her: what I had said to Mia, what I had done with Avery, what was happening inside me now.

I came downstairs early on the first day of June. I'd lain awake all that night, wondering. My body felt raw, exposed, like a body of water raked over by the wind. My insides felt heavy, the way they had when I first heard the news about Riley. But I was starting to think that this might have nothing to do with him, that it might be something happening inside me, something that was only mine. By the time the sky began to lighten, I knew that I needed an answer. I dressed in jeans and a T-shirt, braided my hair. Threw up only once in the bathroom. Put on a face that I thought resembled bravery.

"Where are you going so early, Duck?" Mom and Kaleb were sitting at the kitchen table, drinking coffee, doing the crossword. Like nothing in the world was wrong. Seeing the two of them together made me miss Mia, a sensation that traveled all the way to my fingers and toes, the feeling of having been underwater for too long, of dying for the oxygen you used to take for granted.

"I've got to run to CVS," I said, casting about for a suitable excuse. "There's a rally against fossil fuels. I was thinking of going with some people from Climate Club."

Mom smiled. "Good," she said. "You haven't been to anything like that in a while."

It was true; last year, I had been to a rally almost every weekend. Now it was like I'd been swallowed by my own life, completely self-absorbed. I remembered those long walks with hundreds or thousands of people beside me, Mia and me with our fingertips discolored and smelling of Sharpie. The sense of being good and pure and right. Mia's smile as big as the avenues we walked down.

"I need to get some markers and poster board," I said. "For signs."

Kaleb smiled at me. "Do you want to take my car?"

"We can drive you," Mom said.

My skin suddenly felt itchy. "It's okay," I said. "I can go myself."

"No, it'll be nice," Mom said. "A morning drive."

❖   ❖   ❖

Kaleb drove us to CVS, his hand out the window, the turns he took languid, the movement of the car peaceful. I played a Tupac song on his iPhone: an ode to Tupac's mother.

I remembered something Kaleb had told me a few months ago, when Mom had been low after the San Bernardino shooting. "She's a mystery," he'd said. "Sometimes it hurts to be around her. Like rubbing your hand against a piece of rough wood. The splinters sting then and they sting after."

"I don't know why," I'd said.

"I don't know if she knows." He'd been showing me a stir-fry recipe, chopping up a yellow bell pepper. He'd been taking care of me again.

"But you love her, don't you?" I looked up at his face, nervous. I felt an urge to reach out and grab his wrist, to hold on to him.

"Yes, I love her. She is the weirdest, most wonderful woman. But it's hard to be with someone who is always staring in at themselves, wondering what the hell they're made of. It is a privilege to get to decide who you are. And sometimes I—" He stopped and gave me a thin smile. He wasn't going to say it, whatever it was.

"For now we see in a mirror, dimly, but then we shall see face-to-face," I said.

I knew my Bible verses. Though I'd never believed, I'd always felt that I read the Bible more carefully than Mom did, as if she didn't even want to know what it said. As if she was reading it for some other reason.

"Corinthians," Kaleb had said. "Exactly."

But Mom was not a mystery today. She was not a woman who would give you splinters. Today, she was the strong, bright sun, laughing in the passenger seat, her hand on Kaleb's hand, turning around to tell me something funny, her smile radiant and full, her blue eyes soft as an early-morning sky. I felt sorry, then, for what I'd done. And I felt very, very scared. It seemed impossible that I had ever tried to hurt her.

Kaleb pulled up outside the pharmacy.

"I'll be right back," I told them, jumping out of the car before my mother could think of joining me.

Inside, I kept my eyes on the carpeted floor. The holiday aisle had been redone for Pride: rainbow sunglasses and bandannas. I reached up and touched the rainbow tassel on a party hat. The shimmery, flimsy substance reminded me of Mia: the fluttering, timid feeling she gave me.

I came back out with the paper box double-bagged and stuffed it in my backpack. It was just to make sure, I told myself. There was no way this was what I thought it was.

"No luck?" Mom asked, looking at the place where the small bag had disappeared into my backpack.

"They were out of poster board," I said.

❖   ❖   ❖

On top of managing the shelter staff, Mom prepared and served dinner at the shelter once a week, and I almost always went with her to help, pouring milk into the corn-bread pan, beating the eggs, making classic American recipes for crowds of people, quadrupling the measurements. Sometimes, standing beside her at the long, plastic folding table, I felt so claustrophobic that I could scream. I wanted to run to find someone young and bury my face in the pungent odor of their immaturity, wanted to sneak three cigarettes and leave the stench on the cuffs of my flannel so Mom would smell it when I got home. But sometimes, standing beside my mother, I felt pride rising inside me, like a giant bird in my chest taking flight. The thing between us unbreakable and constant, stronger than any rope or handcuff. Me and her, her and me. I pitied the world that did not have her.

That afternoon, when we got to the shelter, I scanned the room, pretending not to notice Mom's gaze on me. We both knew who I was looking for.

I went about helping set up the plastic forks and plates. Her body next to mine made my skin prickle. It was like a needle on my flesh, her gaze on me, her arm so close to mine. I kept moving my backpack from one side of the table to the other, keeping it close enough that I could touch it with my foot, grab it in an instant. I didn't let it out of my sight.

We worked quietly together, laying dinner out on the table, and then JoJo rang the dinner bell, and Mom began to serve the food, smiling and chatting with the residents. I took advantage of the opportunity and snuck outside, slinging my backpack over my shoulder.

❖   ❖   ❖

The Mississippi Man's eyes were a glint of glass in the dark. *Damon's* eyes, I corrected myself. I knew it wasn't right to call him whatever I wanted, like I was some kind of God.

His long, thin fingers extended a cigarette to me. I shook my head.

"Of course," he said. "The director's daughter doesn't smoke." The Ds rolling off his tongue, the dirtiest of letters.

"Not 'of course,'" I said. "Not all daughters become their mothers."

He looked out across the street, exhaled fumes like car exhaust. There was a piece missing from his nose, on his right nostril, like a chink in armor. I thought of Achilles being dipped into the River Styx by his heel, his only vulnerable part.

On the other side of the one-way street was a parking garage where the woman always waved away Mom's money. But I knew that an ex-con parking a borrowed car there before a job interview wouldn't be as lucky. That's how it always is; when you're up, people raise you higher. When you're low, they rub in the dirt. Mom and Kaleb had taught me that, taught me about Occupy Wall Street and wealth inequality, about the American dream and the American myth, about the criminal justice system, how there were few criminals and absolutely no justice. The prison that most of the men at the shelter had come out of was just around the corner. They still had to walk by those gates most days, no matter how long ago they'd been released.

"You're lucky you're not from here," I said after we had stood without speaking for several minutes, me listening to the sound of his deep inhales.

"How do you reckon?"

"It isn't good to be stuck where you were born," I said. But once I said it, I wondered whether it wasn't worse to be stuck far away from home.

"Who says I'm stuck?" he asked.

He stubbed out his first cigarette and put another in his mouth. I felt slightly hysterical, knowing what I did not know, what I would have to find out. The CVS bag in my backpack. The paper box, white and pink. I watched the unlit cigarette hang out of his mouth, caught on the line where the wet part of his lip met the dry part. It was so careless, so casual.

When Damon lit his second cigarette, it burned the orange of highway cones, made that sizzling sound in the air like a warning. I felt his inhale within my own lungs, the spiderwebs igniting across my body.

His face was like a dog-eared book, a wrinkled bedsheet. It lolled into a smile by accident, unintentional and unfelt. He was, I thought, a life compacted, earned, experienced; he had really lived while I was just beginning. He was not afraid to tell me things—what he had done, who he had been—his fearlessness a contrast to Mom's superstitious avoidance of the past. In that moment, I could have cut out my own liver for him, could have climbed inside his skin. Anything to be him and not me. To be free of the box in my bag, of my suspicion. The fear was like a stampede inside me, my heartbeat like gunshots.

"Actually, can I have one?" I asked, nodding to his cigarette.

He laughed out the carcinogens. "Oh, no," he repeated, "the director's daughter doesn't smoke."

That's what they all thought. They never worried about me falling into this kind of life. People rarely do worry about girls with loving mothers, but wasn't I proof that we could fuck up just as badly? The mistake was in Mom's assumption that the shelter had taught me enough. The runny cough of lung cancer. The toothless grin of meth. The addict's lurch when the heroin hits, knees bent under the weight of their ascendancy. She thought she'd properly scared me, without realizing that fear is another form of desire. Of course I had walked right into the danger. Of course I had wanted it. Didn't she know that too much love could drown you just as well as neglect could? That was what I had done to Mia, how I had lost her. I had loved her too hard, too fast, too much.

I still found it red hot—addiction, desperation, emergency—though I knew it only led one way. That is what is so attractive, the fall we've been waiting for. The release. I longed for the legitimacy of an alcoholic, the inevitability of an addict. A life in which nobody could depend upon you. In which no decision was necessary. And I longed for Damon, so full of lies that it felt like he was telling the truth.

"I'm not who you think I am," I said, still eyeing his cigarette. "I'm not some little girl. I think I might be—"

"Bernie?" Mom was closing the door to the shelter behind her, bag slung over her shoulder.

I swallowed the word, my confession.

"I'm ready," I said, picking up my backpack. It felt heavier than it should.

"You didn't need to come," she said as we got into the car.

"I know. But I was bored at home."

"I don't like you talking to him," she said.

"I know," I said again. I rubbed my pointer and middle fingers together on my right hand, imagining I held a cigarette there. I did not want the cigarette. I wanted the fingers.

❖   ❖   ❖

Back home, my heart raced with anticipation. I would go straight to my room, open the box, have it over with. In less than ten minutes, I would know.

But I'd forgotten we had dinner plans, as had Mom. When we walked in, we found Kaleb at the dinner table talking to a young woman with very curly blonde hair and pinkish skin. She was drinking a glass of white wine, and Kaleb was drinking a can of seltzer. When Mom saw the two of them chattering happily away, she looked murderous.

"You're late," Kaleb whispered as he got up to kiss Mom hello. I wondered if I could slip away, pretend I had some summer reading assignment and creep upstairs, but Kaleb had set four places at the table and was beginning to serve the food.

"Bernie," he said. "I've been bragging to Clarissa about your forays into philosophy."

Which meant I couldn't leave.

Kaleb had made a vegetarian chili, which Clarissa oohed and aahed over even though it only took twenty-five minutes to make and was just a couple of cans of beans and tomatoes mashed around with a wooden spoon. Mom poured herself an exceptionally large glass of white wine and sat down next to Kaleb. I was stuck on the other side of the table with Clarissa.

"Clarissa is studying radical altruism," Kaleb told me. "You know, like Peter Singer."

I made a hum of interest, trying to avoid being rude while also making it clear that I took my mother's side in all things. Except when it was me against Mom, of course. But if she didn't like Clarissa, neither did I.

"What do you do?" Clarissa asked Mom, either oblivious or indifferent to her annoyance.

"I run the Pomona Valley Homeless Shelter," Mom said.

"I think you're forgetting a word." Clarissa laughed. I looked at her out of the corner of my eye. "Isn't it the Pomona Valley *Christian* Homeless Shelter?"

"Yes, it's a bit of a mouthful." Mom's smile was a death sentence.

"Cheese?" I offered, holding up a bag of Trader Joe's cheddar shreds.

"I'm vegan." Clarissa turned back to Mom. "I guess I just feel like religion doesn't really have a place in nonprofit work?" She said the statement like a question.

Mom took the bag of cheese out of my hand and began to load up her bowl with it, making eye contact with Clarissa while the shards fell on top of her chili. She easily used up half the bag. I knew what she was thinking, could feel the fiery reaction on the tip of her tongue. *And what have you done lately for your community? And what is it you believe in?* She was skeptical of anyone who criticized belief when they had none of their own. It was easier, she said, to stand for nothing than to stand for something, for your own traditions, for your own ideals. She had found the shelter through our church, I knew, and she had taken to them both, not as things to understand or analyze but as things to serve, places to carry out her worship without asking questions. "It's not my place to wonder," she'd said to me more than once. "My mind has its limits. It's my place to do what is asked of me."

"Ina is an incredible asset to the shelter," Kaleb said, quickly intervening. "While we academics sit around all day talking theory, she is on her feet making a difference. And I think there's a lot to be said for academics taking a more practical approach, learning from people who are on the ground doing the work."

That shut Clarissa up, and the rest of dinner passed as smoothly as could be hoped for. But when Clarissa finally left, Mom wouldn't speak to Kaleb, except to say under her breath: "What a bitch." Kaleb told Mom she was being immature—he wasn't wrong—and Mom slammed the door to her bedroom, which pretty much proved his point.

In my room, I stalled for a while, doing nothing on my computer. Refusing to unzip my backpack and see what it contained. When I couldn't stand it any longer, I went downstairs for a cup of tea.

From the hall, I could see that Kaleb and Mom were sitting on the couch together. In the half-light, they were intertwined. My mother's head leaning against Kaleb's chest as he stroked her hair. The sound of him laughing, and her talking, and him laughing more.

I stood in the doorway for a moment, watching them.

Back upstairs, I held the tea in my hands for a long moment, letting the mug warm me. I said a Hail Mary, like Mom had taught me, feeling foolish for praying when I didn't believe. Then I went into the bathroom and sat on the toilet, waiting. The bathroom was small and quiet around me, dark and secret and fearful.

I watched the image appear in the fateful little window. The stick balanced on the rim of the sink. The pink cross, like a tiny crucifix.

Why was it that I felt most alone upon learning that I was not alone? When the plus sign appeared, I wanted so horribly to be entwined with someone, to be part of something larger, a family. And yet I was. That was the very thing I was cowering from.

I thought of the thing as an extension of Avery—his persistence, his indecency, the way he considered my body a sheath for his own, a depository. And yet the question at hand could not have felt more remote from him. It would have been like asking his permission to pass a bowel movement, to eat a chocolate cake.

I went into my room, lay on my bed, and googled options. "Climate change will profoundly affect the health of every child alive today," a headline said. Someone in Mumbai was suing his parents for giving birth to him. I remembered what Kaleb had said, that to be able to choose was a privilege. I knew the truth, the one truth, the only truth: whatever I did, I was going to waste a life.

I went back downstairs and ate two grape Popsicles standing at the kitchen counter. Mom and Kaleb must have gone to bed. The living room was empty. I went back to my room. I had always thought that you were a daughter until you were a mother. I had broken it, then, the mold of my daughterhood. I would grow too large to fit the role.

I knew what I would decide, what I had to decide. But it would mean something much more serious than what I'd done with Avery. I'd wanted to push my mother away, but not this far; I knew how she felt about abortion. I could already feel her disapproval like a slap across my face. An icy chill of the severance yet to come. Not the excavation of the fetus—the procedure I would undergo or the pills I would swallow—but the fallout of Mom and me. Two bodies plummeting, an inevitable drop. If she never learned the truth, we would be separated by the secret forever. If I told her, nothing between us would ever be the same again.

PART TWO

Chapter Eleven

1998, Miami, Florida, United States

She stood at the currency exchange desk, her back to me, rummaging for something in her purse. Her hair was long and blonde, with beach-wave curls. Her sweater was yellow. I felt tiny pearls of sweat on my forehead.

When I was standing before her, and she had turned to look at me, I saw that it was not Ina. Her skin was tan; her nose was pierced. Her fingernails were painted red, the polish chipped. And there was something haughty in her expression, something I had never seen on Ina's face. The long arc of her nose and high forehead exacerbated the impression.

"Yeah?" Her American accent was toneless and nasally.

"Sorry," I said. "I've money to exchange?"

I had five hundred British pounds in the pocket of my jeans, money I'd taken from the safe in my father's office. I handed over the tall bills with "Northern Bank" printed on them. And Ina's double handed me back American dollars, thin green sheets of paper that would buy me my new life.

"Thanks," I said.

"Welcome to Miami." She smiled, and I felt my heart flutter as I saw the ghost of Ina's grin on her face.

The first flight out of Dublin had been to New York; the first connecting flight from New York had been to Miami. All I'd wanted was somewhere warm, somewhere distant. Somewhere that would feel like a dream until I had my feet on the ground. In the end, it had been so easy to leave. I wondered why it had taken me so long.

❖   ❖   ❖

The lobby of the motel was painted a greenish brown. The receptionist chewed gum with her mouth open and took the cash I handed her.

"Your name?" she asked, squinting at my necklace. "Ira?"

"Ina," I said automatically. It made me shiver, the name I'd always wished was mine. The person I'd always wanted to be. It felt, oddly, like the truth.

My bed was damp; the motel pool was half-filled with dirty water and debris. The air-conditioning stank of rotten bananas and sour milk, so I left it off, waking in the mornings covered in sweat, with the sound of cars honking outside my window and the smell of water in the air. I slept in Ina's bra and underwear, the same pair I'd worn when I first joined the movement, a pair I washed meticulously in the sink of the motel bathroom, stealing bars of soap off the housekeeping carts whenever someone checked out of their room. The thin white bars made a tub of creamy water in the sink, and I wrung out her underwear again and again.

I took a bus to the ocean, let it lick my feet. The Atlantic was calm. I imagined I could see it stretching all the way to the west coast of Ireland, where it smashed against the rocky shores of Donegal, where Enda might be walking with Siobhán. Tears fell down my face, soft and unobtrusive.

I went to Walmart and roamed the aisles, fingers dragging over patterns of comforters and sheets. Picking up and putting back down different sets of dishes, trash bins, shower mats. I was not looking for anything. I just wanted to touch it all, to feel the mountains of things that seemed to be America. I wanted to become different, to undo who I had been in Ireland. To unravel the clothes of my old self and sew something new.

❖ ❖ ❖

I got a job waitressing at a diner near the motel, a run-down place where the vinyl was peeling off the booths. Bulletproof windows had been installed several years ago, though the worst violence I saw there was an intimate, private violence, the kind that would sometimes occur between men and women as they huddled around a table.

In Miami, the drug wars had only recently ended. People still talked about a time when the city had kept dead bodies in refrigerated trucks because there was no room at the morgue. When restaurants were shot up and people killed in broad daylight. They walked with a jitteriness I found familiar, but it was a different kind of fracture than the one I'd grown up with. I did not see the borders here, the way I had at home. And in my ignorance, I was free from fear, the way Ina had always been.

I refilled the sugar shakers, picked hair out of soup, slid tips into the pockets of my uniform, mopped up the spilled water, sodas, coffee. Men leered, grabbed at my waist, my arm. I learned to laugh, to shake them off.

I watched two women in jean jackets walk into the diner, holding hands. The defiant stare the blonde one gave me, the jolt in my stomach as I bowed my head in deference. One day after work, I went with the other waitresses to a gay bar and saw drag queens sing onstage. I watched in awe, staring at the sequins and the costumes. The tight clothes, the slight shake in someone's hand, the backbone of shame, of fear, of fierce pride.

As I carried hot dishes to tables, balancing them in the crook of my wrist, I remembered the pub in Tyrone, with Ina. Remembered her coming up behind me to scare me, to see if I would drop the tray I was holding. Her sneaking french fries off the tops of orders, chewing with her mouth open, her eyes like stars in the darkly lit room. There was the same bustle here, the same dishes balanced on my hands and wrists and forearms, but where the pub had been dark and intimate like the inside of a fist, the diner was bright and blinding, the fluorescent light on an operating table.

In Ina's clothes, my hair done up like she'd worn hers, I felt like I was keeping her alive. Like a painting of Mary kept Our Mother present, my body became a shrine to my sister. I kept calling myself her name, and every time I heard the word, I felt like she was there with me. Like we were one and the same, united again. I had come to America for the both of us.

I thought about trying to lose my accent. It seemed so easy, in those first few weeks, to slip it off like an old wedding ring, to soften the edges of my language so that it became like that of the girls around me. But I couldn't bear to do it, couldn't bear to lose the part of me that sounded like my family. The way I spoke, and Ina's name, were the only parts of Ireland left to me.

My favorite waitress at the diner was called Maria, and we went out after work some nights. She would call me *amor* and plait my hair like Ina used to. She drank whiskey sours, and her voice was husky and masculine. One night, when we'd both had too much to drink, she showed me her nipple piercing in the bar bathroom. Like the other girls at the diner, she did not ask about my past, but while the other girls were oblivious, I got the sense that Maria knew what it was like to keep a secret.

In March, when I'd been in Miami two months, Maria and I worked doubles all week and went to EPCOT. I held cotton candy in my hand and stared around at the gigantic playground, the absurdity of it, the men and women dressed up like animals. We went on rides; we toured the world. We drank large glasses of beer, and Maria threw her head back to laugh.

At dinner, a man at the restaurant bar kept looking over at us. When I went to the bathroom, he followed me. Leaning me up against the wall of the hallway, he kissed me, pressed his hand between my thighs. I didn't stop him. It did not feel like me he was touching. I went back to our table.

"I don't like men to see me naked," Maria told me that night. We had taken a bus back from Orlando, and it was past midnight. "I feel like they can see everything you've ever done laid out there."

It was hot out even though it was dark. The oppressive Miami night. I held Maria's hand as we crossed the street, like a child clinging to her mother, though I wasn't sure which of us was which.

"Nobody's ever seen me naked," I told her.

"Nobody?" she asked.

"Well, my sister." I laughed. "But not a man."

I would have liked to be close to Maria, closer than I was when we shared our fears, when we pushed back each other's hair and lamented how the other had been treated. I would have liked to tell her what had happened, with the man in the bar, with my family. But I had learned that with the diner women, friendship only happened in the spaces where men weren't. Water filling the crevices of rock. It had become clear to me that our intimacy, however essential, would be dropped as soon as a man came around and then picked back up once he left. Always sacrificed, always returning. I thought of my mother, who I had left alone with only men for company.

❖ ❖ ❖

When I had been living in Miami for three months, I turned on the motel television one morning and watched a blonde American announce the Good Friday Agreement: the peace treaty between the British, the Irish, and the paramilitaries. The old IRA had signed the agreement. The Real IRA had not.

There was peace in Northern Ireland, the newscaster said, and as I heard the words, I felt the vibrations of celebration run through me as if I stood in the streets of Coalisland. I heard the women bang bin lids one final time. Heard the shouting in the streets. The hiss of an aerosol can repainting a mural for a new generation.

To Ma, I knew, this treaty would mean nothing as long as Ireland remained split, shorn down the middle by the scar of partition. But at the pub, they would be singing old republican songs, not yet thinking of the irony. They would mourn those we had lost. They might even say her name. I imagined the faces of the women who drank their afternoons away at Sláns: Susie and Cliona and Eimear's mother, whose name I could not remember. I could see their eyes widen and water with the news: Susie and Cliona had both had family members unmade by the conflict. I could feel the country breathe a sigh of relief to be done with the fighting, even though we had not won. Even though it seemed now like we never would.

The thing I had done had not been enough. My joining and my leaving had both been in vain. History had trundled on without noticing. I could not tell, from my distance, what the change would mean. But I knew that there had been a change.

I suddenly longed for our town, our house. For the wet fields, the bumpy tongues of the neighbor's sheepdogs, the hot, smooth eggs cracked into sizzling butter on a Sunday. For the water of Lough Neagh licking my ankles, Ina shrieking at its temperature. I wanted to look out the window and see Enda and Tad, dressed in yellow and blue windbreakers, their backs spattered by rain, their hair sticking to their heads until they resembled children. The long marron grass and the smell of a fire.

The blonde American had moved on to sports news, and I turned off the TV. I knew the number for our old landline by heart. The phone bill would cost a fortune.

I listened to the long ring, coming down the line from a world away. I waited to hear her voice, soft and strong. I waited to hear her sharp inhale, her exhale, the breaths of the body that had given breath to me.

"Hello?"

Tad picked up on the third ring, and I could tell by the wetness of his voice that he had been drinking.

"It's Bríd," I said. I had not used that name since leaving Ireland.

There was a long pause, and I could hear the television on in the background of the call.

"I want to come home," I said. "I'm after seeing the news. I won't get in trouble now, will I, for running off? Not with Conor and them." I didn't know if I was asking him or telling him.

He was still quiet. Finally, he said, "Forget about Conor so. It's Ma you should be afraid of."

"I'm going to buy a ticket," I went on. "I have the money." I had stretched the phone cord as long as it would go as I reached for the cookie tin where I kept my savings. I wanted to count the bills in my hand, feel my return between my fingers.

"Bríd," Tad said. I drank in the sound of him saying it, his familiar voice. "Bríd, you left," he said. "Just like Enda did. Just like she—"

"Ina didn't—"

"You all left me here, alone. I don't know where you went off to. They said America but—"

"Yes, I'm in Florida," I said. "I'm in—"

He cut me off. "But things aren't good here, Bríd. Ma . . . she was beside herself when you went."

I swallowed. "Is she all right?"

"Yes, she's all right. But she's angry, Bríd. I've never seen her this angry."

I saw my mother again, the way I'd left her. The sting of her last words.

"It's too late," he said. "I'm sorry, but you made your choice." He didn't sound sorry.

I hung up the phone.

Chapter Twelve

2016, Los Angeles County

In the backyard, I pulled a lawn chair into the sun and lay there in my bra and underwear, reading *God Is Not Great*. I had taken off the book's jacket so that Mom wouldn't see the title, but now I put it back on and held it high above my knees so that if she came into the backyard, she would have no choice but to read the four words, to sin in her mind.

I heard her foot on the porch step. She was quiet for a moment, looking at me.

"You're going to get cancer lying there in the sun," she said.

"This is my backup plan. In case the cigarette smoking doesn't kill me first."

"Don't be a smart arse," she said. "I know you don't smoke."

I raised my eyebrows but kept reading. I wished it wasn't true, wished I was bold enough.

"Did I do something?" she asked after a minute. "To piss you off?"

I put down the book. "Do you know what the Bible says about homosexuals?"

She sighed. "It says love thy neighbor."

"It says it's an abomination."

"You can talk to Father Michael about this."

"I want to talk to you."

"We don't have to agree with every word, Bernie. What's important is to believe in Him."

"Then why do we go to church? If God's all that matters."

"That's our community."

"A community that hates women and homosexuals."

"There's a Pride flag outside the bloody church. Nobody hates homosexuals."

I knew she didn't too. I knew she loved me in any form I took. But I could not help feeling like I was too different. Like I had turned out not at all the way she'd expected. I felt sometimes like we really were from opposite sides of the world, thinking things in foreign languages. I felt like I was a secret, kept even from myself.

I sat upright. Somehow, our relationship was now political: talking points on CNN, referendums in foreign countries. Everything I was had become an act of politics.

"If I stopped going to church," I asked, "would you still love me?"

"Of course."

"The same as if I did go to church?"

"Yes, the same." She hesitated. "I might feel . . . further away"—she gestured—"but I'd still love you the same."

I let that sit there for a moment, saying nothing.

"What if I sinned? Did something the Bible says you can't do?"

Another long pause. "Do you mean like . . . being gay?"

"No," I said quickly, blushing. "Something even you think is wrong. Like killing someone. What if I killed someone?"

She laughed. A little, hoarse thing, more like a cough than her usual musical laugh.

"You'd never hurt a fly," she said. "I know you, Bernie. You came out of me, remember?" She turned her back on me and went into the house.

"I'm getting you sunscreen," she called over her shoulder.

The plastic of the lawn chair was burning my flesh in strips, leaving the space in between cool as the breeze. I checked my phone; the air-quality index was at 101, unhealthy for sensitive groups. A new study had found that over one thousand people die in the Los Angeles area every year due to bad air quality. For a moment, I felt like I couldn't breathe, like the smog trapped in my lungs was choking me. Then I remembered what I had to do. I remembered how steely I would have to be to survive, how like a knife: quick and small and deadly. And I felt my breaths steady again.

I was tired all the time. My breasts got puffy, swollen. I wondered about my mother's pregnancy, closed my eyes and tried to picture her, younger and round, glowing like the statue of Mary at our church. I wished urgently that my father was alive. That there was someone else I could go to, someone with softer opinions, someone without a chemical imbalance, someone clear-sighted and undogmatic. Every time I spoke to her, the words I was not saying loomed in the back of my mouth.

"Was I an accident?" I asked one night at dinner. I was chasing steamed peas around my plate with a fork.

"Sorry?"

"When you got pregnant with me. Was it an accident?"

"It was a blessing," she said and stood to clear her plate, leaving me alone at the table, feeling neither blessed nor like a blessing.

I was scraping the last of the mac and cheese into the garbage. It had hardened onto the aluminum tray. There was no sink in the back room of the shelter, so my only option was to use a fork and scrape until the food came free. I'd read that even the smallest speck of food could ruin an entire bin of recycling.

I was determined to clean the dish, but the smell of the old cheese was making me nauseous. I felt shaky on my legs. Food had begun to disgust me recently: the creaminess of dairy, the fattiness of meat. The noodles like worms sticking to the foil.

"Are you sure you should be dumping that?" Damon was leaning against the doorframe, squinting at me.

"It's old," I said. "It's been in the fridge since last week." I felt my hands begin to shake and stopped for a moment, breathing hard through my nose. He didn't seem to notice.

"Isn't everything you feed us old?" he asked. "We're like dogs. You give us scraps."

I didn't know if he was angry or if he was trying to make me laugh. He wasn't supposed to be back here. I studied the rips in the knees of his jeans.

He came closer to me, and I put down the plastic fork I had been using. The prongs of it were warped now. I felt conscious of everything, the long braids in my hair that made me look younger than I was, the naivete of my endeavor with the aluminum, the baby growing inside me, invisible but felt, alive but doomed.

"Are you all right?" he asked. He was standing over me now, and I could see that his eyes were red. He had been crying or he had been using or there was no difference.

"I'm pregnant." It was the first and last time I said the words out loud.

He put his hand on my stomach for a fraction of a second. His fingers were long and hot. I thought of how badly I had wanted those fingers, how I had wanted him to touch me, recognize me, show us both that I was real. I could see the riverbeds of lines in his face. The watery fluid around his eyes. That sense of drowning. Then he put his hand back in his pocket quickly, like I'd burned him. He took a step away from me.

"Accident?" he said more than asked. I shrugged. Of course it had been an accident, but not in the way I'd always expected accidents to happen. I had walked right into this. I had chosen every step along the way.

"I'm getting an abortion," I said. It seemed the clearest answer to his question.

I thought again about the man in Mumbai. I thought about the landfill where the aluminum foil would go if I didn't get the cheese off it. I thought about the boy in the lake, drowning.

"My mother got an abortion," he said. "Before she had me."

I stared at him, imagining what it would be like to know that kind of thing about your mother.

"I always wondered what would have happened if we were switched. If I'd been the one aborted and he'd been the one to live."

"Why did she have an abortion?" I asked. My voice was so quiet, I could barely hear it. I could feel all the parts of my throat, the ones we'd studied in school: larynx, pharynx, epiglottis, esophagus, trachea. I could feel the little hairlike cilia and the mucus that kept the dry air from hurting my lungs. That was what was being created inside me: another body, just as intricate as mine.

"Why does anyone?" he asked. "She couldn't live with it. It was her or the baby."

Then he staggered forward, like he had tripped. I reached out to steady him.

"Are you okay?" I asked. He was leaning into me.

"Fine," he said. His eyes seemed wild, unanchored. His pupils were blown wide: caves in the side of a cliff, the dark hole of the night sky with no stars in sight. He isn't here, I thought. He isn't here.

He steadied himself, pulled away from me abruptly.

"You'll be all right," he said. He looked me in the eye when he said it, and I felt momentarily comforted. He of all people would know what someone could and couldn't survive. He turned around and left the room without saying anything else.

I was lying in bed when Mia finally texted me: do you want froyo? It had been a month and a half since I'd seen her. I let out a long breath of relief, and then my heart began to hammer against my chest. I wanted to see her badly, but I was afraid of what it would be like. Afraid we would feel like strangers. Or, worse, that I would still be in love with her. That the pain of my longing would be unbearable.

"Hey," she said when I found her sitting on our old bench outside the yogurt shop.

She looked smaller than she had that night we'd lain beneath the stars. Her smile was like a shard of glass compared to what it had been; I wanted the whole bottle of wine, the old, stored sweetness. I suddenly wanted to say it to her again; I wanted to keep telling her I loved her until she felt it, strong as alcohol running through her blood. I wanted my love to cure her, protect her, make her feel okay. God, I had missed her.

"How are you doing?" I asked instead. It felt like the only four words I'd been saying to her lately. I would have given a lot to be able to say something different, to be able to talk without thinking, like I used to.

She let out a sigh that was half a sob and half a laugh. "You know," she said.

I nodded.

"This was always our worst fear," she said.

I was quiet for a minute.

"At least he's getting help," I said.

"Yeah." She sighed again.

"Can I get you a yogurt?" I asked.

"No," she said a little too quickly. "I'll get my own."

We went inside, ordered, and returned to the bench with our yogurts. I pretended to eat mine, but the taste disgusted me. It was artificial, milky. I thought of the animals who'd been held prisoner to make it.

"I—" I started to say, wanting to address what had happened to us. "I'm sorry for—"

I broke off again. I didn't know what to say. Was I sorry for telling her the truth?

"It was bad timing," she said with a small, bitter laugh.

"Yeah," I said, relieved that she'd spoken. "It was terrible timing." I laughed.

She was quiet, eating her yogurt. I watched her. The rhinestone of her nose ring against her freckled skin. Her movements slower than they used to be, none of the bubbly energy that she used to carry everywhere she went. Everything felt off-kilter between us, uneven. Like the focus had sharpened on video footage, faces up close and in painful detail. But it was still Mia and me. We had been through bad things before—fights and hard times, bad days and broken bones.

"I slept with that college student," I said. "Avery." I didn't know why I said it. Maybe I wanted to hurt her or to make her feel more comfortable, safe from my desire. Maybe I just wanted to distract her from whatever was happening inside her head.

"What?" she asked, genuinely surprised. Her spoon suspended on the way to her mouth.

"I know," I said. I gave a small laugh to show that I thought it was funny, that nothing serious had happened. Even though, of course, it had.

"How did it feel?" she asked. For the first time since we'd sat down, she looked like herself again. Like nothing had ever gone wrong between us. I knew she'd never had sex; her curiosity about it had always been greater than mine, and it seemed ironic that we should be sitting here, our positions reversed.

I tried to remember how it had felt. I wanted to describe it so well that it would be like we'd been there together. It had felt strange, was the truth, perverse, like driving on the wrong side of the road, like laughing at your mother. But it had not felt like "losing" something. If anything, it had felt like gaining something. I should've known then, I guess.

For a moment, I thought I would tell her everything. About the baby, about next week's appointment. But the air between us already felt so heavy. I didn't want to burden her with yet another sad thing.

"It was interesting," I said, and we both laughed, the sound of it foreign when it had once been so familiar.

"Did it hurt?" She was curious, her eyes searching. We were sitting closer than we had all afternoon. I could tell that the fact that I'd had sex with Avery made Mia feel more comfortable. Her gaze worked its way over me, like she was looking for a change. Like she was trying to see any damage.

"A little," I admitted. "But then it felt fine. It felt—good." Had it felt good? I couldn't honestly remember. I was rewriting the past as I spoke. "It obviously wasn't his first time."

She laughed again, and I remembered being twelve and giggling, how nobody ever seemed to understand what was so funny. Nobody except the two of us.

"Was it romantic?" she asked.

"He didn't know it was my first time," I said. "I didn't want to say."

"Yeah," she said. "I wouldn't have either." But I didn't know if that was true. Mia had always been braver than me in moments like those. She was the kind of person who would look you straight in the eye and tell you the truth, tell you what she wanted, and demand that she get it. I couldn't imagine her biting down on her hand in a dirty dorm room. She would have expected better, would have deserved better.

As we continued to talk about Avery, I wondered again about my mother. Who had she told about her pregnancy? It was strange to think of our shared past. There was knowledge buried somewhere inside me, like genetics. I had been within her all that time. If only I could remember.

When Mia and I said goodbye, we didn't hug. Instead, I stood there awkwardly until she turned and walked away from me, waving once over her shoulder.

It seemed like we might stay friends. Like one day we might even be close again. But, right now, I was still alone.

As I walked home, I passed a group of protesters outside the Episcopalian church. At first, all I could hear was the rhythm of their chants, but as

I got closer I could see the signs they were carrying. Pictures of infants' faces with Sharpie underneath: *I want to live* and *I have a heartbeat.* I stopped in front of them, horrified, searching the crowd. But she wasn't there.

She was sitting in the living room when I got home, watching the news. More about the UK referendum. The anger inside me was like a drug, filling every inch of me, breaking down my inhibitions. The protesters had chosen to make war; they had chosen to fight me where I was most vulnerable. She might not have been there, but she was one of them.

"How's Mia?" Mom asked.

I stood in the doorway. "Did my dad know when I was born? Did you call him?"

She looked at me and then looked back at the screen, at the prime minister's face.

"Mom?" I asked again. "Did he know?"

"Drop it, Bernie," she said finally. "It doesn't matter anymore."

"He doesn't matter?" I stomped my foot on the floor. "Are you serious?"

"Bernie," she snapped. She was looking at me now, and her gaze said I was in dangerous territory. "Stop asking silly questions. The past is the past."

I went upstairs to the cabinet where my mother kept the liquor. She had two open bottles of tequila and a bottle of Irish whiskey that I'd never seen her touch. I took the tequila to my room and began to drink: great swigs of it that burned all the way down into my stomach. I wondered if it would be enough to kill the child, to spare me a trip to the clinic. I drank until I could no longer feel the fear inside me, until all I could feel was the familiar swaying of the room, like a mother rocking her baby. And I lay on the bed and watched the ceiling dance.

Chapter Thirteen

In August, a bombing in Omagh killed twenty-nine people, and all of Ireland turned against the Real IRA.

On the television, I watched the death toll rise. I read the victims' names. I watched their faces appear on the TV screen like smoke signals out of a fire. How they were defined in the end, a single word: mother, lawyer, child.

I knew who was responsible for the deaths. I saw the woman's face in my mind again, the lipstick smear of red over her lips. This was what I had wanted once upon a time: death, destruction, revenge. This was the war I had chosen to join, the cause in which I had believed. I felt sunken with guilt, a waterlogged island. I felt homesick, terrified, uneasy. The men I had delivered the car to, the woman I had obeyed—they were now responsible for twenty-nine deaths. For the pain and misery on my television screen. If I'd been there, would I have been beside them? I had come so close to being guilty not only for the one woman but for all of these people. For this town I had visited hundreds of times.

All over Ireland, there were marches, demonstrations, cries of outrage. Old IRA members, nationalists, activists—the whole island condemned the group responsible. The woman suspected of the bombing was forced out of the border town where she lived, her neighbors turning against her as savagely as animals attacking a weak link. It was clear now that Ireland herself was ashamed of our violence, ashamed of what we had done for her.

It was the first crack in the glass of Miami, an indication that the past would not be forgotten so easily. Again and again, I thought of ringing my mother, of asking: *Are you happy now?* But I remembered the call with Tad, and my heart sank lower in my chest. It was too much to take: my guilt over this newest attack, my brother's rejection.

I was fired from the diner. I'd missed too many shifts. For days, I couldn't get out of bed. I lay on the stale-smelling cot, sweaty in my sheets, watching the time tick by on my alarm clock, watching the world continue turning without me. There seemed to be a bird perched on my chest, heavy, feathery, suffocating. Like a swan lying on the water, holding me down.

I thought about the drive, about the calfskin leather beneath my hands, the sticky steering wheel. I thought about my mother, her tight mouth, proud and demanding, her hair curled out. I thought about that other mother, lain up in hospital because of me. I wondered if her baby had made it. If she were able to hold her own child. And I thought of the woman who had done all of this, her cheeks hollow and empty, famished.

My money ran out, and the motel bill was due. Finally, desperate, I called up Maria. I could have the couch, she told me. I moved my suitcase to her apartment and, while she was at work, I sat at her kitchen table, drank strong tea, and wrote out job applications.

❖   ❖   ❖

A month later, I got a job in housekeeping. I collected my tips to pay off what I owed Maria: backdated rent, the cost of the food I'd eaten from her fridge. At work, I tied the belt of my uniform tightly. I wore ballet flats. My hair was in a ponytail, long now, down my back. My name tag. Ina. I told myself this would be a fresh start. Another one. Slowly, day by day, I built back my life, or some semblance of it. This time I tried to put up guardrails so that I would not fall so far again. I saved my money. I drank less. I took care of Maria's apartment, built a little life making us dinner in the evenings and listening as she talked about her day. I wanted something stable, something constant. Something that resembled the lives that other people made for themselves. A job, a boyfriend. Maybe, one day, a child.

❖　❖　❖

"Hot whiskey, please," I said, sitting down on the barstool.

"What's that?" The bartender had bright eyes, lips quirked into a smile. Curly hair under a backward baseball cap.

"Hot water, whiskey, lemon, honey, cloves." I said it all in one breath. "Just the hot water and whiskey's fine if you can't do the rest."

"Don't think we have *cloves*." He said the spice like it was a disease.

"That's no bother," I said. "How about the rest?"

He moved away from me to make it, and I pulled off my sweater, which was soaked from a sudden summer downpour. I twisted my hair in my hands to wring the water out of it. The air-conditioning was on in the bar. It was on everywhere in Miami. Between the thick heat and the freezing interiors, I was never happy, was always undressing or redressing, always sweating or shivering. The weather had begun to lose its charm by now. The palm trees seemed less exotic. I wondered at the circles of their bark that looked like a rash, the dead leaves that clustered at their heads, just below the green.

The bartender put the drink in front of me. He had served it in a mug, and I put my hand to the ceramic to feel the heat. Then he moved away from me, leaned against the wall, and opened a book he'd stashed behind the bar.

It was a paperback, thick and tattered, and he'd folded it almost entirely in two, so that he held it easily with one hand despite its girth. I could just make out the *M* and the *D* and the spout of a spraying whale.

I thought of the smudged and folded papers I kept in a shoebox under Maria's couch. Articles about Ireland painstakingly cut from newspapers. The uneven edges of each clipping a reminder of how imprecise my knowledge of home was. At night, I would open the box to stare at the sea of my country, the papers scattered like the froth of waves.

"I've never found sea life very interesting," I said to the bartender. "I don't get what the big deal is, with whales and sharks and giant squid like."

He looked up at me. His dark eyes direct and unimpressed. He had a soft face, handsome in a boyish way. Good-looking, Ma would have said. A face that would look well on a child.

"That's moronic," he said, but the words had no heat. "Giant squid are fucking awesome. You're like an ant compared to them. And anyway, this book isn't even about the sea, really. It's about religion."

"Oh," I said. "I didn't know that."

"I mean, sure, there's a whale."

"Right," I said. "Are you religious?"

He shrugged.

"I don't believe in Hell," he said, "if that's what you mean."

I looked down at the bar top.

"I do."

I could feel his eyes on me.

"Is that where you think you're going?" He laughed. I did too.

"Yes," I said after a minute. "I do."

"There is no Hell," he said. I knew he was wrong, but I didn't mind.

"Where are you from?" he asked.

"Ireland." Americans never asked me to specify north or south. It made me feel like the conflict had never existed, like the British occupation had been a fever dream. It made me feel like the place I came from had disappeared.

"That's why you're in a bar." He laughed. "The Irish are always in a bar."

"Ach only in America. We have to drink away our disappointment."

He grinned. "I know what you mean. It's a piss-poor excuse for a country." He looked back down at his novel.

"What about you?"

"Oh, I'm from all over. I was born in Massachusetts. But my family's all in Virginia. That's where I grew up."

"And now you're here," I said.

"And now I'm here."

I took a sip of my drink. Too much honey. He looked at his book again, but his tongue darted out and wet his lips, and his eyes looked without seeing.

"What's Ireland like?" he asked, looking up again like he couldn't take his eyes off me. It made me shiver.

"The air is much lighter," I said. "And people know each other."

"How else is it different?" he asked.

"It's not," I said. "It's the same."

Another pause.

"What are you going to Hell for?"

I smiled. "I didn't listen to my mother," I said.

"Well," he said. "If you want to make something of your time here . . ." He scratched the back of his head and looked around the room like the entire earth was encompassed in this bar. "You know, before eternal damnation—"

I laughed.

"You should come over. I have a pool." He met my eye then.

A life flashed before me: A house. Sunscreen and baseball caps strewn across a deck. A child learning to swim, little floaties wrapped around chubby arms. Smoothies in the morning with fresh berries. Nights in front of the television, him mixing me a drink. That was the woman I wanted to be: A woman with a backyard, with a house of her own. A woman who belonged somewhere, to someone. Who had a place in the world.

"I'd like that," I said.

"Dean Evans," he said.

"Ina."

As I said her name, I thought of how excited she would be to go on a date with a man like this. How she would dress up and do her makeup. She would dream them a fairy-tale future. I wanted to give that to her. It seemed like the right thing to do.

He ripped a page out of *Moby-Dick*. "Don't worry," he said. "It's just a library book." In black ink, he wrote his name and number.

❖ ❖ ❖

When I got home, Maria was lying on the couch in long flannel pajama trousers that were fraying at the cuffs. Her curly black hair fell over her shoulders, around her neck and back like a wave. The curves of her body reminded me of Ina's angularity: her opposite. Ina, too, would sprawl across my mattress, offer up her body like a libation.

"Did you see the tornado?" Maria asked. She was reading a magazine and didn't look up at me or show any sign of moving off my couch.

"Yeah," I said. "Mad."

I had seen it from the bus window on the way home. Something black and ominous, disjointed from the hope in my chest as I clutched Dean's number.

"You don't have those in Ireland, huh?"

She still hadn't turned, and I stared at the mass of her hair. It was thick like my mother's. Nothing like my thin, stringy brown. I thought about my sister, wanted to lie down and lean into Maria and pretend she was the same. The way that schoolgirls always talk of becoming twins or cousins, of inventing blood ties. The way they cut themselves and touched palms to swap blood, as if that were all it took.

"You have a bed, you know," I said.

❖ ❖ ❖

I shaved my legs, sat on the floor of the shower as the hot water began to run cold. I was not thinking, was not moving in straight lines to answer some articulated question. But images came to me like soft rain, the water from the faucet running down my face. Ina's body wrapped around her boyfriend's years ago now, the heat that radiated off them, the way their bodies orbited each other when they thought you weren't looking. The cold bend of a body at Mass, the sweaty condemnations of sin, the prickle at the back of your neck, the lurch toward the confession box as to a toilet in which one must vomit.

Later that night, I went into Maria's room where she was sleeping. For a long moment, I stood over her, feeling something I could not put into words. Her hand was lying next to her face on the pillow, her breaths coming in little puffs, blowing across her fingers. I thought of small blades of grass in the wind. I wanted to touch her hand, to run my fingers over the skin I knew was extraordinarily soft. Wanted to feel the little holes that were her pores, to try to fill them with the tip of my finger, to see them overflow. I remembered kissing Ina as a child, thinking I could take a part of her away with me. I couldn't stand the strength of the feeling, the pull of my memory. I backed out of Maria's room.

The next day, I rang Dean. We went to the movies. His laugh was infectious. His hand traveled up my thigh. We went out five nights in a row. On the fifth night, I slept over.

At work, I folded the corners of the clean bedspreads carefully, tucked them, smoothed them down. I wrapped the mattress tightly in its clothes, as if holding it there, imprisoning it. I hit the pillows. I fluffed the comforter. I was a tamer of inanimate objects; I was communing with the world of furniture; I was one with the structures that held people, the containers they lay in, sat on, and then left behind.

And all the while, projected onto every hotel room I entered, was the image of the other room, destroyed. As I made bed after bed beautiful, I thought of the one I'd made terrible. The sheets waving like so many ghosts in the wind.

Chapter Fourteen

2016, Los Angeles County

Mom came home from work one Sunday to find three jumbo garbage bags filled with my old clothes and old toys.

"What's all this?" she asked.

"I'm giving it to children who need it," I said. My lower back ached, and I paused to massage it with my thumbs. That morning, when I'd looked in the mirror, I'd been surprised by my own beauty; I looked radiant, electric.

She rummaged through the open bag, the one I was still filling. "I don't think any children need your underwear."

"I'm giving up fast fashion," I said.

"What's that?"

I rolled my eyes. "The way we all shop and then throw out our clothes when the seasons change. It's ruining the world."

"So you're throwing out your clothes on the off-season?"

"No, Mom," I said, annoyed. "These don't fit me."

She picked up an old doll, soft-bodied with yarn for hair. "What if you want to give this to your child one day?"

Mom was obsessed with saving things for my children, cramming boxes with my old artwork and baby clothes so that one day I could show my own daughter. She, of course, had nothing from her own childhood.

"I'm not going to have children," I told her. "I don't want kids."

She sighed, tucking the doll under her arm. "You're too young to know that," she said.

I looked at her for a long time. It seemed impossible that she did not know, that she could not read something so total and altered in my face. I had never kept a secret like this. If it's even called a secret when you want so desperately to be found out. And yet, her face was blank. She was rummaging in the garbage bags for other sentimental objects to save from charity.

I sat down on the sofa, suddenly exhausted. Mom went to make a pot of tea.

"Do you have your period?" she asked when she came back into the room and offered me a cup.

"What?" I hated when she talked like that, when she acted like my body was a shared object, belonging to both of us. As if I just happened to be its custodian at the moment.

"I saw a bunch of pads. In your room."

"Yeah," I lied. "I have my period."

"Has it been a bit irregular?"

I didn't answer. I had read online that you should stock up on pads before an abortion.

"Are you sure you're getting enough iron?" she asked. And then, without waiting for my reply, "I'll get you some tablets at the store."

"Okay." I took a sip of my tea and leaned back against the arm of the couch. I closed my eyes. Mom took my feet in her lap and began to rub them.

As she rubbed my arches, my heels, a thought slithered its way inside my brain, a predator, an intruder: what a terrible mother I was.

❖   ❖   ❖

At dinner, Mom put a plate of chicken and broccoli in front of me.

"What, are you on hunger strike?"

"I'm vegetarian."

"So eat the broccoli."

"I don't like broccoli."

She took my plate away and sat down to eat her own dinner.

"Since when?"

"Since when what?"

"Since when are you vegetarian again?"

"I watched a movie."

"About animals?"

"About the world."

I took a box of Cheerios down from the cupboard and began to eat them out of the plastic bag with my hand.

"Do you want milk with that?" she asked like it was the biggest chore in the world. Like it was her job to remind me that cereal went with milk. She looked just as exhausted as I felt.

"Milk's not good either," I said.

"Grand." Her Irish always came out when she was annoyed. The sometimes-subtle accent growing stronger, the colloquialisms shooting up out of her speech like sprouts in soil. It was like anger pulled her back to that old home.

❖   ❖   ❖

As I waited for the day of my appointment to come, I all but stopped eating. Food made me feel ill. Whenever I looked at it, I thought about animals living in their own excrement, about carbon dioxide floating up from farms, trapping heat, warming the earth.

Mom tried. She made me eggplant cooked in marinara sauce. She bought almond milk, until I told her that almond milk was killing the bees. I didn't even get a bite of the eggplant before I had to run to the bathroom to puke. That night, I opened a bag of baby carrots but was alarmed at how artificially cute they were. I ate an adult carrot instead, holding the stick in my hand like Bugs Bunny.

Mom thought I was acting out. Kaleb thought it was a political statement. My GP, when Mom called him, suggested that I might be anorexic.

I couldn't listen to people discussing food, couldn't be around anyone eating. As soon as you become disgusted by food, you start to realize that the language is everywhere. Don't cry over spilled milk. Butter wouldn't melt in his mouth. Bring home the bacon. She's a bad egg.

I kept thinking of the child inside me, its small fingernails, its sinews. Did a fetus have wrists? Eyelashes? I thought about finding the group of protesters, asking them. It would not change my decision, but I wanted to be aware.

I stopped to pet dogs on the street and felt their joints, armpits, haunches. I could see on them the pieces of chicken that Mom served for dinner. The drumsticks of their legs. I cried over a Yorkie one day, crouching down to pet the puppy on Harvard and Bonita. Its owner smiled at me, the kind of smile I saw people give the shelter residents, and dragged the dog away, its leash taut. A mother's tug.

That Thursday, I went to the animal shelter just to stare through the bars of the cages at the pit bulls. I wanted to lay down my body and let the animals feast on it. I wanted to make up for what I was going to do to the creature inside me. The child I would never name, birth, raise.

By the weekend, I began to feel weak. My legs shook when I stood. Mom's nervous eyes raked over my body, and she ordered me to bed. I thought about what Damon had said, how Mom's disease might be coming for me. I told her I was fine, kept getting up just to prove to myself that I could, that I was not like my mother.

But, finally, standing was too much. My head swam just walking to the bathroom. My thoughts were a blurry haze: animals and babies and Damon from Mississippi. How Riley would have looked, bile leaking from his lips. Mia's eyes full of fear when I told her I loved her. I got back into bed. I curled into my mother's side and tried to cry, but nothing came out, like I had nothing left inside me.

Chapter Fifteen

2000, Miami

I woke in the middle of the night to pee. Dean was standing at his bedroom window, staring out. In the darkness, the bulb of his Adam's apple seemed giant. I thought of the thing he had swallowed, the thing God had warned against. He reminded me of Conor then. The way his face seemed like a weapon at odd angles. Like Conor, he magnified things. He made me feel the possibility of reinvention. I wanted to dig up old bones. I wanted to plant something new.

Dean did not have a private pool, like I'd imagined. He did not have a house with a deck and a room for a baby. What he did have was a small apartment in a housing complex and what amounted to a communal, chlorinated bathtub. But I had nothing. And I desperately wanted something, anything, that was mine.

Soon, we'd made a small life together. I decorated the apartment with colorful cushions and plastic plants. I cooked dinner on Fridays, and Dean brought home pizza on Saturdays. We watched *Survivor* on Wednesday nights and *ER* on Thursdays. We went to the bar with his friends, drinking enough that I lost hours of my memory. We went to the beach, and I watched him swim, his body a small dot among the waves. When I got the flu, he cleaned up my vomit, brought me soup. And while the word *love* never crossed my mind, I felt close to him, grateful for him, the way one is grateful for a midwife or a flotation device.

❖   ❖   ❖

We sat on opposite ends of the sofa in the living room, watching each other. The couch was not large, and our feet touched uncomfortably every so often, before we pulled them away again. I did not know what he would say. My teeth were latched on to my lower lip to stop a smile. I had bought a bouquet of tulips for the kitchen table, and I thought I could smell them, even from this distance.

"Okay," he said. He was twenty-two. "I can drive you."

"Drive me?" I asked. He was silent for a long minute, in which I understood.

"No," I said, feeling sick. "I could never."

He just looked at me.

"I'm sorry," I said, and for a moment, I was.

We sat in silence for several more minutes. Outside, a small dog yapped. The clock on the wall clicked by the seconds. Then Dean got up, slipped his bare feet into his Reeboks, grabbed his keys from the table on which the television stood, and left the apartment. The little bell I'd hung from the doorframe tinkled.

I made myself a ham sandwich and drank a glass of white wine. One glass wouldn't hurt the baby. I could hear my ma saying that. *One glass, you'll be grand.* I lay across the sofa, occupying the space that minutes before had held all of our tension.

Dean woke me when he got back. It was dark out.

"Did you mean to?" he asked on an exhale. He looked so young then. I didn't know what to say.

"I didn't mean anything."

"Okay," he said. "We'll deal with it."

The word was like a stone in my stomach. *Deal.* Like a discount on a product. Like the cards they hand you when you gamble. Like a pact you make with the devil.

The seed was planted then, the seed of my anger. What had felt to me like a door opening had felt to Dean like a dead end.

❖   ❖   ❖

But I was not one to give up. I was my mother's daughter. I buried my anger. I knew I needed Dean. I needed the structure of him, the figure of a man. I did not need a perfect marriage, a Hollywood love story, but even my mother had had a husband. I could not manage a birth, a baby, all alone.

We got married a month and a half later: a small ceremony at my old church. I wore a loose wedding dress. Afterward, we drove the four hours south to Key West, the edge of the country, and spent three nights in a motel there. The beach was outside our door, curtains flapping in the sea breeze when the windows were opened. In the early mornings, before Dean woke, I slipped outside and walked along the beach for miles. It was still dark out, and the crash and roll of the waves, the white foam bright in the light from the setting moon, made me feel like I was walking on another planet. I was afraid of the ocean—the dark depths of it, the certainty of its currents—and this fear felt to me like wisdom, not cowardice. I had tried to tell Ina this: it was good to be afraid. She hadn't listened, but my daughter would.

When I got back to the hotel, the sun rising over the water in violent yellows like a two-day-old bruise, Dean was just beginning to stir. I lay beside him, watching his eyes move beneath his lids.

Finally, he opened his eyes. He looked at me. "Good morning, Ina Evans," he said. His smile almost looked genuine.

I laughed. It was a beautiful name. When he said it, it sounded real.

I thought back to the first few months of our relationship, when I had been giddy to see him, always rushing out of Maria's apartment to spend time at his. My hair unruly from lying in bed with him all day, from the ocean, from sitting on the steps of the pool with a beer. I remembered how his mouth had felt on my neck, back when it was still a shock to feel it. And how we'd laugh at our own jokes like schoolchildren. I remembered those moments like they had happened to a different person, and I wondered if it would ever be like that again or if I had gone too far, if I had broken the small, fragile thing we'd had.

❖   ❖   ❖

The air-conditioning in Dean's apartment was no match for the weather. I bought sunflowers as often as I could to offer a bit of color. From the window, beyond the light wood fence that delineated the complex, I could see a dense thicket of palm trees and the nearest petrol station.

Dean got a better job, one with benefits and health insurance; I bought new kitchen appliances. They sat on the counter, price stickers against the cream-colored kettle and the bloodred toaster. The tags reminding us that the appliances had been bought on credit, were not yet paid for. It made everything feel temporary, as I, too, felt temporary. As if my tag were still attached, my return-by date inching ever closer.

It was during the early months of my pregnancy that I began to return obsessively, almost longingly, to the car-lit road, the headlights searching, the whir of the tires over smooth pavement, the tightness in my chest that told me I was living. I thought of it constantly, closed my eyes and I was back there. My head leaning back on the sofa in Dean's apartment touched the leather of a car seat in Ardglass.

My new beginning with the baby seemed to require a reckoning, an ending, a truth telling. And yet anybody in the world who could have told me what had been in the boot of that car would die with the secret. I had to hold the not knowing inside me, like the hollow space of the boot, like the empty bottles I had saved for Conor all those years ago. Containers for destruction. Vessels I had offered without ever asking to see the end result. The rag dipped in petrol and lit on fire. The innocent object turned weapon. I had decided not to know. Now I had to live with it. I applied for a green card, and I considered the fact that I might never go back to Ireland.

❖   ❖   ❖

As the baby grew inside me, Dean slipped further into despondency. I saw it happen, and panic rose in my stomach like the feeling of little legs kicking. I felt seasick with it. He would come home late, hours after his shift had ended, and even when we were both home, we didn't talk over dinner anymore. We watched the local news while he thought of other things. I watched him until he couldn't stand my gaze and went to take a shower or lie in bed with his eyes open and his back to me. My reliance on Dean had become a noose for both of us. The more I needed him—the more I asked him to do the dishes when my feet ached or listen to a list of baby names—the more it strangled him. The more he fought the rope, the tighter it held me. For the first time since seeing that small pink cross appear, I was terrified. I did not know how to do it alone.

Dean took two days off work and went to Fort Lauderdale with his friend Roger.

"But I'm pregnant," I said.

"Six months pregnant."

"Six and a half."

"It'll only be four days."

"What if something happens?"

"Nothing will happen," he said. "You have my car."

He had no idea how dangerous I could be behind the wheel of a car.

❖ ❖ ❖

They drove off on a Friday, Dean's right hand raised in a half wave and his knockoff Ray-Bans covering his eyes. As I watched them go, I could feel the baby kicking, her legs weak but insistent. It was starting. It had already started. The bond between us had been created, cemented. Nothing could undo it now. I put one hand on my stomach, holding her. I put the other hand on my lower back, where the pain was.

I drove into Miami to call home from a pay phone.

Far away, I heard the house phone ring. Imagined it was me on the other end hearing it, leaning down to pick it up. It was almost dinnertime there. I counted the hours out on my hand, and I waited for Tad to answer.

"Hello?"

Her voice was as smooth as a pebble. A low note from a cello.

Tears formed in my eyes. I took a deep breath to control my voice.

"Ma?" I asked. It was all I could come up with.

There was silence on the other end of the phone. Silence traveling across the ocean to get to me.

"How are you doing, Ma?"

I imagined her pushing her chin up, pulling back her shoulders.

"Aye I'm fine, Bríd," she said. "How are you?"

"Grand, yeah," I lied.

Again, the silence.

"I've some news for you," I said. I tried to sound cheery, like I was any other daughter calling home. Like she might have been expecting it.

"I'm married," I said. "I'm going to have a baby."

Still, she said nothing.

I thought I could hear her breathing, but it could have been the blood pounding in my ears. I was afraid she was going to hang up on me.

"I thought you might have some advice about the birth," I went on. "It's getting closer now."

She made a sound between a laugh and a sob, the same sound she'd made for Ina. Again, the silence stretched on.

"Do you remember your sister's birth?" she asked finally.

"Flashes of it."

"It was a bloody war," she said. "And then out she came, the most beautiful girl I'd ever seen."

I closed my eyes.

"You left the room when I screamed," she said. "I'll always remember that. The first scream of labor, and you were out the door. Went and sat in the waiting room." She paused. There was the edge of hysteria in her voice, of anger. "I mean, you were only a wee girl, I know that, but I had a feeling it would always be like that. That you would always be one to flee."

"I don't remember that, Ma."

Silence again.

"You wanted advice so? Don't be a coward this time—that's my advice."

The line went dead.

It was raining when I left the phone booth. The street was practically empty. The storm made the city feel wild, uncertain. A woman passed me on the street as I walked toward the car, and she smiled at me in that way that people smile at expectant mothers: a pat on the back after a sports accomplishment, a gold star at the top of your exam. I nodded at the woman but was careful not to be too friendly. I didn't want her asking me questions, bending down to touch my stomach.

The words Ma had said to me echoed in my mind as I got into Dean's car, hair damp from the rain, shivering slightly. I could imagine my mother standing in her room, her hair, distressed from tugging, falling out of the hair band meant to secure it. I could hear her voice, a blade, a shard of glass. I knew she wanted to hurt me, but that didn't make the hurt any less.

I had longed for her for so long, for her advice, for her voice. And this was what she gave me. The woman who was all I had left in this world, the woman who was as fickle as a teenager. It had been the best decision I'd ever made, leaving her.

I coddled my fury all the way home, but in the early hours of the morning, when I woke to the pain of my first contraction, gripped with the terror that I would miscarry and the taste of copper in my mouth, I knew my mother had been right: I had run away from everything. I could not run away from this.

Chapter Sixteen

2016, Los Angeles County

When I was twelve, I became a vegetarian. I made the announcement over a breakfast of scrambled eggs, pushing away a plate of turkey bacon.

"Well done," Kaleb said. He was fiddling with the coffee maker.

"If you're going to be a vegetarian," Mom said, "you should stop eating eggs."

"No." I had a forkful of scramble raised to my mouth. "That's a vegan. People who don't eat eggs are called vegans."

"Well, eggs are baby chickens," Mom said. "Why would you eat baby chicks and not adult chickens? Do you think the babies deserve to die?"

"But they're just eggs," I tried. "They're not chicks. They're still in the shell."

"Would you eat a baby out of its mommy's stomach?"

"Ina," Kaleb said, "you'll scare her."

She pretended he hadn't spoken. "Because there are people who kill babies while they're still in their mothers' tummies. Even though that's where they're supposed to be safest."

I put down my fork and stared at the creamy eggs, pastel yellow. She seemed calm, and yet I could hear the shiver at the back of her voice.

The waiting room was blue. The doctor's office was yellow. The sun was muted, as if in winter. I clenched my fist as I waited for my turn, and I imagined her hand was in mine, something to squeeze, someone to hold on to.

I hadn't been able to eat breakfast that morning or much dinner the night before. Mom had made me a smoothie before school, but under the berries, I could taste the yogurt and could not help imagining the cow's udder being rubbed raw by the farmer's hands, the calves going without their mother's milk.

Inside the room, I put my legs in the stirrups and, inverted, thought of riding horses two summers ago when I'd gotten a job at a stable. The pulse of muscle between my legs, violence beneath me. I felt too still, flexed my foot to remember movement. The nurse felt my stomach, gently. Mom would have had the same exam, the same light pressure on the place where I had lived. But she had made the other decision, the kinder one.

The doctor came in, face obscured by beard and glasses. He ran the ultrasound probe over my stomach, cold gel sliding against me. I was thicker than I had been, but not noticeably so. I felt, more than saw, the difference.

He examined my uterus then, pushing his gloved fingers inside me. I was amazed that the touch, sexual and intimate, could become something entirely different here. It seemed impossible that this clinical intrusion could ever be pleasurable.

When he was done, he looked down at me sternly. I felt awkward, still lying exposed on the table.

"Are you sure about this?" he asked. His voice was softer than it had been before. Like he was trying not to wake someone.

I stared at him with hollow eyes. I was sixteen; I was not sure whether I liked boys or girls. Not sure where my family was from. The only thing I was sure about was that I wanted to save myself with a fanaticism I had never felt before.

He prescribed pills, wrote out instructions. The first pill would stop the baby's growth. Then, I'd take a set of eight pills up to forty-eight hours later. They would start the abortion: heavy bleeding, cramping. It would take several bedridden hours. I would need to find a time when my mother was not home.

"Take the first one when you're ready," he said. "A day from now, a week from now. That's fine. Once you take it, there's no reversing it. You have to be sure."

❖　❖　❖

Outside, in the sunlight, I saw I had two missed calls from my mother.

"Bernie?" she asked as soon as I picked up. "Are you okay?"

Fear flooded through me.

"Yeah," I said. "What happened?"

"I've been calling. It's been an hour. Where have you been?" Her breathing was heavy on the other end of the line.

"Sorry," I said. "I didn't mean to scare you."

"Are you sure you're okay?" she asked. The old panic creeping into her voice. Her at the window staring through a crack in the blinds and worrying about a police car idling out front. Her in the doorway of my kindergarten classroom in the middle of the day, just checking to see if I was all right.

I was quiet.

"Bernie?" she asked again when I didn't reply, her voice more urgent now.

I thought about her recounting my birth story when I turned sixteen. She always said she had been put on earth to do one thing, to make me. Like her worth depended on being my mother. Which meant my worth depended on being her daughter. I saw her bent in front of a statue of Mary, Mom's dark hair and Mary's white shroud. Her blue dress the color of Mom's eyes. She worshipped mothers; she worshipped

178

children. The former remade by the innocence of the latter. An innocence, I thought, that I was getting ready to kill.

But even if it was murder, it was a murder I could live with. To protect not only my life but hers. To protect the home we had built and the uneasy peace we'd earned. The future she had dreamed for me and that I'd dreamed for myself. Some part of me believed that there were certain things worth killing for. Certain deaths you had to live with.

"I'm coming home," I said. I fiddled with the instructions in my pocket, the wall I'd built between us, the line I'd drawn in the sand. Like we were foreign countries separated by a militarized zone, a border. I stopped at the pharmacy on the way home, picked up my prescriptions.

Chapter Seventeen

2000, Miami

Whatever Ma had said, I could remember only flashes of Ina's birth.

I never knew why my mother brought me, but I suppose she wanted me as witness. Da stayed at home with the boys. "He doesn't like blood," Ma had said to us at dinner. He'd turned red and, later that night, taken his anger out on Enda.

As far as I remembered it, I had sat in the waiting room for many hours, and then they brought me in to see my little sister. I remembered only the color of her, really. Pink like a sky at dawn. Her tiny fists flying in the air. She had come out fighting.

"Ina," my mother said, and I thought I saw the baby smile.

It had been a hard birth ending in a cesarean, and they kept her for three nights in hospital. I watched Ma lift her shirt and unhook her bra to give the baby her sore nipple, her swollen breast. I could see the pain on her face, the ache of her full breasts. I remembered her hunched down over the baby, her chest and arms protecting. Her body like the mouth of a cave. Was she protecting her from me? I stood a little ways away and watched her, feeling suddenly separate from her body, suddenly alone.

How horrible birth had seemed to me then. The fistfight that a woman has alone, that screaming match with only the walls to hear you. The little girl who comes out of you, a small pink pig, a wailing bloody thing, covered in brown fluid. A love so strong, it feels like fear. What greater penetration is there? No wonder it was only mother and daughter in the end. Mother and daughter, at war in a hospital ward.

❖ ❖ ❖

I felt like I was being sawed in half, split down the middle, severed. I had been a volunteer in the Irish Republican Army, but I had never known hardship like I did in that small room with the single bed and the midwife's steady, calloused hand. I was being destroyed, blown apart. And I thought of Ina then. I saw her dancing at the club before it happened; I saw her yellow dress spinning out around her, and I saw the explosion: her unraveling.

And then there she was: Bernadette, Bernie. She was light. Light as air, the poor premature thing, a waif of a child, the inkling of a human girl. But also *light*, the beam of it, the full glare, an unsheltered bulb. The first thing that God commanded into creation. I looked into her face and was forgiven.

❖ ❖ ❖

Dean got to the hospital twenty-four hours after Bernie was born. Upon seeing him that first day, when I was still hooked up to an IV, still lying in the adjustable hospital bed, I felt relief wash over me. The same steady relief of the machine rehydrating me, knowing that my face was going from wan to colored. I was not relieved to see him; I was relieved because, upon seeing him, I knew I no longer needed him. He had made sure of that: taught me not to depend on him. I had found a way to go it alone. The whole time I had been in labor, I had never once asked them to call him, had never wanted him there.

He was as handsome as ever, his young, worried eyes eager as he looked at me, looked around for the child. He did not yet know where she was, and I could see him begin to wonder if something had gone wrong, if I had lost her. I could see his fear and also, I thought, his hope. A furtive wish that we would not have to raise a child, that he would not be a too-young parent like his own mother.

I suppose he found a different woman than the one he had left. He asked again and again if I was okay, if something had happened. He could not work out what had changed, even when he stared through the glass at her, her little eyes so concentrated and serious, as if she knew how hard she had to work to stay alive.

My face, of its own accord, turned away from Dean, turned toward the window. I knew then that I could do it—had already done it—alone. Everything in my body hurt, but I was free.

❖   ❖   ❖

Born ten weeks early with a lung complication, Bernie was transferred to Mercy Hospital's NICU after a week. I rode with her in the ambulance down to the city, siren blaring. Dean followed in the Hyundai.

Her face was placid as we sped along, red and yellow wires attached to her chest to monitor her heart rate, a tube down her nose to help with breathing. She was red and blotchy and too small. My chest ached. My throat was thick as if coated with honey. I loved her, my strange girl, my own child. She had different-colored eyes: one green and brown, one blue. Here was my trinity at last, all the points of me.

She stayed at Mercy for thirty-seven days. Thirty-seven days of feeling like my heart was split in two, of being ushered away from her by a nurse as soon as visiting hours were over, of haunting the hallways of the hospital like a ghost, of crying all the way home and into the night until I could return to her again. Thirty-seven days of pumping milk only to flush it down the sink, praying that it would keep coming even though there was no child in my arms to drink it. The plastic suction that was meant to mimic her soft lips—lips I had felt only once—and the loneliness that threatened to drag me under. Thirty-seven days of thinking I would get a call any minute, any hour, any day, telling me she hadn't made it.

Thirty-seven days, and, finally, we took her home.

Dean drove, and when we parked outside our apartment, I found that I was surprised to be back in the housing complex, as if I had expected the tall elm tree and chipping stones outside my parents' home.

Bernie had a phlegm build-up in her lungs, a condition that made her vulnerable to other sicknesses. A flu, a cold, could kill her. For many months, nobody was allowed to visit the house. I washed every surface that Dean touched, made him shower as soon as he got home from work, stood outside the bathroom and counted to twenty while he washed his hands. It was like having two children, trying to explain to Dean what the consequences would be if he accidentally passed germs to Bernie. He didn't believe it would really be that bad, couldn't think of himself as dangerous, as a threat. For me, it was the easiest thing in the world to believe that my own body might be fatal.

Bernie was everything I had been searching for. The family I had left behind, the home. The warmest moments of my childhood grafted onto her. Everything I had believed in, been ready to die for. She gave my life structure, meaning, purpose. The same way the paramilitaries had years ago. But this time she was all mine: not my mother's, not my sister's, not my country's. Bernie: her sweet-smelling skin, the slight jaundice of her face. I needed no life outside of her, wanted no life outside of her. She was the sun around which I spun, and I was happy to orbit her, to protect her, to shield her from the outside world, the night sky. I would never let her go.

❖ ❖ ❖

Money was tight now that I wasn't working. The impossibility of life in America began to weigh on me, the fact that mothers were bankrupted by childbirth. Dean was our sole lifeline, and he came home smelling of whiskey, the scent unbearably familiar, his unshaven cheeks reminding me of my father. He worked for us, "provided," as if we were two baby birds requiring regurgitated food from his mouth. As if men could operate only in the world of materials and transactions.

I watched him from across the room, his back ramrod straight, his long fingers hovering by his sides, his hands like hardback books. He stood at the window with eyes unfocused, and I wondered what it was he was not saying. He loved Bernie. I knew he did. I could see it in the way he closed his eyes when she lay on his chest. The way he would look at her sleeping and his usually mobile face would fall entirely still. But his love was quick to ebb, to turn to anger.

"Do you know how hard I work?" he yelled at me one night. "I'm not on vacation!"

I turned my back on him, slamming the door to the bedroom as hard as I could, so that the entire wall seemed to shake. The sound made Bernie cry. I held her close to me, her sobs my sobs. And when she finally calmed herself down, lay with her wet face against my chest, I was comforted too.

❖ ❖ ❖

When the doctors confirmed that Bernie's lungs were as healed as they ever would be, I rang Maria. She met me after her shift at the diner— she was a manager now—looking me over with a kind of familial distaste. I felt comforted by her appraising gaze. Like a sister, like a mother.

We walked in the dying light, Bernie in her stroller. She had never been this far from home before, and it filled me with excitement, possibility. I wanted to go farther and farther, until I could no longer remember the smell of mildew and the stains on the living room couch.

Maria thought a girl shouldn't be named Bernie and called her Bernadette. She made me feel, by lessening it slightly, the loneliness that had permanently settled on my chest. As I complained to her, she smoked American Spirits, blew the smoke away from the stroller, and nodded, offering no solutions. She seemed simply to agree that this was how men were, this was how marriage was. There was nothing to do for it except to walk for miles with another woman and complain. We did not mention the months I'd spent on her couch and my sudden decision to leave her. But it hung over me, the mistake I had made in choosing him.

Bernie grew. She crawled to me. She said "mama" and then "Ina," and when she said it, it was like the three of us were in that room together. She held my hand with little fingers. I pushed her around the housing complex in her stroller, and I dreamed of going away.

A few weeks after Bernie's first birthday, the United States categorized the Real IRA as a terrorist organization, the word smoldering like ash on my forehead. I saw the article buried in a newspaper Dean brought home from the bar. In the bathroom, I punched the wall hard enough that two of my fingers broke. When Dean found me there, my knuckles bleeding, my mouth a rosebud of silent agony, he didn't yell. He said, very quietly—so quietly that at first I'd thought I hadn't heard him correctly—that he was going to move out for a little while.

❖   ❖   ❖

The phrase *a little while* shifted in meaning, depending on how I looked at it. It seemed at first like he would be back momentarily, as soon as I got my temper under control, and then, later, it seemed like he was gone for good.

The idea grew on me. I wanted Bernie to myself, even if it meant she would have no father. I envied the Virgin Mary, she whose child had been between her and God. Again and again, I heard Dean's words. "We'll deal with it." It would be better, I thought, to be the two of us. I wanted to get on a plane with her, to vanish so completely that he would come looking for us and find only an old pair of flip-flops. I wanted to go home. It had been three years of displacement; I wanted to become Bríd again.

I went to the passport office with Bernie strapped to my chest. Men held doors open for me, waved me to the front of the line. I handed over Ina's passport, my green card, Bernie's and Ina's birth certificates. The fact that I looked enough like Ina to pass no longer gave me the same thrill. I felt itchy under the fluorescent lights, Bernie gurgling against my chest. It felt like a game: playing Ina, playing wife. The reality of Ireland loomed in the back of my mind: a landscape dark and profound and real. Home was like an ocean I wanted to swim in, was afraid to drown in.

Of course I couldn't just leave. I had vague ideas about kidnapping, leaving the country with an infant. Dean's name wasn't on the birth certificate, but the last thing I needed was a warrant out for my arrest. I needed to know that he would not come after us.

Nothing with Dean was simple. It never had been. He went one week and then two without answering my calls. Then he showed up out of the blue to take Bernie for such a long walk that halfway through, I set off after them, certain he had decided to leave with her. One night, he suggested a divorce—yelled it in the heat of an argument—but he never brought the papers that he said he would. Bernie's passport arrived: a dark-blue vinyl booklet that looked nothing like Ina's blood-colored red one. On my nightstand, they sat together like unread novels, containing worlds I hadn't yet seen.

By the second week of August, I had gone four weeks without hearing from Dean, the longest it had ever been. Because we had never gone to court, no child-support payments had ever been mandated, and I had been relying on his general decency to bring me money of varying amounts each month. But when August came and went without so much as a word, I swallowed my pride and called him. The phone line, the operator said, had been disconnected. Panicked, I drove to the condo that he had rented in central Miami, only to find that it was empty; he had left, the superintendent said. He hadn't said where he was going; there was no forwarding address.

❖ ❖ ❖

I went home, a strange mixture of relief, elation, and fear running through me. I had just enough money for a plane ticket, with nothing left over. Over that next week, I packed our bags.

Bernie and I spent our last night on the sofa, watching TV and eating crisps out of a jumbo bag I'd bought at Costco. I made us tea because I couldn't sleep, pouring it into Bernie's sippy cup when it had cooled enough. As I mixed a spoonful of honey into the water, dark from the seeping tea bag, I remembered the house, a dusty gray morning by the fire, in the month before winter became spring. My sister's boots clattering on the stairs as she ran up and down, changing outfits until she found something Ma would deem appropriate. Ina was magnetic, face flushed with exertion. A girl of fifteen. Sometimes you looked at her and the sight made you want to get down on your knees and pray.

Bernie was glorious like that. A face tipped upward toward the sun. The smell of her gave me goose bumps, the soft newness of her skin. The way her wrists and ankles stuck out of her pajamas as she sat on the couch, the shape of her small body beneath the fabric. The cold black stare she gave to strangers. And her smile, scrunching her face into an alphabet of joy, her own language of happiness.

She would never really know her father, the smart, self-destructive, curly-haired man who had kissed her forehead so gently the first time he held her. Maybe some part of her would remember the smell of his chest as they lay in bed together, her tiny body atop him like a bird perched on an elephant's back. But she would never put a face to that smell, would never see him drunk and be afraid, would never hear him tell a joke and laugh uncontrollably.

We would be home soon, there for the changing of the leaves, the snow if it fell, the holidays. I finally fell asleep on the sofa, lulled by the sound of children's television. Bernie slept beside me, oblivious, unknowing.

❖ ❖ ❖

The radio was not on in the taxi. I kept my hand on Bernie in her car seat and watched the palm trees pass, the rush-hour traffic. At the airport, the doors opened automatically for us, and I remember Bernie's awe at that magic. There was a television near the check-in gates, and a man stood in front of it, crying. We walked toward him. We were not the only ones. People moved as if in slow motion toward the screen, eyes glued to it.

I held Bernie as we watched the second plane hit the towers. The blackness spread from the top of the buildings down. At first it seemed like it was only their color that was changing. Then I could see that they were falling, imploding. I thought they would topple to the side, but they crumpled inward, received themselves. And I saw the shapes falling, tiny and black, petals from a flower. The bodies.

The smoke spread, a nuclear cloud, slow and physical, huge over the men and women running, their suits and ties pathetic as their faces contorted with fear.

Though we were a thousand miles away, I thought I could smell burning, thought I could hear the noise. Wondered if that was what it sounded like to die, a suck of sound. If that was what Ina had heard.

The towers were gone so quickly, gone and it seemed like they had never been. The sky outside the sliding doors was bright blue. A beautiful September day.

We were standing in a crowd of people now. Over the loudspeaker, a woman announced that the airport was closing; all flights were canceled. On the television, the headline said this was terrorism. That word again. The growl of the *R*s. There was something coming apart inside me, and I knew I could not go home.

PART THREE

Chapter Eighteen

2016, Los Angeles County

My morning sickness only got worse after the appointment. Maybe it was the knowledge of what was to come, the pills in my nightstand. I missed the last three days of junior year, tossing and turning in sweaty sheets instead of doing whatever our teachers had planned to waste the final hours away. I still wasn't eating; I still hadn't taken the pills. On the fourth day, Mom told me to get in the car. I hobbled downstairs on her arm to find she'd packed a bag.

"What's up?" I asked, looking around suspiciously.

"Not much."

"Like, where are we going?"

"You'll see."

"Can't you just tell—" I said at the same time as she said:

"Do you not want a sur—"

"No."

"No?"

"No." My legs were shaking, a slight tremor behind the knee.

"I thought we'd have a girls' weekend," she said. She never said things like that.

Last summer, we had gone to Joshua Tree for three days, staying in an Airstream trailer we'd rented. There was no reception at the campground and, except for the dull toothache of missing Mia, it had been lovely, open, free. The cool desert air at night and Mom and me foraging in the nearby pharmacy for microwavable meals. Giving each other facials with Mom's exfoliants and creams and listening to U2 on the CD player Mom still used. But she had never called it a "girls' weekend." And we had planned it together.

"Are you taking me to the hospital?"

She didn't respond.

"Mom?"

"No, Bernie, I'm not taking you to hospital. I'm taking you to get some rest. To get your mind off things so you can start to *eat* again."

How I'd learned to hate that word.

"What things?" I asked.

"Get in the car," she said.

I felt like I was about to collapse, so I got in.

She took me to a "rehabilitation and luxury spa" by the ocean. In the parking lot, we sat in the car.

"Mom?"

"Bernie."

"I don't need rehab. I'm not an alcoholic."

"Think of it as recovery," she said. She had that look in her eye that she got when she was too far gone on an idea to be talked out of it. "I read their website. It looks amazing. I'm coming too. It will be like a slumber party." She was keeping her tone light, but I could see the worry between her eyebrows, the creases of her forehead.

"I don't think they appreciate parties in rehab."

"You worry too much," she told me. "Let's go fatten you up." She opened the car door.

I felt like a farm animal, raised for the slaughter. She wanted to stuff me full so she could stop worrying. But she didn't want to tell me anything, didn't want to treat me like someone who deserved to know her own past.

"Mom, what the fuck?" I felt numb, but I was yelling. "I'm not going to rehab."

She shut the door again.

"It's not rehab," she said. "It's a spa."

"It *says* rehabilitation." I pointed to the sign. I was going to cry. I wanted to grab her and shake her. My body was seized with anger. Anger that she would not treat me like a woman, that she did not know what I was going to do. Anger that there was something I still didn't know, something she would not tell me. That she was trying to treat me, to fix me, when it was she who needed fixing. She who needed to sort out her problems. I was, I suddenly realized, fucking starving. That fact made me even angrier somehow.

She rummaged in her handbag and held up several mini bottles of white wine and a few airplane-size Kahlúas. "It's not rehab for us, okay?"

I stared at her.

"I can't stand this," she said, suddenly serious. "I can't stand seeing you in pain. I need you to get better."

When she said "pain," I saw the packet of pills I'd hidden in my backpack. I saw Mia getting to her feet, saying she had to go. I heard her voice through the phone when she told me what had happened to Riley. I couldn't think of a retort.

❖   ❖   ❖

Once we got into the center, I saw that she was not entirely misled. It was primarily a spa, the rehabilitation only extending as far as optional AA meetings and sober-lifestyle meditation classes. In the cafeteria—which was entirely silent to encourage meditation—I began to eat again. No solid foods, just soup and smoothies. I felt like a child. I spit out chunks of carrots from my vegetable soup. Mom didn't care, kept saying fluids were the most important thing anyway, which I didn't think was actually true. The longer I ate an all-liquid diet, the more convinced I became that if I ever did bite into a veggie burger again, I would choke on it.

Mom had packed for me and had exclusively brought clothes that were either too tight or too childish for me. I bought a baggy green jumpsuit at the gift shop. It was woven from organic cotton. I wore it for the whole weekend, even to sleep. Mom called it my prison uniform.

We got facials and back massages.

"Can we afford this?" I asked.

"For two days, sure," she said. I figured Kaleb must be paying.

We got pedicures. We talked about the upcoming election. We talked about Brad Pitt. We talked about the forest fires. We talked about Kaleb's aunt, whom neither of us liked. We talked about boys in my class. We talked about college. We talked about David Bowie dying. I could tell we were building up to what we really wanted to say; we were treading water until we got the nerve to dive.

"I told Mia that I love her," I said.

We were in the hot tub at the spa, hair held on top of our heads by towel wraps. I had waited for the other bather to step out, to leave the locker room.

Mom looked at me, and I knew what her gaze meant. She wanted to know what kind of love I was talking about.

"That I'm in love with her," I said. I was staring straight ahead, fidgeting with the towel on my head. "She said—well, she didn't really say anything."

I turned to look at her.

"Oh, Bernie," she said, and she put her hand against my cheek. The softness of her voice made me want to cry.

"And then Riley—" I said, unable to hold back now. "God, I was so scared. And Mia wouldn't talk to me, and then you got . . . you got low, and I thought you would be next."

Her eyes were filling with tears; mine did the same. She hugged me for a long moment, held me against her in the water. I wondered if this was what it had felt like in her womb. The warmth of her embrace, wet and safe. It felt almost too intimate. I wondered if she could feel the hardness of my stomach, the change in it. If she could sense the thing that had come between us.

"You know every time you go for a drive," she said, "even if it's just down to the pharmacy or to see Mia or whatever . . ." She looked away from me, to the wall at the far end of the room. "I always think you're not coming back. I always think . . . every single time, I think you're gone. I'm sure you've been in an accident; I'm sure you're dead. And I go up to my room and I get ready for the call telling me what happened. And then you walk back in the door like nothing happened, maybe looking a little worse for wear recently"—she gave a watery laugh—"and you say, 'Hi, Mom,' and you have no idea that I'm beside myself with grief."

❖   ❖   ❖

That night, we drank the mini bottles of Kahlúa and white wine. Mom's phone was playing CNN, but we talked over it. She produced a bottled Green Machine smoothie and made me finish it. While I drank the smoothie, she took out a full-size bottle of wine and poured herself a glass.

I had made my decision. Mom knew something was wrong. For all I knew, she might have guessed it already. She seemed so open today, so forgiving. It was time, I knew, to tell her.

I had opened my mouth to speak when her eyes darted to the phone screen. There was a Breaking News banner at the bottom of it. She reached for the phone and turned the volume up. I swallowed my words as the newscaster's voice got louder.

"A shooting at a nightclub in Orlando, Florida," the newscaster was saying. "So far, there are reports of over thirty fatalities. Police are still at the scene of the crime."

"Jesus Christ," I murmured.

We both watched the phone in silence. Footage of the crime scene: dark night and flashing lights, first responders moving quickly in and out of a building.

"This is awful," I said. I looked over at Mom. She was quiet. Her eyes were unfocused on the phone screen. She looked shell-shocked, frozen. Fear gripped me, like cold water drenching my body. What was wrong? I stared at the screen, wondering if I was missing something. If there was some connection I wasn't making. I'd been born in Florida—was that it? Did this feel too close to our old home? Did she know someone who lived there?

"Mom?" I asked. "Are you okay?"

I took the phone from her hand and turned the volume down.

She was still quiet, still not looking at me.

"Mom?" I could hear the urgency in my own voice.

"That's how she died," she said after a long minute.

"What?" I asked, my mind racing, trying to place the pronoun. She?

"My sister," she said. "My sister, Ina."

"What?" I asked again. The name ringing in my head. The three letters that had always meant only one thing: her. I looked down at her necklace, where the word was spelled out. I wanted to grab for it, to ask her what it meant.

"That's how she died," she repeated.

Her face looked very fragile, as if it would collapse at the slightest of disturbances. She was still staring out at nothing. Somewhere, in the back of my mind, I was trying to make sense of the situation. To put things in boxes, to sort out the jumble. The word *aunt* came to me, a word I'd never thought much about.

"The night she died, she was wearing yellow," Mom said. "They threw out the dress when they buried her. It was closed coffin. They said it was all torn up, couldn't be salvaged."

"The body?" I asked.

"The dress."

"How did she die?" I still did not understand what had happened, how she and my mother shared the same name. It felt like she was dying again now. Like we were moving back in time together.

"Dancing," my mom said.

I could feel her moving away from me, knew she would not keep talking for long. But something about being here, something about the rehabilitation center and her determination to heal me had changed everything. It was healing her too. Even with this awful thing, this time, she was pulling closer instead of drifting further away.

"Her name was Ina?" I asked carefully.

Finally, she sighed, looked at me for the first time.

"Yes," she said. "That used to be her name. I took it from her. When she died."

My heart was pounding in my chest.

"What's your real name?" I asked slowly. I tried not to make it sound like an accusation.

It felt, somewhere inside me, like I had known all along. Known that something this fundamental was a lie. I couldn't swallow; my throat was too dry. Everything was spinning.

"Bríd," she said.

"Bridge," I said, leaning into the sound, wanting to get it right.

"Bríd," she corrected.

The way she pronounced it, it sounded more like *breach* and less like *bridge*. But still, there was a *g* sound.

"How do you spell it?" I'd have an easier time if I could imagine the letters on the page, if I could know her that way.

"B-r-i-d. The *i* has an accent. Bríd Kane."

So Evans had been my father's name, I thought. I wanted to ask for his first name, wanted to demand to know, but I was afraid she would shut down forever if I did. She had always said she couldn't bear to talk about him.

"Okay." I kept my tone as level as I could, like balancing a pencil on my finger. I did not want to frighten her. I needed her to keep talking. I felt angry and confused, frightened and relieved. Like a soldier coming home from war to find her home feels foreign. All I could focus on was discovering what there was to know. Being free, finally, from the burden of these secrets.

"When did your sister die?" I asked.

She lay down on the pillow next to me.

"1997," she said. "She was fifteen. Younger than you are."

It felt like she was drifting away from me, back to the past, a place I couldn't reach her. She looked at me then like I knew everything that she knew and this comforted her. I didn't want to remind her that I was her daughter, uncomprehending, uninitiated. Born too late to know Ina, to know her. I felt simultaneously closer to her and further away. Like it was only now that I realized we had miles between us, but at least now I knew. At least I could see her now, in the distance, and know what I was running to.

We fell asleep like that, our faces turned toward one another.

Chapter Nineteen

2000s, Los Angeles County

When Bernie was nine, four men were found guilty of the 1998 Omagh bombing in a civil trial. Among them was Aidan, who'd been second-in-command to the woman. He was one of the men I'd delivered the car to in Donegal.

It felt like an indictment of me. I would have been arrested, too, I thought, if they had known who to look for. If they had known where to look. If I had stayed, I might be hearing the knock on my door even now, feeling the ice of the handcuffs around my wrists.

Bernie and I had been in California for five years by then, the most stable years of her life. Before California, it had been motel rooms and temporary housing, quick stays in cities that we never got to know. Now Bernie had her own bike. She knew her way around town. It was starting to feel like home.

I went to confession. I hadn't been since I left Ireland, feeling that what I'd done was between God and me, that including a third person would only complicate things. "I came not to send peace, but a sword," Jesus had said. Back in Tyrone, Father Jim had been as much a part of the conflict as any of us. He had spoken during Sunday Mass about defending your people, about Moses freeing the Jews from Pharaoh, about Jesus's love of the righteous. He had quoted Matthew to us: "I am come to set a man at variance against his father, and the daughter against her mother." He had wanted us to fight. When I clung to Catholicism, it was really Irish Catholicism I was holding on to. It was the liturgy and dirge of my homeland; it was the familiar rhythm of the text more than any individual words. American priests, I thought, would not understand.

But now my thoughts felt heavier, darker. I wasn't as able to carry them alone. I had a daughter to look out for, and I thought that confessing might fix me, relieve me, absolve me. It was the first time I said out loud what I had done. The first time I heard it, the narrative of my own actions. Everything I'd done in Ireland I'd done in silence.

The priest had teeth that glinted through the thatches of the confession box. He was like a doctor or a magician, extracting the story from me. I tried to remind myself that God was here, that His presence was stronger in this upright coffin than it had been in the car I'd driven to Donegal. But it didn't feel that way.

"And what happened to the pregnant woman?" the priest asked when I had finished my hazy confession.

"I don't know," I said. "I never knew.

"There's something else I have to tell you," I said. And I recounted that night with Ina: how I had scoffed at her. How she had thrown her makeup bag at me. How I had known where she was going, known it was dangerous. How I had let her go. How, deep down, some part of me had always resented her, had always been jealous of her. How at times I'd wished she would disappear. How much I missed her.

Afterward, I lay with my head against the car steering wheel, feeling a weight on my back as if Bernie were strapped to me, remembering my forehead pressed against the wheel the day I witnessed the destruction at the hotel. The day I'd driven to the hospital and seen the victim's face in the paper. The priest had asked for Hail Marys, and I said them, crouching in my bedroom, knowing God's eyes were on me.

Trouble the Living

Confession did not absolve me; it terrified me. I had said the unsayable; I had unstopped the dam. Everything, now, could be told. What if, under examination, Aidan remembered my name? What if the priest went to the police? I stayed in my bedroom for weeks on end, watching cars pass with mounting terror. Sure that I was about to be arrested, Bernie about to be taken from me. I kept praying to God, but it felt as though He couldn't hear me. He was like my mother, turning His back on me, and I was sure then that I was damned. That I could spend the rest of my life trying to make up for what I'd done and never get any closer to forgiveness.

It was worse than it had ever been, worse than the days I'd spent in bed in Miami, worse than the nights after giving birth. And, this time, I had a daughter who was depending on me. Bernie sat in my room while I lay in bed, scribbling in her school notebooks. Her handwriting looked like stray hairs across a page.

I knew that every minute I lay there aged her. Every time I told her to turn off the lights and watch the window, I was breaking the thing between us, bending it until it would snap. And yet I could not get up, could not help my own daughter, could not lift the weight off her and shoulder it myself.

❖   ❖   ❖

In the end, it was a nun who saved me. Sister Josephine had a wide, round face and a mouth that always looked a little too red to be natural. I met her volunteering at the church one day, and she gave me the phone number of the director of the homeless shelter.

"If you're going to do God's work," she said, "you might as well get paid for it." And she laughed her throaty laugh. "Your girl won't get fed on her own."

I'd been working at a hotel near town, but I called the shelter director as soon as I got home. It had been a long time since there had been something, apart from Bernie, that felt meaningful. Something I could believe in.

The director was an ex-alcoholic and, after he hired me, he brought me to my first AA meeting. I had asked about it, not because I thought I was an alcoholic but because I thought the iron taste of honesty might help me, the community of sinners. At the meeting, neither of us spoke. A woman with a hoarse, painful voice told us that she had cirrhosis of the liver and at most five years to live if she never had another drink. Two nights before, she'd drunk a handle of vodka, and her neighbors had called an ambulance for her, ready for her to die.

A young man with tattoos across his arms and chest had been on a seven-day bender. He had broken six months of sobriety and was close to tears. "Where did I sleep?" he kept asking us. "During that time, where did I sleep?" As if any one of us might have the answer.

Afterward, when I stepped out into the sunshine, I felt something heavy in my own stomach, as if I, too, had liver damage. The moments of levity had been therapeutic, just as the moments of despair had been cathartic, but still I felt vaguely nauseous from the whole thing. At the end, when we'd said the Lord's Prayer, it was like I was hearing the words for the first time in a long time, even though I said the prayer with Bernie every night. "Forgive us our trespasses," I thought again and again.

As I got into my car and started the engine, waving goodbye to my new boss, I thought about what one man had said. "I was sixteen when I had my first drink," he'd told us. "And I knew, I knew from that moment, that I would be an alcoholic."

I knew what he meant, that sense of predestination. Of there never having been another way. I remembered that afternoon in April when Ma had brought us to the border, how the rocks had slipped beneath my feet. It had been a crooked line from there to the accelerator under my foot, the velvet night sky, and the unknown burden in the boot. I thought of Ina's head falling onto my shoulder, thought of her falling;

her death had deserved something terrible and beautiful in return. The fragmented hotel, bedsheets swirling in the wind like the white of waves at sea.

That night, when Bernie fell asleep, I opened a bottle of Southern Comfort. I only meant to have two or three drinks. My hand shook on the pour. Bernie found me in the morning, passed out on the sofa, the trash can by my head. I was fine, I told her. I sat up and asked her to get me a Coke, but she couldn't reach the shelf in the fridge where they sat. I stood and got one for myself, poured it over ice, and drank it slowly while Bernie watched me.

❖   ❖   ❖

I kept going to AA. The room we sat in was tight, signs hanging precariously off the wall, literature stuffed onto shelves, knees stepped over, someone's breath at the back of your neck. When you talked, you looked at the floor. When you listened, you did the same.

There was a lot of talk of blackouts, and I thought I knew what they meant. It wasn't just a night of heavy drinking; it was your brain acting of its own accord, wiping the hard drive, denying you the truth to save your sanity. It was when you looked down at your hands and genuinely did not know what they'd done, what they were capable of. It was looking up at a building turned to ruins and wondering if you were the one responsible.

I kept drinking, even as I went to the meetings, but, if anything, the alcohol made me feel closer to the group. After my first meeting, I had sworn to myself that I would never talk, never stand up and expose myself, but very quickly, I began to speak regularly.

I talked about my father, the fear I had felt around him, about my brother getting married and going off, about a death in the family for which I felt responsible. I talked about deserting my mother, about being left by Dean. How I'd packed our daughter into the back seat of a car and driven west. I knew I was supposed to be talking about alcohol, about addiction, but once I'd opened up, I couldn't stop. I talked about mistakes I'd made, people I'd hurt, relationships I'd sacrificed, and I let them assume that it had been alcohol driving me all the time, when in reality it had been revenge, doctrine, belief. In reality, it had been guilt and fear and grief, the thin line of my mother's smile, and the blossoming of Ina's skirt as she spun.

❖   ❖   ❖

I met Kaleb when Bernie was twelve. He went to AA once a week on Thursdays, and one week, when I had to miss my regular meeting, I joined his. He sat with his head tipped back, the crown of it pressing against the wall and his eyes closed. He didn't speak, except to say the traditional "Hi, John" or "Hi, Liz," and even then, he didn't open his eyes.

I spoke. It was my three-year anniversary with AA, though in actuality I'd had a margarita the night before. Still, I had to keep up appearances, and so I stood and acknowledged the milestone.

After the meeting, I pumped myself a cup of coffee from the plastic canister, and he came up behind me and asked my name.

"Bríd," I said. "Ina," I corrected. "Ina Brigid." He'd caught me off guard. I had been feeling too much like myself.

He gave an easy laugh. He had dark-brown skin and tightly curled hair. "It's a pleasure to meet you, Ina Brigid," he said. "I'd like to take you out for a drink. I'm dying to know why someone would pretend to be an alcoholic."

At the bar, where he ordered a soda water and I ordered a vodka tonic, Kaleb told me he was a professor, writing about the morality of lying.

"I'm particularly interested," he said, "in the ways in which our lies can get us closer to the truth. You are not an alcoholic," he continued, "and yet you were telling the truth when you spoke in the meeting. I could hear it in your voice."

"How did you know?" I asked.

"I was at Rosita's last night too," he said. "I saw you order a margarita with two shots."

"I could have just slipped up," I said. "How did you know I was lying?"

He thought about that.

"The way you talked in the meeting," he said. "I know we're not supposed to discuss these things out here." He made a gesture with his right hand to encompass the bar, the outside world. "But you talk like a person who has only ever done what they meant to."

"That's—"

He held up his hand to stop me. "I'm not saying you don't have any regrets. You obviously do. But alcoholics only ever choose one thing: drinking. Everything else just happens to them. You made all your own choices. Even if you wish you hadn't."

I stared at him, said nothing. We took another sip of our drinks.

The next week, Kaleb came by the shelter and helped me prepare and serve dinner. He took me out for another drink. If he was attracted to me, I thought, he was attracted to the darkness. Even if his own life was conducted in the daylight.

Chapter Twenty

2016, Los Angeles County

A week after our spa weekend, I came downstairs to find Mom standing in the kitchen, listening to the radio.

It had been a good week. We had been more relaxed around each other after our time at the spa. We'd gone to the movies a few times and cooked dinner like we used to. We'd listened to the radio—a pop-music station; she hadn't wanted to hear any more about the shooting—and Kaleb had come over for ice cream sundaes, all of us eating so much that our stomachs ached. I'd felt, finally, full.

Mom was still calling herself Ina, but she had told me more about her life. She was from the north of Ireland. Her mother's name was Aoife; her father was Sean. She had two brothers, still living, Tad and Enda. Ina had died in a bombing, a civilian casualty killed by a British paramilitary group. Only when I asked her why we had never visited, why she had left and never returned, did she get that distant look in her eyes. "They're hard people, my family," she'd said.

I was still planning to tell her about the pills, to ask for her help. It only seemed fair. If she had lost a sister, she had lived with harder things. I was just waiting for the right time.

"You're up early," I said now. Usually, the yellow pills she took every night made her sleep in late, through her alarm, so she was always rushing to work, a mug hastily stowed in the car cupholder. Sometimes, on her days off, I'd climb into her bed in the early afternoon and take a nap beside her, with her still asleep.

"They voted to leave," she said quietly.

"Who did?" I asked. I had forgotten what day it was. What she had been waiting for. It felt too foreign to be worried about what was happening across the ocean.

"England," she said, and I remembered the Reddit threads on her iPad and her nights spent in front of the news.

"What will happen now?" I asked. She was still staring out the window. I felt frustration rise in me and then sadness. Things had been so good between us; now she had reverted to that old remoteness, like she was the faraway land we were discussing. I could feel her body beginning to sag; she was going back underwater.

She sighed. "I guess, I guess they'll start withdrawal negotiations."

"Sounds like a drug thing," I said. I moved toward the kettle to pour myself a cup of tea.

She didn't laugh. "The North voted no," she said. "The North wanted to stay." For a moment, something passed over her face. I could see it, even from the side.

Once, when I was little, before I knew that consumerism was deadly, we went to a department store together to visit the makeup counter. Mom let me sit on the counter itself, while a gorgeous, plump lady did her makeup, painting over spots on her face until her skin was all one color: a rosy white, like a slab of wood. I watched the woman spread blush across my mother's cheeks, watched her flick the mascara wand over her lashes, and, before my eyes, my mother's face became that of a stranger's. That was what it felt like now, like seeing someone else hidden in the folds of her features, someone buried underground, trying to dig herself out.

"You left," I pointed out. "You wanted to leave too."

"It's one country!" She yelled it so suddenly that I jumped, my hand on the teakettle shaking violently so that I nearly dropped it. "They can't just lop off the head and call it something else. They're connected, North and South. You can't go and build a bloody wall!"

She slammed her mug down on the counter, and it made a loud clunking sound and then a grating while it scraped against the stone of the surface. It didn't break; it was IKEA sturdy.

"What are they going to do to Belleek?" she went on. "Will they check your passport on the way to the shop so?"

I didn't say anything. There was nothing I could say. I didn't know what Belleek was or where the shops were. Maybe that was where she had grown up. Belleek. I liked the sound of it.

"It's this small part of England that wants it," she said, "and now they're dragging all of us along with them." I wondered at the pronoun she'd chosen. "Us." I wondered if "us" included me.

She sighed heavily. "I think I'll go back to bed," she said. Her face was suddenly placid, still as a pool of water, shallow as a puddle. I watched her turn away from me again. I wondered what her face looked like when I couldn't see it. Was it any different? Did my gaze change her, even as it sought her out?

❖　❖　❖

I went for a bike ride. I needed to get out of the house, stale with the past she'd dragged us back to. I biked to the shelter automatically, taking turns without seeing them. My eyes a fog of frustration. Just when things had been okay again. Just when I'd been about to tell her.

"How's the baby?" Damon asked. I'd found him in his usual spot behind the shelter. He'd been rolling down his sleeve, and I caught a glimpse of the marks up his arm like hairs. I wanted to reach out and touch them. I didn't know if he was talking about me or about the fetus growing inside me.

"Fine," I said. "It's almost over."

He looked at me with those watery eyes. Did he know what I was saying? Did he even remember?

He nodded, looked out at the road behind us.

"What's your story, then?" I asked. "Do you have a family?"

"You think I'd be here if I did?"

I shrugged. "Some people leave their families," I said. "Or they're made to leave."

"That's what I mean," he said, "by not having a family."

We were talking in circles. He had the same faraway eyes that my mother did. I suddenly wanted to get out of there, away from him. Why had I come?

"I'll see you," I said, turning to go.

"Did you ever find out about your grandparents?" he asked.

"What about them?" I turned back around.

"If it's genetic," he said, and I remembered our conversation about my mother. It made me feel the slightest bit less alone, knowing he had been listening.

"No," I said. "But I found out what happened. Her sister died."

"How?" he asked.

"A bomb," I said. "My mother took her name, actually." I gave a strange laugh, not sure if I thought it was funny or sad. "I never knew her real name until, like, a week ago."

"Why?" he asked.

"I don't know." I shrugged. "I haven't gotten that far," I said. "I'll tell you next time."

He nodded, and I left him there, leaning against the wall, feeling the rush of his own body. I biked home, feeling the wind against my face, remembering the rolling of Damon's eyes. I imagined Mia beside me, her hair whipping around, her laugh as she yelled back at me to race her, her strong legs pedaling faster and faster until I lost her entirely.

Chapter Twenty-One

2016, Los Angeles County

The decision was an old wound reopened. It was a thin blade down scarred skin. Everyone was surprised, except anyone who had lived under occupation. Except Kaleb, who kept saying that Donald Trump would be president. Except anyone who'd grown up in the North and saw how little we mattered.

It wasn't that I didn't love Bernie, or Kaleb, or the house, or even California, warm caress that it was. It was that I missed my home. I missed my island in its entirety, the oaky smell of pubs, the cawing of seagulls, the patchwork of green, the bushes, the shrubs, the smell of the air—fresh like the sea—the stars scattered across the sky like broken glass, the clear note of a soprano singing a folk song, the strum of a guitar, fingers tugging out the longing deep, deep inside me.

I had always hoped that I was innocent, but now I wanted to be guilty. The anger of this June separation brought me back to that old December, the dance club, my Ina. And what I wanted now was to look inside the boot of the old car and see the bomb, small and wiry, like a child tied to tubes, like Bernie. I wanted to be the one who'd broken the bones of the old hotel. I wanted to have made my mother proud.

I felt like I had lived through every occupation, every bullet in a man's chest, every schoolchild taught the names of kings who were not her own. I wanted violence, more and more violence, and it terrified me.

I stayed in bed for a day and a half. I drew the covers up to my chin like a straitjacket, as if the flimsy cloth could hold me. A useless gesture, like drawing a line on a map and expecting it to stick.

❖ ❖ ❖

On the second day, Bernie got in bed next to me and opened a book about the climate crisis. She looked pained as she studied the words and, for a minute, I felt responsible for all of this, as if I had done her a great disservice by giving birth to her sixteen years ago.

I wrapped an arm around her stomach, nestled my head against her shoulder. She smelled wonderful, like honeysuckle mixed with the rich smell of a barn in summer. Her skin was warm, and her body felt wild and strange, not at all like the girl I'd given birth to. It was as if her insides were restructuring her, were creating a new woman from the flesh and bones my body had produced.

I stared at her collarbones where they lay above the tight band of her tank top. Her skin was darker than mine, the bit of Dean still in her. Her hair up in a loose ponytail. She still wasn't eating enough.

"Mom, stop staring at me," she said, and I managed a laugh, closed my eyes again. But I kept my arm around her like a seat belt. I wanted to protect her from the wreckage. She didn't know what I'd done, my sweet, justice-seeking, morally resolute Bernie. I would never tell her.

I fell asleep like that, holding her.

❖ ❖ ❖

I dreamed of a small boy, curled up in the boot of a car. Lying in the fetal position. A sheen of sweat on his pale forehead.

Then my father was holding him under one arm, casually, precariously, and I was watching, filled with a terror that Da would drop him, knowing—in the illogical way you know things in dreams—that if he fell, he would die.

It was the same feeling I had gotten when I watched Bernie on the monkey bars as a child or now when I saw her drive off in Kaleb's car. The feeling of living on a bridge between two worlds—one in which she was swinging, laughing, and the other in which she had fallen.

Bernie woke me up at 5:00 p.m. A gentle hand on my shoulder. A cup of tea.

"We've got to go," she said. "To the shelter. Please, Mom."

I stared at her. My daughter, acting like my mother.

"It's been two days," she said. "You have to go to work."

I squeezed her hand. I got out of bed. I let her take the driver's seat. I was shaking with the same anger I'd felt all those years ago, when my hands on the steering wheel had meant revenge. I had done terrible things behind the wheel of a car. It was safer, I thought, for her to drive.

When we got to the shelter, I knew something was wrong. Evenings were usually hectic as people lined up for their dinners or stood in groups outside smoking. The beds were all supposed to be set up by 7:00 p.m., though sometimes it was nine before we started unfolding them. But that evening, there was nobody standing outside smoking. The air around us felt compounded, charged with movement. We hesitated for a moment on the threshold.

The giant, high-ceilinged hall was lit up with the overhead lights and the last rays of the day's sun. There was the familiar smell of powdered coffee, of sweat, of Lysol and antibacterial wipes. But the bodies were not spread out like usual in evenly spaced beds or assembled in a chaotic line for food. They were all crowded around the bathroom entrance, a mass of frantic movements. I walked quickly, Bernie behind me, pushing my way past several people until I found Dan. Dan had been at the shelter for as long as I had worked there. He was tall, with deep-brown skin and a scar beneath his left eye. He had served in Vietnam.

"What happened?"

Dan stood, facing the bathroom with his eyes closed.

"Damon," he said without opening his eyes.

I looked at Bernie to see if she had heard. "Go wait outside," I told her. I saw her begin to protest, her brow twisting to argue with me, but I shook my head and turned away from her, pushing forward into the crowd. I joined the staffers at the mouth of the men's bathroom. There were two women on duty that evening.

"What happened?" I asked in a low voice.

Mariana, our youngest employee, was only a few years older than Bernie. She looked up at me with black eyes, and I saw tear tracks on her face.

"We were about to call you," JoJo said. "We called 911. They're on their way."

"What happened?" I asked again. They didn't reply.

I pushed past them, like a swimmer fighting a tide. Finally, I was in the bathroom, alone. There were four stalls and three urinals, and next to the urinal on the far right was the body. Someone had covered it with a bedsheet. I pulled it down to see his face.

I had never seen Ina, after. The coffin had been sealed shut, mahogany, shiny wood. Only my mother had seen her before they covered her up. Only she had to live with that memory. I had seen other bodies, of course, but they had been old, at rest, laid out in their beds, their hair done and their faces made up. None of them had been violated.

They had cut him down from the ceiling. I wondered which of them had done it. JoJo, I thought, or one of the other residents. The belt was still around his neck, but it was loosened now. There were bruises around his throat, like a necklace. And his face was swollen, reddish.

For a moment, I thought there must have been some mistake. This was not how I'd imagined his death. I'd imagined a needle in his arm, his eyes rolled into his head, his fragility chemical, not emotional. When I had told Bernie to stay away from him, I had thought I was telling her to stay away from a liar, an addict. But I had been telling her to stay away from the darkness, from a man who saw too far down into the abyss. She was my daughter. No wonder she had loved him.

I heard the door open and turned.

Chapter Twenty-Two

2016, Los Angeles County

At the far end of the bathroom, Mom was standing over someone. Two boots poked out from either side of her. The sole of one boot was gaping open.

She started and turned around. For a moment, I had a glimpse of a body, something purple, a green hoodie, and then she pulled a sheet over it and held out her arms in a T to block my view.

"Bernie, get out of here," she said, her mouth a snarl. "Get in the car and go home."

"Is it him?" I asked, my voice a knife edge of panic. "Mom, is it him?"

"Bernie, *go*." Her face was contorted. I thought she was going to vomit. "Ring 911 for me. Tell them we need an ambulance."

"Okay," I said. I took my phone out of my pocket.

"Outside," she said. "Ring them outside. And then go home."

"Will you tell me?" I asked her. I was thumbing the volume switch on the side of my phone. "Will you tell me what happened?" I couldn't keep my eyes off the shape beneath the sheet. I wanted to run to him, pull it off him, see his face. But I was afraid to look, afraid of what I would see.

"We'll talk when we get home," she said. "But go, Bernie; please go."

Sitting in the car, I called 911. They said there was already an ambulance on the way. Mom's colleagues must have called before we got there. She had just been trying to get me out of the shelter, pretending I could be useful. In the distance, I heard sirens. I felt the cold wash of my fear, and I started the car. This was what Mia must have felt like, I thought, finding Riley. It was like a punch to the stomach, imagining what she had gone through. I wanted to drive to her, to run up the stairs to her room and hold her. But she didn't want me. Feeling like a coward, knowing I was not as brave as she was, I began to drive.

❖   ❖   ❖

I threw up when I got home. Kaleb wasn't there. I felt weak, but there was nothing I could even think about eating. I'd go to his office and tell him what had happened. He had another class at six or seven, a nighttime seminar.

I walked to the Africana Studies building. Normally I would have biked, but I kept seeing spots in front of my eyes. When I knocked on Kaleb's door, I heard him call from within. I pushed it open. Kaleb was frowning at me. In the chair opposite his desk was one of his grad students.

"Bernie?" He looked concerned.

"Something happened," I said. I felt like I was going to cry. There was a strange, distended silence.

"I'll go!" The student stood up and tossed her bag onto her shoulder. She had very long and very curly blonde hair. It was Clarissa. "We'll find another time, Professor."

Kaleb seemed to be having a hard time processing. I pushed past Clarissa and collapsed into the chair she had vacated.

"Something happened at the shelter," I said. I suddenly felt very tired. I could barely keep my eyes open. I put my fingers on either side of the bridge of my nose to keep my face alert.

"What?" Kaleb asked when I was quiet for a moment.

I was having trouble saying what had happened. I didn't know. The memory was a chain of shocks, like a prolonged electrical current, the flash of different colors, drawn faces, the army of empty beds in the center of the hall.

"Everyone was scared," I said. "They were all by the bathroom, and someone was on the floor in the men's room. I think it was the Mississippi Man."

"Who?"

"His name was Damon," I said. "He was my friend."

Kaleb frowned. "Was he hurt?"

"I think he was dead." I thought I knew what had happened, but I didn't want to say it. It was only my paranoia making me think that. It was only everything that had happened with Riley, with Mom.

Kaleb took a deep breath. "Did they call an ambulance?" he asked. "Is your mother still there?"

"Yeah," I said. "She told me to call an ambulance, but when I did, the operator said they were already on their way."

Kaleb picked up the phone, called Mom and then the shelter. Mom's phone went straight to voice mail; the shelter line was busy. He typed out a text and then switched on the kettle.

The tea was chamomile. "He didn't believe in the moon landing," I said after a minute. "Damon."

Kaleb squeezed my hand.

"It's going to be okay," he said. It felt like everyone was always saying that, and it had never yet been true.

Mom was peeing in the upstairs bathroom when I shoved my way inside and closed the door behind us. She didn't say anything to me, and I didn't say anything to her. She was sitting with her head bent, looking down at her knees, holding a piece of toilet paper in her right hand. I stood on my tiptoes to see my full face in the small mirror and began to braid my hair.

When Mom finished peeing and flushed, she stood to pull up her underwear and sweatpants, tying them slowly at the waist. All her movements seemed labored, as if her clothing were heavy and hard to manage. I watched her from the corner of my eye as I pretended to watch myself in the mirror. She sensed my gaze and looked up at me for the first time.

"Damon died," she said. "I can't talk about it now."

Then she went into her bedroom and closed the door. I looked down at the toilet where, just a few weeks ago, I had taken the test.

When Mom wouldn't answer any of my questions about Damon, I got into her car and began a circular pilgrimage up and down Foothill Boulevard. I thought about what she'd said at the spa, how she thought I would die whenever I went driving. It served her right, I thought, for telling me nothing.

I didn't believe that Damon was dead. He was so bright in my mind, the end of his lit cigarette, the two parallel lines of his fingers. He felt like something just around the corner, something I was driving toward.

I stopped at Mia's house.

I'm outside, I texted her. Want to go for a drive?

Five minutes later, she came and sat in the passenger seat. She smelled the same as always, like peppermint and grass. Her hair was in a bun on her head, and she was wearing a sweater over an old pair of overalls. I could remember when she'd bought the overalls: we'd been at the mall together, squeezed into the same changing room, giggling like little kids.

"I can't stay long," she said. She seemed out of breath, harassed.

"Everything okay?" I asked. On the car stereo, the Beach Boys were singing. I imagined I was a sixties teenager, taking my girl out for a spin.

"My parents." She sighed. "They're driving me crazy. They want to treat Riley like a kid. They think that's going to help him."

"Maybe you should let them," I said. "It isn't your job to take care of him."

That was the difference between Mia and me: she had parents to look out for Riley. Mom only had me.

She gave me a hard look like she was going to yell at me. She didn't get angry easily, but I could see that she'd been pushed too far tonight. I wanted to bite my tongue. I remembered my confession to her. I had thought that nothing bad could come of it. My feelings had been so strong, so pure, so good. But the force of them had pushed her away. Just as Mom's love could feel like grasping, so could mine. I had learned to love at full speed and never to slow down. I hadn't considered that she might not want to hear it.

Then she sighed.

"How are you?" she asked.

"I'm fine," I lied. "I'm fine." I wasn't going to give her another thing to worry about.

❖   ❖   ❖

I didn't think the casket would be right there. The room in the funeral home had looked like a reception room, harmless, an antechamber. But the body in its coffin was off to the side, and I caught it in the corner of my eye. A face waxy with embalming. That nose with the nick on the side of it, a chink taken out. The thing I imagined when I thought of the word *cocaine*.

"Why are you sitting over there?" my mom asked. I didn't know where I should be sitting. "Why don't you get a doughnut," she said.

I got a doughnut from the refreshment table. I poured her a cup of coffee. When I tried to hand it to her, she shook her head and didn't look at me. There was no sleeve for the paper cup, and it burned my hand. The doughnut was melting in my fingers, getting sticky. There was nowhere to put it down.

In the corner of the room, a blonde girl was crying. She had filled-in eyebrows. Hoop earrings. I watched her frame shake as if with hiccups. Her breasts moved in her shirt like the churning of waves. She looked overtaken.

"That's his wife," my mom said.

"Wife?" I asked.

"He left her in Jackson," my mom said. "Six months ago."

I felt the shock of it. He had said he had no family.

The woman had stood up and was walking toward the casket. I could see, under her tight black dress, the parts of herself that she probably hated. Saw her pinching her arms and stomach in the mirror.

In his coffin, Damon looked flattened. I thought about how Mom had called him a liar. Was this the real man, then? Was he telling the truth now, looking two-dimensional with his eyes closed? Or was this another lie? I thought about the fetus I was carrying. I'd always felt the two were connected, the baby and the Mississippi Man. He was the only one who had known about her, after all. The only one who had touched my stomach, like the baby's father might have done, like my father might have done.

When I looked back at her, Mom was sitting down. Above her head and through the window, I could see the first spray of rain, hard and deliberate like pellets from a toy gun. A summer storm. Mom's hands were cold; her cheeks were flushed. I touched her, moved away.

We had looked through Damon's things at the shelter. His notebook filled with sketches. There had been one of me playing tic-tac-toe. My face was glowing, and my eyebrows were furrowed, ecstatic and attentive.

"What's her name?" I said now as the girl from Jackson placed her forehead on the rim of the coffin and took back up her crying.

"Nancy," Mom said. She watched me with close eyes, like a bird of prey.

❖   ❖   ❖

"Did something happen?" Mom was standing in the kitchen, facing me. The kettle roared to life behind her, like the sound of the white noise she slept with at night.

It was a ridiculous, stupid question. We had just come from the wake of a man we'd both known. Of course something had happened.

"What do you mean?" I asked.

She sighed and turned away from me, as if I had disappointed her. I felt the sour turn of her shoulder. She was angry with me somehow. Or was she sad?

"You're not saying something," she said, and I could hear the fracture behind her voice, the pain. But at the same time, I felt the heat of anger course through my spine like fluid. I was not her mother. I could not put her fractures back together.

I didn't respond. There were thousands of things I was not saying. I didn't know which one she meant.

"Did something happen with Damon?"

I opened my mouth and then closed it. Nothing had happened in the way she meant it, but there had been something between us. Something real and important. Something like the truth. He was the only person in the world who knew what I'd been through.

"Did something happen?" she asked for the third time, and her voice was the crack of an iceberg, the sink of a ship. "Bernie, do you not trust me anymore?" Her face was a dark forest. Who was she to be talking about trust? She had lied to me all my life.

"I just don't want you to be angry."

She gave a bitter laugh. I felt the rage leap inside me like a wild animal. I could have killed her.

"I slept with someone," I said, knowing the words would land hard as a punch. "I slept with my friend Avery."

Her face contorted, a quick clenching and unclenching. I was happy to see her confused, in pain. It was what she deserved. What she had coming. *Bríd,* I thought, the name foreign and cold.

"You don't have a friend named Avery," she said.

"I do," I said. "You've just never met him. We're not that close."

She gave a short snort, the sound a horse makes.

"You're close with him now," she scoffed.

The words made me feel dirty, ashamed. I remembered our bodies pressed together, Avery's intrusion, the slimy feeling of disgust I'd had afterward. She was making me feel it all over again. I wondered if she meant to.

She was silent for a long minute, looking into the distance. I couldn't stand this anymore. Her sullen silences, her mistrust.

"And, Mom," I said. This was not the right moment, but the right moment wasn't going to come. I was ready for her to know. Ready for it to be over. Once she knew, she would have no choice but to help me. Once she knew, I could take the pills. I could end this.

She held up her hand to stop me.

"I don't want to know," she said. "I don't want to know any more." She was backing away from me, like I was contagious. The look in her eyes terrified me; it was like she was looking at a stranger. She left me standing there, alone, with the words on the tip of my tongue.

I went to my room and knelt by my bedside table. The position felt right: a shape of shame, of penance. The pill was round and flat and white in the palm of my hand. It reminded me of holding my baby teeth as a child.

I thought of Damon, asleep in his coffin, quiet now. I thought of my mother's anger, the cold turn of her shoulder. Until now, I had been holding out hope, even without admitting it to myself. Believing that she might be there for me, that I might be able to tell her. I had been waiting, I realized now, for the right moment. Avoiding taking this pill so that she could help me through it. But I knew the truth now: I would need to do it on my own. I would find a way to be alone two days from now. And then I would be finished. I would put it all behind me.

I gritted my face like a soldier. I thought of my father going off to fight his war. I swallowed the pill.

❖   ❖   ❖

Twenty minutes later, I was lying in bed listening to Bright Eyes. The book I was reading about climate change was open on my chest, but I couldn't focus. I kept thinking about what Mom had said: "You're close with him now." The disgust in her voice. I kept thinking about how she'd looked at me, how foreign it had made me feel. Like we were standing on different sides of a border. Like I was something to be ashamed of.

There was a knock on my door.

"Wake up," she said. I was not sleeping.

"Mom?"

"I need you to get up," she said. "My dad's died."

"What?"

I sat up. I tried to study her face, but there was no emotion there. It was so blank that I thought she must be in shock. She looked a little pale.

"Can you pack a bag?" she asked.

"I'm sorry," I said.

"Just basics. Let's say for a week. Kaleb's not here. I'll text him to let him know."

"Okay," I said. "Where are we going?"

"To the funeral," she said, and then she was gone from the doorway.

I packed quickly, fog-headed though I was. Was this how I would finally see Ireland? To mourn a grandfather I'd never known? Another death, like it was a catching disease. Like the darkness I'd been afraid of had finally come for me. I thought about the men I dreamed about: shooters in masks with guns as big as the children they shot. In the end, death had snuck in in other ways, surrounded me. It had caught me off guard.

I packed two sweaters and my rain jacket, jeans, a pair of boots. A beanie, a few T-shirts. A long black dress with full-length sleeves that Mom said made me look like the Wicked Witch of the West. I changed out of my sweatpants, picked up my backpack, and went downstairs.

Mom was already standing by the doorway, holding a cup of black tea and a bag of cheese sandwiches. I could smell the tea, strong in the air between us. I gave her a one-armed hug, wary of the mug she held. She was moving slowly but purposefully, like she was fighting her way through a dream. She did not look like she had cried, but it seemed like something had permanently altered in her face. Like she had taken on something that had not been there before.

She squeezed me. "The car's here," she said.

It was not until we were speeding down the freeway that I realized: I would be with her when I took the second dose. I would be away from home, with nobody to help me if something went wrong, with nowhere to hide. I felt for the foil in my backpack pocket; the pill packet was still there. My heart beat a funeral march, slow and heavy, a stomp of dread.

PART FOUR

Chapter Twenty-Three

2016, County Tyrone

I'd found out from a Google search after Bernie and I fought. Her words still in the back of my head: "I slept with someone." Like it was as casual as brushing your teeth or tying your shoelaces. As I sat and thought, I'd absent-mindedly searched Coalisland on my phone. I'd been doing it more and more lately, keying in the names of my family members. Looking back to wet black leaves, drafty rooms, the woodstove.

And then there it was in little blue type. A death reported in a local news outlet: Sean Kane, aged 58, died from liver cancer at his home in County Tyrone. He is survived by his wife, Aoife, and three children.

Da. The smell of him, like wet cardboard and a pack of Majors and the day-old lager he'd reach for in the morning when he had a bad night and woke up on the sofa. Da laughing at something I'd said, surprised by his own reaction, looking at me like, *Where the hell did you come from?* Da, the boy just out of school who'd gotten down on one knee when Ma told him she was pregnant. Who spared her a trip across the sea to England, who spared her shame and blood between her legs, and losing her first baby, losing Enda. Who spared her—if she hadn't been able to stomach England—some institution. The "cold climates" where women were locked up, used and abused, buried in a mass grave. My own country doing to itself what the Brits had always done to us. Da had saved her from all of it, and he had regretted it all his life. Stuck with a family he'd never wanted. A woman who made him feel small.

I remembered the only time he'd ever hit me. I was eleven, and he'd been walking up the stairs when he slipped and fell. He'd probably been drunk, but I didn't know that at the time. It was a comical fall, the kind when time seems to be suspended. He lurched and grabbed at the air. I couldn't help it; I laughed.

I quickly stifled the sound, running up the stairs to where he was. "Da, are you all right?" I asked. I should not have gone to him, should not have asked.

He was fine, good enough to stand, but his face was red. With one backhanded slap across my face, he pushed me down the staircase, my head bumping along the steps. My face stung. My neck twinged from the angle. My arm throbbed. He had broken it. Or it had been broken. The way things just happen to you, in the passive voice. The way you bring them on yourself.

Da drove me to hospital. He bought me an ice cream on the way home. Put me up on the couch with my new cast and covered me with a blanket.

"That's you sorted," he said. "You'll be grand in no time."

The fall was almost worth it for that moment. My arm slung in a cast and my father's hand on the back of my head. The next time he made a fool of himself, I averted my eyes. It was better to leave him alone; it was what he wanted.

I looked back down at the screen, read the sentence again. Though I had not thought of him much over the years, though it was to my mother and not my father that all my thoughts led, I could still feel the loss of him somewhere underneath my skin. Another piece of my home gone forever. Another person I couldn't say goodbye to.

And her name was on the screen like an order. I would go to her, my mother. Before it was too late. Before I lost her too.

Asleep in the car, Bernie looked six, not sixteen. Her face was soft, a little sad. A frown etched on her forehead, like she was still thinking, even unconscious. What would my mother think when she saw her? Bernie was almost the same age I'd been when I left. Older than Ina had ever been. I wondered if Ma still thought of me as an eighteen-year-old with too-pale skin and acned cheeks or if I'd become, in her mind, a stranger with a blank face. Or did she not think of me at all?

Bernie woke up as we were passing the *Los Angeles Times* Building. She rubbed her eyes and looked out the window. I remembered when her hair poked out in two little pigtails, hair so short it stuck out like antennae or antlers. Her yellow rain jacket, her big eyes that always looked slightly bruised. Blue and green and brown.

She took my hand, and the gesture felt like a return.

❖ ❖ ❖

My right hand shook as I held our passports out to the TSA agent. I remembered the day we had gone to get Bernie's. How I had held this moment in the back of my mind: something as fragile as a butterfly wing. Not daring to let myself dream but wanting her to have the papers all the same. To be able to run if running became necessary. To be able to come home.

The agent scanned Bernie's, then my own. It felt like he was taking forever, staring down at Bernie, looking back at the photograph of her. I had not traveled internationally in eighteen years, and I was terrified that there would be a flag on my passport, that I would be pulled into a small room for questioning, wrenched out of my life and into one of my nightmares. For the first time, it occurred to me that this could be the end of everything. That in the split-second decision I'd made to go home, I had sacrificed my life with Bernie.

Bernie yawned, oblivious. The agent looked at my face, at the face in the passport. Blank stare as he scanned without seeing. The accepting beep of the machine when he held the barcode over the reader.

"Ma'am," he said. He was holding out our passports and boarding passes. I had been waiting for him to tell me there was a problem, to call over another officer. I had not realized he was motioning us through.

Bernie took the documents, smiled at him, and I followed her into the line for security. She took my hand again then, as if she knew.

❖　❖　❖

It was a ten-hour flight to Dublin, and I couldn't sleep. Behind us, Irish Americans talked loudly about the Guinness Storehouse and Temple Bar, the Cliffs of Moher, and trad sessions. The woman in the aisle seat had fallen asleep to *Keeping Up With the Kardashians*. I couldn't tell if the episodes were repeating or if they were just too similar to tell apart.

"Mom?" Bernie took off her headphones, the big over-the-ear kind that made her look like a helicopter pilot. She had been sleeping intermittently, her light breathing occasionally catching in a snore. "What happened to Damon?" she asked.

I had forgotten that she still didn't know. She must have guessed. Surely she'd heard whispers at the wake, had intuited from the glimpse of him she'd had in the bathroom.

"He took his own life," I said. "God rest him."

I remembered the slumped body, the wet patch at the front of his jeans. Alive, he had been suave, slim as a knife, the kind of man who could seep through the crack in a door. It had been horrifying to seem him like that, bloated and messed. Unrecognizable. His coolness turned to a hot grotesqueness, the face of a marionette.

"I'm sorry, love." I could not read her expression as she looked down, fiddling with the wires of her headphones. I tucked a wisp of hair back into one of her plaits.

"How?" she asked.

I didn't respond.

"Please," she said. "I need to know."

The worst thing was that I wanted to tell her, to make her share my pain. It hurt to know a thing that Bernie didn't. After all these years of hiding from her, I couldn't bear to add another secret. Couldn't stand for there to be anything else between us.

"He hung himself," I whispered, thinking about the other passengers, the noisy tourists behind us.

She winced. "Hanged," she corrected.

"What?" I asked.

"It's hanged. Not hung. I mean, grammatically."

"They say it's one of the quickest ways to go. Practically painless."

"Good to know." She snorted.

"Stop it," I told her. "Cut it out."

"What did he use?"

"What?"

"Was it his belt?"

My stomach turned over.

"Yes," I said.

"The brown one?" she asked. "Thick?"

"Bernie." I didn't want to do this. "Bernie, stop it."

"Please," she said again.

"I don't remember," I lied. "Okay?" Then I said, "Yes, I think it was the brown one." As if I could forget.

She sat back in her seat and put her headphones on.

❖   ❖   ❖

We landed at Dublin Airport. Disembarked. I felt the ground leaning away, falling slowly out from under my feet. The carpeted walkway to customs seemed to teeter as I walked it with Bernie. Each step held the fear that they would be waiting. That my name, on some list, would have raised the alarms. Any minute now, I might feel the cold metal of handcuffs on my wrists, see the last glimpse of my daughter's face as they hauled me away. But nothing happened. Nobody called out to me. My foot met generic carpet, and Bernie hummed something softly to herself. I had made it back unscathed.

We waited at the car hire. The humdrum banality of the other commuters was jarring, as if this were an ordinary day. But the air kissed me like a mother; the accents grew around me like the shrubs of a childhood home.

It was late afternoon when we arrived in Coalisland. The town was identical to my memories, and yet everything was new. A Chinese restaurant. A nail salon. I kept driving until we got to the old pub.

"Is this where your house is?" Bernie asked.

I looked up at the window. I could see a girl's face as she looked out at the water.

"Are you hungry?"

We climbed the stairs. I looked at Bernie only out of the corner of my eye. She was a blur of movement, a swoosh of long hair. She who had not existed when I had left. Who could never know the girl I had been. I did not want my memories to be overwritten by her. I wanted to be quiet, to stop walking, to stand in the dark staircase and think of Ina.

Gold light when we entered. Warmth like the most glorious foliage in autumn. Hard, angular vowels. Voices melted together, but the sounds jutted out at me. Tears rose. I looked around, checked the faces to make sure I would not be recognized. But they were strangers, all of them.

We sat at the window, where I had never sat with Ina. Bernie ate a veggie burger, solid food. I felt the relief of her being nourished. Saw again the doctor coming in to say her lungs were damaged but she would make it. I was quiet as we ate, looking out at the lough. She watched me with wary eyes but said nothing.

❖ ❖ ❖

I left the pub with the old fear. It crept into the car as the sun sank in the sky. I would have to tell Bernie what had happened. She was not an idiot; it would be obvious.

I wondered about old neighbors. The people I would pass on the street, sit next to at the funeral Mass. They were the ones who would not have forgotten, who would see me and remember. Who would know that I had joined the rotten movement and then left it. There was no stopping the knowing from spreading, recognition a contagion, memory an illness. An illness that could get you driven across the border, shot in the head, and buried in a bog. It was a worse fear than I'd felt at the airport; the Real IRA would not be as kind as the authorities. They dealt with traitors in one way: with brutality. And I was not only a terrorist, according to the governments of both countries I called home. I was also a traitor, according to the men and women who'd once been my comrades.

I tried to recall how I'd been taught to cope in the old days. The process of compartmentalizing, stowing fear in your gums and carrying on. You didn't say anything, didn't answer even the most banal of questions. If you gave them none of yourself, they could not take more.

"Every person in this country has to make a little sacrifice," I remembered Ma saying when I was a child. Bernadette Devlin had just been shot nine times in her home, in front of her children. She lived only a road away from us. Somehow, she'd survived. I remembered the fear I'd felt when I'd heard about it. Remembered the raw excitement. Ma's idolatry of Bernadette, of her sacrifice.

I was not facing a threat, I told myself. I was facing my daughter. I was facing my mother.

"Are we going?" Bernie asked. My hand was on the key, but I hadn't started the car. I looked over at her in the passenger seat; something about her seemed feral. Her skin was wan, her forehead damp with sweat. I wondered if she was getting sick again.

What better place to tell her than a car, where it had happened? Where the seeds for our lives had been planted. I remembered my mother driving Ina and me to the border. Her boots in the mud.

"I need to tell you something," I said.

"Is Bríd not your name either?"

"Bernie, please be serious."

"Be serious about what?" Her voice was raised.

"I was a different woman before I had you. Before I was a mother. I was something else."

"What were you?"

"I don't know. A daughter, a sister."

She nodded for me to go on.

"You know that Ina was my sister's name. I took it when I left Ireland," I said. "I needed to become someone else."

"Why?" she asked.

"Because I'd done something."

I hesitated.

"What?"

"It's hard to say," I said. I thought of saying something else but didn't.

"Well, are you going to tell me?"

She looked greedy for it, rising up out of the leather of the passenger seat.

"I don't know exactly," I said. "I volunteered for the Real IRA."

"The IRA." She said the three letters carefully, holding them apart from each other. Like she was trying to remember what they stood for. "That's, like—are they terrorists?"

I paused for a moment, unsure how to answer that. "They . . . weren't called that at the time. There were two groups. One that wanted peace and one that wanted to keep fighting. The Real IRA . . . later, after I left, yes, they were called terrorists."

She gave a short nod. She was expecting more: an explanation, an apology.

"I wanted to get revenge for what happened to my sister," I said.

Somehow, this seemed like an oversimplification. It left out the giddy, gummy pleasure of it. How strong and lovely I had felt, being capable of war.

"What did you do?" she asked.

I ran my pointer finger across the hired car's steering wheel.

"I drove a car," I said.

We were both quiet for a moment. I felt the ocean wave of shame, of regret. I saw the boy from my dreams, curled in the boot in the fetal position. If I only knew what I was guilty of. If I had blown apart a hotel room. If mother and child had survived.

"There was a woman," I said finally. "There were several people injured. Including a pregnant woman."

"Injured how?"

"In a bombing, right after I drove the car."

She stared at me, like I was speaking another language.

"It is likely," I said calmly, remembering the only other time I had said these words, how easily they had come when the priest asked for them, "that I was responsible for the bombing. It is likely that I was responsible for her getting hurt."

Bernie let out a shuddering sigh, a sound I'd heard her make when she watched the news, when she learned about new tragedies. It was her instinctive reaction to injustice. She was looking at me like I was BP, like I had poured oil in the Gulf of Mexico. Like I'd shot up a school.

I could feel the other car's leather under my hands, tan-brown, sticky, the indentations on the inside of the wheel. I felt like carefully balanced stones were falling. The meanings I'd attached to objects were slipping. Labels falling off things like rain, the melting down of everything solid. The wheel was slipping out of my hands; they were wet, too wet to hold it.

"Mom?"

Bernie had unclipped her seat belt, and her face was inches away from mine.

"Do you need some water?"

My chest was heaving. Nothing had happened, and I was undone by it.

"I need to see my mother," I said. I ran my hands over my face, sat up straighter, took a deep breath. I started the engine.

I kept checking the minutes on the car clock. Each change in the number made my heart sink further into my stomach. Or was my stomach rising to meet my heart? Eighteen years, and I was fifteen minutes away, my fingers inches from the flame. I was desperate for that first gleam of recognition. How long had it been since somebody had seen me for who I really was? I could not help the grin that tugged at the corners of my mouth, the strange whirring feeling in my temples.

I stopped the car momentarily by the big elm. It was the first spot on the driveway from which you could make out the outline of the house. The first view that proved it was still there. It was lovely. Much grander than our house in California. The most beautiful place I had ever lived.

"This is it," I said to Bernie. "This is where I grew up."

I drove past the fence that had been erected my last year at home—Tad and my father working long summer days with their shirts used as sweat rags. The house, as I got closer, looked different, though everything about it seemed to be the same. It was serene in its emptiness, in the absence of dogs barking and children fighting.

I parked the car.

"Will you wait here?" I asked Bernie.

"What?"

"Let me just say hello to her first. Then I'll come get you."

"You don't want me in there?"

I sighed. "Of course I do, Bernie. It's going to be a shock for her is all."

"Whatever." She turned her back on me, an awkward angle in the passenger seat, and stared defiantly out the window, looking off at the empty fields, watching nothing.

"I'll be right back," I said. I took a deep breath.

❖ ❖ ❖

I knocked three times on the red door, thinking it strange that after the hundreds of times I'd opened the door for my parents' guests, for Conor to collect our bottles, I would be the one to knock. The one to be seen through the peephole, analyzed, sized up. The blinds were closed. I imagined her face pressed against the wood to see through the crack, her eye straining to make out my features, seeing and not believing.

The door opened. Dark, wild hair. The same eyes enclosed in new wrinkles, like a fresh envelope around an older letter. Aoife.

Her gaze was level with mine as I stood on the second step. We stared at each other.

"Brigid."

"Ma."

"You're back," she said. The mouth that had ruined me, again and again. The woman I had run from, run to, run from.

"I'm back," I said.

There was a very long pause. Finally, she stepped back and let me into the house.

❖ ❖ ❖

It smelled of lilies and smoke and something I could not name; the scent brought me so forcefully back to being small that I could almost feel

Enda's arm around me, guiding me through the woods, could almost smell Ina's hair when she let me braid it. I looked around at the couch we had lain on to watch TV, the kitchen where Ma had cooked and cleaned, the long dining room table where Da had taught us to be silent until spoken to. But the sense of it was different, emptier. Somehow the sight of the furniture made me want to cry, like looking at a grave.

I followed Ma to the kitchen for a cup of tea.

The kettle was new, and it made a different noise when the water boiled. An unfortunate wailing, a whine. The old one had sounded inviting, a steam horn out at sea. The kitchen seemed smaller, darker. The intermittent buzz of the radiator. At least that was the same. It sounded like crickets.

I opened my mouth to say something, wondering where to begin.

"And where the fuck have you been?" Mom asked suddenly, turning from the kettle to look at me. I closed my mouth.

"You know where," I said. "I rang."

"You rang." Her mouth twisted. "You rang *twice* twenty years ago. Do you know how long I've been looking for you?"

The air between us felt solid.

"What do you mean?" My skin prickled suddenly with heat. I had never imagined this. Her, looking for me.

"I rang again and again, trying to find you. Called the hospitals, the courthouses."

She seemed like she was out of breath, and I remembered panting the night that Ina died, feeling like my grief was a marathon I'd just run.

"They told me they'd no record of a Brigid Kane being married." She gave a harsh laugh. "But they had an Ina Kane, in the time period I was asking about. Typical Brigid, I said. Never could be happy with herself. Always running off to find something better."

Her voice was husky. I felt the sudden urge to hit her again, or to leave. I thought of Bernie in the car, and I kept my feet planted on the ground.

"The number Tad had for you went out of service. Still, I tried looking for you. Ina Kane. Ina Evans. It's not a very common name, but I couldn't find you. Eighteen years, Bríd. Where the fuck have you been?"

"Ma," I said. "Ma—" It was like that was the only word I had left. I could not order my thoughts. I felt seasick, borne on churning waves. My face was hot. Her anger scorching. We both stood there in silence.

"Why don't you go see your da," she said finally. "That's why you came, isn't it?"

I did not want to go. I nodded.

❖　❖　❖

Walking up the winding staircase, I remembered the hundreds of ascents of my childhood. Bringing Ma up a tray on a Saturday morning, the only morning she got to sleep in. Ina running up and down these stairs, the way the ruckus of it seemed like applause.

He was in Enda and Tad's old room, laid out on Enda's bed.

It was cold inside, and it smelled strange in that it smelled like nothing.

Da looked—there is only one way to say it—like a corpse. His remaining teeth were bared out of his mouth, yellow and reedy, midsnarl. His eyes half-open, gray. His irises dried out like thin paper, warped and withered and puckered. His face was a mask of a man. I had not expected him to seem so dead.

I sat down beside him. My hip bone touching the side of him. "Hi, Da," I said. "It's me."

It was eerie, him lying here and nobody to attend him. How red he would have turned if he'd been here in life, how embarrassed and angry he would have been. On a nearby table, a candle had been placed, as well as a pot of tea. Ma must have imagined guests and mourners would perform a vigil here. But Da was alone.

I picked up the beads on the bedside table and began to say the rosary. Its prescription was easy, but the words felt thick in my throat. It had been years since I'd said it. Though I'd never stopped going to Mass, I had sunk into the background of my faith. I had not prayed at home much. I had preferred a crowd, preferred a single Hail Mary or Our Father. The meditation of the rosary overwhelmed. Now, when I stumbled on certain words, I half expected Da to correct me. I thought he would find my mistakes insolent. But he just lay there and bore it.

I put down the beads. I closed my eyes and tried to remember Da in life. This dead man looked nothing like my father. His face was a puddle, like he had drowned inside his own body. I couldn't remember my father's face; I saw instead the blur of him as he yelled at a football team on the television, as he took a swig of his drink. The shaky, stuttering step of him, the gummy smile. Ma was right; he had always been a coward. But how could you blame him? We had all lived with our terror in different ways.

Chapter Twenty-Four

2016, County Tyrone

I had felt no side effects from the first pill. Or maybe they were just lost in the flashes that followed: Mom's hand on mine in the car, the breadth of the plane's wings as we left California, the memory of Damon's belt that, as I slept and woke from fitful dreams, became first a snake and then a long braid of hair. And then: the new light of the country where we came from, the green out the car window, and Mom's revelation, the one I had been waiting for.

Her secret felt like a loss. A dizzying feeling, like hanging upside down from the monkey bars. My mother had been a terrorist. That was my lineage, my history. The highway I had been speeding down, looking for answers. I was so used to thinking of her as someone to be saved, someone helpless in sheets that smelled like her sweat. It had never even occurred to me that someone might once have needed saving from her. That she was capable of harm, the same way I was.

I was not afraid, but it did occur to me that I could have been. That someone else, on discovering that their mother had been involved in a violent paramilitary movement, might open the car door, run in the opposite direction. But where could I run to? We shared the same blood, the same hot desire to change the world. Of course I'd turned out the way I had.

I texted Mia, Guess where I am, just to see the three dots as she typed her response. When I told her about my grandfather, she seemed sorry, concerned about me. The thought of her at the other end of the phone made me feel steadier. Made me feel like I might have something to go home to after all. I imagined her sitting on the windowsill in her bedroom, where she liked to read, wearing her overalls, her body twisted like a pretzel and her head bent over the phone, thinking of me.

As we drove from the pub to Mom's old house, I leaned my head against the window and looked out. Fields of green—flush and nourished and not dying of thirst—sheep with their wool dyed, elms and hawthorns on the side of the road, the swoop and rise of the car like we were moving not only forward along the road but deeper, across planes of memory and time. Stones arranged in circles or poking out of the earth like graves, moss covering the walls and little yellow flowers bright as sunlight. It felt forgiving, this landscape, and pure. Like cell phones and factory farming and sexual assault could not exist here. Like a criminal could find absolution in these dark hills. Looking out at the reaches and dips in the horizon, I felt different than I did in California. I could feel the damp of the place on my skin, worming its way inside my body, all the water we were missing back in LA. This was a place that could still grow, a soil in which you could still plant something. I felt it could hold me.

There was graffiti spray-painted on brick walls and bridges. BRITAIN'S BERLIN WALL and NO BORDER. Again and again those letters: IRA. Down one side street, I saw a mural of two hulking men, painted in black and white, four times their true size. They were holding AK-47s, faces masked in balaclavas. I thought again of my teacher's faulty barricade, of my fear at movie theaters. Had she given me this, my mother? This edginess, the constant searching for masked men on my periphery? I had always blamed the place I'd grown up: arid desert and homegrown terrorism. I had not known that it had come from her, too, that it was in my blood.

❖ ❖ ❖

We parked in front of my grandmother's house, and Mom went in alone. I sat in the car, running my fingers over the pack of hexagonal pills. Throughout the plane ride, I had imagined that I could feel the child inside me. Imagined that we'd shared the same shudder when Mom said that Damon had killed himself, the thing I had known and not known, been afraid to look directly at. High over the Atlantic Ocean, pressed between my mother and the hollow-seeming plane walls, the child was moving for the last time, its heartbeat slowing to a stop. And nobody in the world knew except for me; the only person I had told was dead.

Now it had been twelve hours since I had taken the first dose. The baby was no longer growing in my uterus. It was suspended in the fluid of me, waiting for its end. I had left it until the very last minute: a week later and I would have needed to go in for the operation. I wondered if some part of me had been putting it off because I did not want it done, my subconscious programmed to protect the child. I tucked the pills into my pocket, looked out at the fields again. It had been fifteen minutes since Mom had gone inside. I got out of the car, stretched. The feeling of the air, clean and soft against my skin, surprised me once again. I went up to the door, just like my mother had, and knocked.

She appeared in the doorway, brown hair grown gray at the roots, blue eyes, a look on her face like a warning. I had never met anyone, besides my mother, who looked like me. It felt like staring into a pond, a warped reflection. Like looking into the future. The left side of her mouth twitched, a half smile. I had felt my own face do that. I wanted to reach out and touch the lines around her lip. Even from here, I could smell her, like a forest after a rain. A little bit like my mother.

I had always wondered if I would recognize my family, if I happened upon them on a Los Angeles sidewalk, at a café. Would I know immediately, a deep wave of recognition? Or would it be one glance, another, thinking there was something strange about them, not knowing what, walking away?

But now I knew. I would have known her anywhere. She would have stopped me dead in my tracks. I could have seen her out of the corner of my eye, and the whole world would have shrunk to the blur of her. I had been looking for her all my life.

Chapter Twenty-Five

2016, County Tyrone

When I came back downstairs, Bernie was sitting at the table with my mother, a cup of tea in front of her. They were talking quietly, and my mother had taken one of Bernie's hands in her own. I joined them, feeling both of their eyes on me, feeling the two different women I was to them: a daughter, a mother.

"You met," I said. Neither of them replied. Ma let go of Bernie's hand.

"You look healthy," Ma said to me. "You used to be all skin and bones. I suppose it's the California sun."

I looked down at myself, tried to remember what I had been like the last time I'd been home, the night I'd slipped out the door like a ghost.

"When will the Mass be?" I asked.

"Tomorrow."

"Will the boys come?"

"Enda will. And his two boys."

"And Siobhán?"

"Dead," Ma said. "Breast cancer. Must have been a year ago now."

"God rest her," I said.

Ma said nothing.

"Tad?" I asked. "Will he come?"

"I doubt it."

I remembered Tad in the weeks following my conversation with Conor, taciturn and stubborn. The way he had gotten into Da's habit of blowing out all candles, that fear of flame.

"They had a terrible row three years ago," she said. "When Tad told us the news. That, well, that he's gay now." The word in her throat sounded like a gulp.

I thought back to Tad as a teenager, the way the girls had worshipped him, the way Da had always found something to dislike in him. I realized that I was not surprised, that some part of me had known it all along. I should have been there, I thought, when he told Da. I wondered how many years he'd spent hiding, wondered what his life had been like, pretending to be someone he was not. I should have thought to ask. I looked at Bernie, tried to tell her I loved her with my eyes.

"You were always the one who got between them," Ma said, standing up. "D'you know that? It was always you who could stop them fighting."

"It was Ina, Ma," I said. "God rest her, it was Ina who always made peace."

Ma shrugged. "If she did, it was because you told her to. The minute you left, the house became a war zone." Her eyes raked over my body again. "But you seem to have done fine."

"Ma—"

"Your father's on ice," she said. "It has to be changed every three hours or the body will start to decay. It'll be better if you're the one to do it; I'll show you how. I don't want to be touching him anymore."

Bernie looked at me. I could feel her gaze on the side of my cheek.

"Why's he on ice?" I asked. I thought back to the wakes I had been at as a child and teenager, the bodies I had seen. They had always been embalmed, cared for by a funeral parlor.

She sneered. "You want me to put on some makeup? Smooth out his wrinkles?" I had forgotten just how relentless she was. The blade of a paper cutter slipped under your skin.

She went to the freezer and reappeared holding two flat packs.

"Will I show you?" she asked.

"I'll be right back," I told Bernie.

In Da's room, we stood over his body. The women who had served him his dinner. I could still smell my old fear, feel the shake of my hand, my nerves making me as unsteady as the drink made him. The urge to laugh at him, the reflex to cower.

We were alone together again. With everything we had and hadn't said to one another.

"I didn't know you were looking for me—" I began. I had a headache in my temples; I was trying to stop myself from crying.

"He's heavy," Ma said. "We need to lift him up enough to take out the packs that are there now."

I rubbed my hands over my face. She watched me. Then I nodded.

I stood by his head and shoulders, one hand scooped under his neck to protect his head, one under his shoulder. His body was stiff, leaden. I could feel the bone of his shoulder blade beneath the hard, compact flesh. He was very cold.

"Ready?" Ma asked.

Together, we pushed and lifted until Ma could reach under his lower back and extract two ice packs just like the ones she had carried into the room. I took the fresh packs, propping up his upper back with my shoulder, and slid them into place.

When we were done, I stared at his face. I had the urge to laugh. I looked up at her.

"You're a free woman, Ma," I said. "Like you always wanted. No husband to hold you back."

She laughed. "Free for what?" she asked. "It's all over now. I'm old."

It was true: there was nothing left for her to fight for.

"Why didn't you ask me to come home?" I asked. "When I rang you in Miami, when I said I was pregnant."

She looked away from me, away from Da, out the window, and over the green fields.

"I remember when you girls were young," she said. "You were like swans. In the lough, over the fields. Running, laughing. It always looked to me like you were flying. And it was always the two of you, following each other. Singing to each other."

I stood there, bereft.

"Swans mate for life," she said. "You never see one without the other."

"We weren't swans, Ma," I said finally. "We were girls."

"Well, there you go. For a long time, I didn't want to see you without her."

"And now?"

"I thought I'd lost you, Bríd. I thought you were as good as dead."

"I'm sorry," I said. I wanted to tell her about that last night with Ina, how we had fought, how I had known where she was going. But I was beginning to realize that I might never be able to tell her. That if she knew what had happened that night, it would be the end of everything.

She nodded. "Why don't you show Bernie where to put her things?"

Bernie and I stood in the doorway to my old bedroom. Ina's old bedroom.

"Make yourself comfortable," I told her.

I went back downstairs to find us something to eat. When I came back up—a packet of crisps and a box of digestives in hand—Bernie was sitting on Ina's old single bed wearing sweatpants. She didn't look at me.

I sat on the foot of the bed. She kept her gaze above me, refusing to look.

"Bernie," I said.

"You should have told me," she said. "You should have told me something. Where you came from, at least. What your name was. It's like I never even knew you."

I nodded. I moved closer to her, to sit next to her. She moved away from me. She stood up and paced the length of the room. She looked like a sailor walking a gangplank, from sea to land, from land to sea. Her feet measured the length of the room, the fact of my old life.

"You made me tell you everything!" she yelled suddenly. "All my secrets! You asked me about my, my periods and my nipples and you talked like you *owned* me, and all along you were lying to me! All along I never even knew your name!"

She had been holding on to this anger ever since the night at the spa. She'd kept it tamped down for weeks, letting me tell her my story in pieces. She'd swallowed it as we'd mourned Damon, as we'd fought, as we'd gotten on a plane and left California. She could be rash, my Bernie, but she was also careful. She took her time to decide what she felt. She had decided now.

I got up. I moved toward her, wrapped her in my arms. I remembered when she was a child. When she would get so angry that words wouldn't come. She would be mute for minutes, eyes forming tears of rage. Now she was fully grown and still a child and I only wanted to protect her. It was all I had ever wanted. We stayed like that for a while. She was crying. My hand was on the back of her head. I thought of the ways in which I had failed her. The weight I had tried to lift off myself in order to love her better. The illness it was impossible to shake. I thought about how hard I had tried, put all my energy into her. Some days, the effort only amounted to lying in bed. Some days, it had been all I was capable of.

And then she pulled away and dried her eyes. We got into Ina's old single bed and leaned against the wooden headboard. We shared the bag of crisps.

"This is all—" she started after a long silence, gesturing around at the room. "Your mother, and—"

I tried to see it from her eyes. I wondered if it looked drab and gray next to the golden haze of her home.

"You took her name," she said finally.

I nodded.

"You must have been so sad."

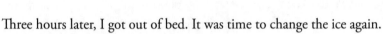

Three hours later, I got out of bed. It was time to change the ice again. Bernie stirred and then opened her eyes.

"What is it?" she asked.

"Go back to sleep," I told her. "I just have to change the ice."

Her lips disappeared inside her mouth. "I'll come," she said. "I want to come."

Chapter Twenty-Six

2016, County Tyrone

The house smelled of flowers, of burning wood, of saltwater. It was larger than I expected: cherry wood on the walls and floors. A long dining table, dark-red linen tablecloth. I wondered if it was the same one my mother had eaten on as a girl, the same table she had bent her head over to say grace. The high ceilings made the room feel empty, vacated. Photographs hung on the walls: women on beaches that looked cold and rocky, men posing in sports jerseys, children in christening gowns. Crucifixes everywhere. I tried to imagine my mother here as a young girl. I saw her darting out of the room, the swoosh of a skirt disappearing behind her as she ran to some hidden place, somewhere adult eyes couldn't find her.

A winding staircase led upstairs; a sliding door opened onto the fields beyond. I noticed myself locating the escape routes and wondered what about the place made me want to flee. I walked to the window, looked out at the green fields, at the trees that bordered the area like sentinels. I thought I could see this house years from now when it would belong to no one but the hills and forest. Covered in ivy and vines, roots cracking the floors. Even now, I thought, the house felt wild.

In the room where my grandfather was, it was cold. I stared at his face. He looked like the animated skull in some movie, exactly how you'd imagine the dead. His fingers were too long for his hands, extended like talons, gripped around an imaginary object. His toes were bent at strange angles, also too long, too clenched.

I searched his face for what I had seen in my grandmother: myself. But he had sunk too far into death for any feature to be recognizable. I thought of Damon again, how he had been all quick movements: the quirk of a smile, darting glances, his cigarette arcing a glow against the darkness. How still and flat he had looked in his coffin. My grandfather must have been that once, too, and I wondered if my mother could see it when she looked at him lying there. Or if he was buried too far back in her memory.

"Try to lift more," Mom said.

"I can't; he's too heavy."

"Then I'll take the head."

"No, I got it," I said. "I want the head."

"Then lift him higher."

"I'm trying."

"Just let me do it, Bernie. I want to be done with this."

"That's not fair—I never even got to meet him. I should at least get to do the head."

"Oh my God." Mom laughed quietly, moved toward his head. "Please, Bernie."

I moved to the hips. I didn't really want to touch them, kept wondering what his shriveled penis would be like. I felt his butt as I lifted him. It was compact and bony but heavy.

"I can't get this pack out."

"One sec—I'll lift him more."

"Maybe you should go on the other side," she suggested.

"Jesus fuck he's so heavy."

"Please be careful. I don't want anything to happen to the body."

"What do you mean? What could happen?"

"Is the pack under him?"

"Yeah."

"Both of them?"

"Yeah," I said. "Check the placement."

"Ach I think it's good. Those are his kidneys, right?"

"I think so."

"Will you find him socks?" Mom asked.

❖   ❖   ❖

In the bathroom, we washed our hands. I ran the cold water over my wrists, the way she had taught me to do during heat waves. The cold against my blue veins settled me. We shared the mirror, and I stared at her reflection. Ina Evans. Bríd Kane. I thought I looked more like my grandmother than my mother. Had she always thought that, looking at me?

I had been trying to understand if what she had done was moral or not. If Peter Singer would approve of her joining the IRA, lying about her name. But I was starting to doubt if it was even the right question. I wondered how she could abet an act of terrorism but condemn an abortion. I left the bathroom.

"Bernie?" she asked when she came into the room we were sharing. I was already lying in the twin bed. "Bernie?" she asked again, but this time I could tell from her voice that she wasn't expecting a reply.

❖   ❖   ❖

At three, Mom's alarm went off, and we went downstairs to get new ice. We didn't speak except to negotiate the movements of the body. It was easier this time, but I was still alarmed when we saw the death mask on his face again. I felt nauseous, but I couldn't tell if it was the medication I had taken or the knowledge of what was happening inside me or the sight of the corpse.

When we finished, I didn't go back to the bedroom. Instead, I went downstairs and outside, walking out into the fields behind the house. I stood there in the darkness, looking up at the stars. In the faint light from the moon, I could make out the angular shape of a fence. I could see the tall grass blowing in a light wind. The shape of the hawthorn trees, their crooked branches. The air smelled different, saltier, damper, older, and somehow more sincere. It was like hearing a minor key for the first time, having lived all my life in major. I could still feel my grandfather's body on my hands, the grain of his skin. Could hear my mother talking about chickens all those years ago: "That's where they're supposed to be safest, in their mothers' tummies." I had twenty-three hours left, the time counting down in units of three. Every time we had to change the ice, the baby got closer to Damon, to Ina, to my grandfather.

Chapter Twenty-Seven

2016, County Tyrone

The voice belonged to Enda. I could tell from the top step of the staircase, and it made me falter. I hadn't seen him since that day in Donegal when he'd told me to run. I was sure he hadn't meant like this.

When I reached the last step, Enda was watching me, sitting on the couch just like he used to all those years ago when he got home from school. But his back was straighter, his eyes narrower. His forehead disturbed by age.

"Bríd," he said finally. He had been staring at me long enough. He said it like he was christening me with the name. Like I had not been Bríd until he called me it.

I nodded and tried to smile. He didn't reach out to hug or shake hands, no gesture of intimacy, no touch. I felt a stab of vertigo.

"I was so sorry to hear about Siobhán," I said. "She was a wonderful woman. The world's poorer for it."

Enda nodded, looked away from me and out the window.

Ma came into the room, put a teapot and mugs on the table.

"Everything's all set, is it, Enda?" she asked.

He nodded.

"Da's in his coffin. Cousin Ted and Neil will be carrying the coffin with me and some of Da's colleagues."

Ma gave a thin smile, and then she turned her back on us. She picked up her tea and began to walk upstairs.

"I'm sure you two have lots to catch up on," she said. She did not turn around.

I tried to think of something to say to him, but I could not decide whether to address the present or the past. I felt like I was being pulled under the black water of the house, the silencing of it, the drowning. I opened my mouth to speak, but the words didn't come, and the old house seemed to settle further into itself.

"Ma told me you were here," Enda said. "She called me this morning." I nodded.

"I'm not that surprised," he went on. "I always thought you would come back one of these days."

I nodded again, not sure what to say to that either.

"Was Da sick long?" I asked finally.

He shook his head. "It happened like that." He clapped his hands together, and the noise startled me.

I wanted to say something real, wanted him to know that I'd thought of him often. That sometimes I looked out at the ocean and imagined him on the other side. But I didn't know how to say any of it. He wasn't even looking me in the eyes.

Just then, the door opened, and there she was. Jeans and an orange jumper, a red rain jacket, her hair in two plaits. Her face pink with cold, eyes fresh, so fresh, so sweet and young. My Bernie.

She had been out in the fields, examining everything. I thought of the way prisoners describe memorizing each inch of their cell, day by day, so as not to lose their minds.

Enda stood to shake hands, and I stood too. I wanted to embrace her. Five minutes with Enda and I needed to touch her skin, feel the heat of her.

"Enda, this is Bernie," I said. I walked over to her, careful to make her feel like she belonged in this room. Her skin was cold when I touched her cheek.

"Hi," Bernie said.

"Aren't you the spitting image," Enda said. He threw a glance at me out of the corner of his eye, like the football we used to pass back and forth in the fields. "Ya look just as much a rebel as your mother ever was."

Bernie smiled, looked at me with a little frown between her eyebrows.

"Me?" I laughed. "A rebel? Sure I was the good girl."

Enda let out a laugh, a real one, surprisingly sharp and familiar all at once. "Good girl my arse. You near enough sent those nuns into retirement. Always talking back and asking questions."

I tried to remember it: afternoon light slanting through a classroom window, maps of Ireland hanging on the walls, and children's handwriting filling in the county names. Drawings of saints hung around the room like Christmas decorations. I tried to remember being brave, speaking up. The way it felt to have my classmates laugh, like applause, like approval. The way it felt to sit by myself in school: no mother, no sister. A room of people who knew me just for who I was.

"I've two boys," Enda was saying. I wasn't sure if it was to Bernie or me or both. "They'll be at the Mass."

The three of us were quiet for a minute. I poured Bernie a cup of tea. Enda was looking out at the driveway. Then he stood up abruptly. I watched the liquid slosh dangerously in his cup.

He gave me one more discerning look, and I thought that this time, he would surely say something real. But all he said was: "You look different."

I nodded, unable to speak.

"I'm going to go pay my respects," he said, and then he turned his back on me and walked up the stairs.

Bernie was lying on Ina's old single bed.

"Was this one yours?" she asked.

"No." I pointed to the other one, drab with its faded pink sheets.

"Oh," Bernie said, but did not move. "I wish I could have met her," she said.

I sat down on Ina's bed, beside her.

"She was a bit like you," I said.

Bernie smiled.

"Do you think you can forgive me?" I asked.

She was quiet.

"I need to ask you something," she said after a moment. "And then I need to tell you something."

I didn't say anything, but I looked at her. She looked away, straight at the wall in front of her. Ina's Take That poster was still taped there, the right-hand corner curling with age.

"Is it true?" she asked. "What you told me about my dad?"

I let out a breath.

"Please," she said.

"I'll tell you about him," I said. "Let me just get through the day." She nodded.

"Do you think you can forgive me?" I asked again.

❖   ❖   ❖

At the church, we sat all the way on the left, in the middle of several deserted pews. The place was packed with neighbors, friends, strangers. I watched the older generation hobble in, some just a touch slower than they used to be, bent a head lower. Others with canes or walkers. Faces I recognized, more women than men, some absences more noticeable than the presences. The men whose wives walked alone. Forty-five-year-olds whose eyes I remembered from twenty-six. Several times I had the urge to jump up and greet them, ask after girls I had gone to school with. But I stayed seated, looking, as best I could, like another war widow.

I did not stand with my family; it would have felt like a lie. I could see where Enda stood at the head of the coffin with his two sons—tall, lanky boys who took after him more than their mother. Next to them were the priest, Cousin Ted, and my mother. I watched them greet the mourners, my mother's face a mask, never breaking into even the slightest smile.

Conor O'Malley was sitting near the front of the church. He looked older, but his lips and nose were still just as striking, and his eyes, even from a distance, seemed to menace. The burn on his cheek had mostly disappeared, but it still hung there like a memory. I looked away. More than anyone, I did not want him to see me. I no longer thought I was in real danger from him, but I did not want to find out if I was right.

I turned to see a latecomer entering the church and felt the air seep out of me. It was Tad, my little brother, walking up the aisle.

He didn't look at me as he walked. He didn't look to either side, kept his gaze straight ahead, and walked to the coffin. I watched him wait his turn and then look down at the closed coffin, saw the twist of his smile as he whispered something through the wood to our father, saw Enda's surprise as he shook our brother's hand, Cousin Ted's earnest greeting, Ma's face finally registering something, something like love, or anger.

Then he walked down the steps, into the left aisle, and sat down one row ahead of us. I did not know if he saw me or if it was a coincidence that we had both chosen the periphery.

"I'll be right back," I whispered to Bernie, who glared at me.

I sat down next to Tad without saying anything. I stared straight ahead. He looked at me for a long moment. He did not gasp or do a double take. He just looked at me, and then he turned and looked straight ahead again.

"You cunt," he said.

"Arsehole," I said.

The music began; the priest assumed his place at the pulpit and began the service. Tad offered me his hand, and I took it.

❖ ❖ ❖

The priest praised my father for his commitment to public service. His pacificism during the conflict. He mentioned the child Da had survived—my heart panged with the sound of her name—mentioned his loving wife, his devoted children. There was not a person in this room who did not know that Da had been a paranoid and violent man. And yet they all stood for the Eucharist.

"Remember your man Conor?" Tad whispered to me when we sat back down, gesturing toward where Conor was. He didn't wait for me to respond; of course I remembered.

"He's a counselor now," Tad said.

"A counselor?" I turned to look at him, ready to laugh at the joke. Tad nodded. "Troubled youths," he said.

"You're fucking with me."

"Swear to God."

I began to laugh. Silent giggles. Then the laughter grew inside my chest; I was shaking with it. I turned my head into Tad's shoulder so nobody would see. I laughed hard enough that tears formed in my eyes. It suddenly seemed like the funniest thing in the world: Conor, a bloody counselor. Conor—who I had been terrified would see me here, would treat me to a traitor's death—helping troubled youths. It took a long minute for me to get myself under control. I wiped my eyes, turned back toward the priest. Hoped that anyone who saw me would assume I'd been crying.

The service ended, and the pallbearers began to carry the coffin back down the aisle.

"What did you say to Da?" I asked Tad. "I saw you whisper something when you went up to pay your respects."

Tad smiled, the old mischievous smile, but more wicked, more sinister. "Thirty years too late, you bastard."

I looked behind me for Bernie, but she was already halfway out of the church.

Chapter Twenty-Eight

2016, County Tyrone

The day of my grandfather's funeral was the day of the final dose. I brought the pack of pills with me to the church, just in case, tucked in the pocket of my blazer. Hardly anybody spoke, which made things easier. Even Mom and I were quiet in the car as we made our way to the church. I looked out the window, and I wondered how I would feel, hours from now, when it was all over.

I had never been to a funeral Mass before. Damon had not had a funeral. Or, I should say, they had not had a funeral for him. There had only been the wake in which we sat around the coffin and watched the corpse fail to wake. This was the opposite of that. Instead of eyes lowered to the ground, eyes were raised to the altar, to the gold of the cross, to the sunlight through stained glass, to the priest's arms, spread wide as if he were preparing for his own crucifixion.

The hum of the church reminded me of wasps: an insistent, predatory droning. I looked from face to face, trying to spot a resemblance to mine, to work out who was family. I imagined Mom coming here as a girl, how she would have been swept up by these people, the whirlpool of them, their currents of conversation. The meaningful nods and serious gazes. The belief as dark as the leather bindings on the Bibles. Everyone here came from the same town. Everyone belonged except me.

Mom was holding hands with her brother in the pew in front of me, and I wanted to break the two of them apart, snap their link. Her brother looked like her mirror image, her face but cast in shadow. I couldn't stop my feet from bouncing on the floor, like my body was preparing to run. I remembered sitting in church all those months ago and texting Mia, her telling me about Riley's party. I'd had a confession to make then, too, but it had been an innocent one.

I thought of Kaleb. I wondered if he knew her real name, her guilt. I missed him, his solidity. The acai bowls he made on weekend mornings. I missed Mia, the sound of her laugh, her sneaker kicking me under a desk. I missed Mom's bedroom, the light through her window, and the frozen yogurt shop.

I watched my grandmother out of the corner of my eye. Her sharpness quick and thorny but undercut by a humor nobody else seemed to understand. Mom thought she was hard all the way through, but I knew that half the time, she was laughing even through her anger. She had suffered all her life, it seemed; there was nothing left to do but laugh.

We knelt to pray. I watched my mom release her brother's hand and become just herself again, bowed in prayer. My body became convex too. I looked down and into my stomach, felt the center of myself. The smallness of myself. Poor baby, I thought. Poor girl. Suddenly, I wanted to cry.

When we stood for Communion, I left my pew, went out into the fresh air.

I was alone outside the church. I knelt on the steps, resting my forehead against the concrete. I wondered if I had been right about this country, if it could hold me. I thought of what I had to do before the end of the day, imagined locking myself in the bathroom or staying in bed and refusing to get up. Whatever I did, there seemed to be no way to keep my mother from knowing, from discovering what I had been hiding. And yet the world in which she knew seemed impossible, unimaginable. I could not picture the two of us discussing the death inside me. I could only see the steel in her eyes as she'd taught me about baby chickens, as she'd told me how my birth had saved her. I had learned that she was not who I thought she was, who I had wanted her to be. But I didn't know if we could survive it happening the other way around.

I sat up, took out my phone, and read through the list of symptoms again. Nausea, dizziness, tiredness, diarrhea, vomiting, fever, cramping, bleeding, bleeding, bleeding. I could hear music coming from inside the church. The Mass was almost over. I got up and began to walk.

There was a cemetery behind the church, and I pushed open the wrought iron gate. Rows of graves laid out in avenues, last messages carved into them. I took my time reading the names, the dates. The world had slowed to this moment. I could feel it in the air: quiet and heavy with anticipation.

Ina's grave was toward the back of the cemetery. The open plot next to it made it conspicuous. When I knelt in front of the headstone, my knees were soaked immediately by the dew on the grass. There was moss covering the base of the grave, and I reached out and touched it, soft and supple but springy, ready to bounce back. It was strange to kneel there, thinking of a dead girl I did not know. I didn't believe she was looking down on me. I didn't say anything to her; she couldn't hear me.

All I knew—my fingers tracing the letters of her name, the way she must have written them on the top of her homework every night—was that this stone had built the path I walked on. Ina had been a part of making me, and she would be a part of this undoing too.

Chapter Twenty-Nine

2016, County Tyrone

We drove back to the house with Tad. Rain had started coming down hard. We stayed in the car for a minute, the engine running, the heat strong and consoling. Then, without talking, we opened the car doors and went inside the house. Emptied of parents, it felt like ours.

Bernie went upstairs to shower. I boiled the kettle.

I could hear the water moving in the pipes, the soft sound of it splashing off Bernie's body and hitting the tiled shower floor. Otherwise, the house was dead quiet. The kettle whined, and I turned off the flame.

Tad and I drank our tea standing at the counter. He looked out into the fields, biting his lip. He had aged more than anyone else I'd seen, even Ma. He looked ashen as he stood there, the cold light from the rainy day draining him of color. I remembered the glow of him as a boy, the feel of our feet in those fields, the movement.

I walked to the back door and opened it.

"Where are you going?" Tad asked.

Outside, the rain was thick and heavy. It soaked me easily, quickly. There was no other way. I began to walk into the field, past the garden in which we had played as children. I stood there for a long moment, looking out at all the green, at all the memories.

❖   ❖   ❖

Enda and Ma were late in coming home. They had been at the parish hall for the after-funeral gathering. Tad and Bernie sat at the table and played cards while we waited. From the kitchen, I could hear them laughing.

"You're funny," I heard Tad tell her. "Reminds me of your ma when she was your age. God, she was a laugh."

"What was she like?" Bernie asked. The slick of crisp cards being dealt.

"Ach she was a good craic. Whenever I brought a friend round, she'd have some wisecrack about his hair or his music taste. But God, did she have a temper." He paused for a moment.

"I remember one time my friend Eddy made some comment. Something real nasty like, about her needing a proper lay. We were thirteen only. He might not have even known what it meant. But your ma was on him in a minute, yelling so loud, she was practically spitting. I thought I was going to have to pull her off him."

Bernie laughed. "She's still kind of like that," she said.

"I'm sure she is," Tad said. "When the boys come calling."

A breath of a pause. I wondered if they knew I could hear them.

"I'm gay," Bernie said. The word came out like an inhale, like she was trying to suck it back in even as she said it.

Tad gave a short laugh: surprised, happy. "Well, fuck me, then. Welcome to the club."

Tires on the gravel outside. I could feel Tad sit up straighter. I was tensed, too, ready. I heard a chair scraping back as Tad got to his feet. I joined him and Bernie, and we watched them from the window.

"Thanks for the help," Enda said to Tad when he opened the door. He looked murderous and exhausted. He'd had to do the work of all Da's children, greeting every mourner, bearing their painful attempts at small talk. Ma looked like she was coming home from war.

Bernie's eyes flicked from one of us to the others. She had stood up at the sound of Enda's voice, as if she expected violence and wanted to be ready.

Nobody spoke. Enda slammed the box he was carrying down on the kitchen counter. The wood split down the middle, but the box stayed closed.

"Mass cards," he said. Bernie moved farther away from him.

For a moment, we all stood there. My mother and her three surviving children. Our family, reunited. I wondered what on earth to say.

Tad was the first to move. He got a bottle of whiskey off the shelf. He laid out five glasses, poured the amber liquid into each. The clink of the bottle on the rims of the glasses. The glug of the glasses filling. I remembered the last time we'd shared a drink of whiskey. The ringing sound in my ears. My heaving chest.

We took our glasses dutifully. Even Bernie. Tad lifted his.

"To Da and Ina," he said.

"To Da and Ina." Our voices pronounced, discordant.

We drank it down, the offering. The liquid burned and soothed the back of my throat, and, for a moment, I could feel her forehead pressed against mine once again, sweaty and creased from laughter. My sweet sister. She was the sun removed from orbit, and we were falling stars. I had to tell them what had happened that night. Ina deserved it: the truth, spoken aloud.

"I could have stopped her," I said.

They all looked at me. Their eyes like torches seeking me out.

"I knew where they were going," I said. "That night. I knew they were going to that dance club. Ina told me."

They were still looking at me. I felt like I was spinning too fast, like I was the one who was dancing, twirling in the center of the crowded club.

I looked at Bernie, and I could see from her face that she understood. Her stare had something hard in it. Something just as bruised as this moment was. And also something soft, and supple, and safe.

"I told her not to go," I said. "But I could have—I should have stopped her. She was so angry at me, she—" I broke off.

There was a clink as Enda put down his glass. He started to walk back toward the door, swinging his car keys between the fingers of his right hand, looking down at them as if he were alone. As if I hadn't spoken.

"Are you going?" I asked. My voice louder than I meant it to be.

He stopped at the threshold of the door, turned back to look at us.

"It's over," he said. "The boys are waiting for me in the car." He paused. "And I'm not living in the bloody past anymore." He took a deep, steadying breath. "It was good to see you, Bríd," he said. "And to meet you, Bernie." He looked at her, and I thought I saw his face soften the slightest bit.

And then he walked out the door without looking back, just like he'd left us all those years ago, moving away from the North, moving somewhere safer, somewhere free.

I turned back to Ma. Her hand was shaking. She put her glass down on the counter. She was looking at me but not seeing me.

"Ma—" I said.

She raised her hand to stop me. Like a sleepwalker, she moved to the stairs.

"Ma—" I moved to follow her.

"Brigid," she said. Her voice quiet but forceful. "Just let me be."

I watched her back as she retreated upstairs, the stiff set of her shoulders, the soldier's stance.

I sank into the sofa, feeling like I was falling into water.

"Another drink?" Tad asked finally. Bernie had come over to me. She sat on the sofa beside me and squeezed my hand.

"Sure what's the harm," I said.

He poured us each one. He still wasn't looking at me.

"You know I don't care, Tad," I said. "About you being gay."

He gave a little laugh. "Sure I'm not worried about that."

"You were so angry with me," I said. It had been something I'd wanted to ask him for years. "When I called from Miami. Why were you so angry with me?"

He looked at me, and I could feel him moving backward through the years, to that time.

"You think you had it hard?" he asked. "Going away to some other life? Imagine staying here. It was just me to take on all that responsibility. All their anger. I had to bear the brunt of it, all alone, while you were in bloody Florida. Remember how mad we all were at Enda when he left? And he only went to fucking Donegal."

"I'm sorry," I said.

"Da could barely stand to look at me," he went on. "And Ma wasn't much better. Once her golden child ran away."

"Golden child," I repeated bitterly.

"You know she died," he said. "That pregnant woman in Donegal. And the baby. The ones in the hotel bombing."

The flesh above his upper lip twitched. There was the tiniest hint of pleasure on his face. He was thinking that it served me right, that I ought to know, to suffer.

"How do you know about that?" I asked. I'd told no one at the time. Nobody except my mother.

Tad shrugged. "I got to hearing about it. Bits and bobs at the local. One day, I went to see Conor myself. It was after you'd left. I'm sure he didn't see the harm in telling me that you'd given a hand, driven a car for him. After that, it wasn't hard to put it together. I remembered that bombing, of course, and I remembered the way you were after it." I tried to imagine Tad standing in Conor's doorway. Tad's sulky frown and Conor's bravado.

I looked at Bernie, the pain on her face that she was trying to hide. I thought of her in the Miami hospital. Her small, small face held against my chest. The tubes and wires wrapped around her like ivy. How her long plaits framed her face now. The flush of her cheeks. Her eating a whole veggie burger after months of me worrying. My child, at least, had survived. In the end, that was what mattered.

They were both watching me. I looked past them, out to the green fields.

"It might not have been me," I said after a minute. "They didn't tell me what I was driving." But even as I said it, I remembered seeing the hotel that day, the sheets as white as swans. The ghostlike room. I remembered the little shiver of pride, like the lurch of flight, knowing I was connected to what I saw. To all the women I admired: Ma and Ina and the woman who had given me my orders.

"I saw you afterward," Tad said. "I remember your face when you got home. All that week, you couldn't get out of bed. You looked like Da when he woke from a bad night and remembered what he'd done. You looked guilty as anyone I'd ever seen."

I bowed my head, looked at the floor. It was true. I had been bedridden. I had starved myself like a hunger striker. Like my daughter had all this month. I looked over at her, though I still couldn't meet her eye. She reached out and took my hand, squeezed it again. Her face was calm, like it was not unusual to learn that her mother was a murderer. She was as much a soldier as her grandmother, I thought. She could stand much worse than I could.

I drank the rest of my whiskey down.

❖　❖　❖

I was in Ma's room, like I had been all those years ago. Ma was sitting on her bed. We stared at each other, and then out the window, and then back at one another. She was still so young—not yet sixty—but she had the air of a much older woman about her. She looked bled dry, exhausted.

"Brigid," she said finally.

I remembered Bernie saying her first word, the jolt of someone being mute one moment and verbal the next.

"You shouldn't have left."

There was a very long silence between us, distended, pregnant.

"Did you know she died?" I asked. "The woman in Donegal?" My voice cracked the way it couldn't with Tad, when I was still defending myself. I could admit my guilt only when I was with her, the woman with whom I shared responsibility.

She looked away.

"I was just a girl," I said. "I had to live with that."

"I would have done it," she said. "If I could have."

"What do you mean, if you could have?" I could feel anger seep into my voice like a tea bag bleeding into hot water. "When did you ever listen to Da? When did you ever respect his wishes?"

"You're not the only one to fight, you know," she snapped. "I was a woman before you. I had a life you know nothing about."

She went to the mirror and pulled up her hair.

"Look," she said.

She was pointing to a place on the back of her head.

I walked over to her. In the mirror, I could see my face hovering above hers, like we were a two-headed beast. I looked at where she was pointing. There was a scar there, curling like a blade of grass. A place where no hair grew. I tried to remember if I had noticed it before, as a child. She had always worn her hair down. I touched it with the nail of my pinkie finger, so softly that I wasn't sure she could feel it.

"A bottle on the back of my head when I wasn't looking," she said. "Almost killed me so it did."

I stared at her. "Da did that?" I had never seen my father be violent with her. I'd hardly ever seen him speak to her disrespectfully.

"It was before he got bad with the drink," she said. "And I think he felt guilty for it for the rest of his life. But he made his point all right, and I knew I couldn't go back. He was a tolerant man most of the time, but he couldn't stand the IRA. I think they made him feel small."

I was quiet for a long time. Ma had let her hair fall back down.

"Did he know?" I asked.

"Know what?"

"About me. Joining."

"Ach by that stage, he was gone, Bríd. I mean, after Ina, I don't think he was ever right again."

There was a pause.

"Did you mean what you said to me?" I asked.

She froze, her eyes finding mine in the mirror.

"What?"

"What you said to me before I left."

She didn't say anything.

"How could you have said something like that?" I asked. "To your own daughter. Everything else, I can understand. Once I had Bernie, I understood. But that, that I've neve—." I shook my head.

"I had four children," she said. "And none of them saw the world the way I did. Except for you. Since you were a child, you had something inside you that I recognized. I just knew—"

"You don't know me," I said, louder than I'd meant to. "You never knew me."

"But I was right," she said. "Look how you've lived. Your whole life, you've lived like a soldier, running from place to place, trying to survive."

I said nothing.

"Will you be staying?" she asked. "Now?"

"Staying?" I asked.

"Here," she said. "Will you be staying here, in Tyrone?"

I took a deep breath. She was going to make me say it.

My exhale felt wet with unshed tears. I wanted to tell her I was sorry, but I couldn't.

I shook my head. "I'm going home," I said. "With Bernie."

I remembered her face again, when she came back from seeing Ina's body. She'd looked the way the world would look, I thought, in a hundred years when it had all been burned and ruined. She'd looked like she'd left her own body.

"You're okay, Ma," I told her. I moved toward where she sat in her chair, embraced her from behind. "You're going to be okay." She was awkward in my arms, and she would not give in to me. But still I held her.

Chapter Thirty

1998, County Tyrone

Brigid was knocking, the delicate sound of her knuckles on my door, her hand making contact with the threshold between us.

"Come in," I called.

"Can I talk to you?"

I handed her the hairbrush. We sat on my bed. Me with my feet on the floor. Her with her legs in a V shape, hugging me from behind. She was gentle with the brush.

"Did you hear about Donegal?" she asked. The pinched sound of her voice. My body went stiff.

"A pregnant woman, Ma," she said. "She's in hospital."

Always that worship of the mother. How I'd hated being full with children. Always filled and gaped at and condescended to.

"Sure she'll be all right." I was iron in my defense. I was ready to talk her down from any heights.

"It could have been me! I've no idea."

My hand gripped the duvet. I could feel myself shaking, trembling with the anger that had been inside me ever since that day. Ever since the priest had come with the news, ever since I'd seen her body laid out on cold metal. Her face the same, the rest of her warped and mangled. They had taken my daughter from me.

"It's not your job to have ideas," I said. He had said that to me once: it isn't a girl's job to have ideas. "It's your job," I continued, "to punish them."

"I've done my part," she said. "I got revenge."

One small explosion on the coast, when they had stolen our whole world.

I scoffed. "You think that's enough? You think that's all she's worth? You've only gotten started, Bríd."

"Ma," she said. "I think I need to go."

"Don't be silly, girl." I moved away from her hands abruptly, and she dropped the brush. It hung from my hair as I turned around, and I pulled at it too hard, feeling a few strands tear at the roots.

"You can't be leaving, Bríd. It wouldn't be fair."

"Fair?"

"Why should you get to go," I asked, "when she can't?"

I could feel the heaviness of my own words. Like a body in a bog. Down, down, down. I felt her eyes on me, was conscious of the curve of my neck as I hunched slightly. The stretch of my shoulders. I felt old.

"And how is that my fault?" She was yelling now. She had always been such a quiet girl.

It was the moment that changed things. Futures branched out like the arms of the elm tree. I could have said something else, but I'd made my decision.

"It should have been you," I said.

For a moment, she just stared. Then she slapped me clean across the face.

My cheek was still stinging as she stood and walked away from me, closing the door behind her. The feeling of my daughter's palm on my face, the last place she'd touched me.

Chapter Thirty-One

2016, County Tyrone

It was time.

In my mom's old bedroom, I put my hand against my stomach, tried to feel if there was anything there. The baby was quiet under my touch. I wondered what would happen if I didn't take the next set of pills, if she would stay half-formed inside me forever. Would it kill me to hold her like that?

He had said not to wait more than forty-eight hours; it had been thirty-eight. I would do my best to stay out of Mom's gaze, but the rest was, as she would have said, in God's hands. If he wanted to punish me, here was his chance.

Eight pills in my right hand. I put them in my mouth, one by one. Nudged them between my gum and lip, where my mouth was hottest and wettest. Waited for them to dissolve. Eight times they became mush and then powder in my mouth, sinking into my bloodstream through my saliva. It took longer than I'd thought it would, left me thinking the whole time of what it would do to the child inside me. What she would feel. What was coming for us both.

I went to the bathroom to wipe my mouth clean of the chalky residue. Mom came in after me; she had been down the hall with her mother. She looked bruised, sullen as a child. I almost asked her what was wrong, but I was afraid that if I opened my mouth, she would be able to see the white smear of the pills.

"Let's go for a drive, all right?" The way she said it made it sound like a plea.

I didn't know how I could refuse. I nodded. Kept my eyes on my reflection. It was almost evening, but the sun did not set until nine or ten here. I wondered when I would start to feel something, tried to distract myself by counting things. The steps down to the first floor. The kilometers ticking up on the odometer. The speed limit signs we passed, the sheep.

❖   ❖   ❖

We went as far as the road would take us, all the way up the coast, past the harsh break of water on rocks. We stopped once at a pub she used to know and listened to a group of musicians getting ready for the evening. They sang as naturally as rocks echo, nothing like the musical performances I had seen back home. They were wild, native singers, like this was their first language. The song carried me on rolling waves, and I could feel the heave and lift of some ancestral vessel. I wondered when the pain would come, when the blood would start.

We kept going—up and down a mountain, summer rain lashing against the windows, Mom's shoulders slowly loosening—and I thought I could begin to feel something happen inside me. Something as rocky and violent as the ocean meeting the shore. Mom sighed twice and then again. Six times, the man on the radio said "Brexit" before Mom changed the station to soft, instrumental music. I thought I could feel the baby swaying inside me as three songs played.

"You know," Mom said suddenly, her voice startling me. "You're almost the same age I was when I left here."

I looked over at her: frown line between her eyebrows, eyes focused on the road like she hadn't spoken.

"Do you feel sad?" I asked after a minute. "About your father?"

She glanced at me, quickly, and then looked back out the windshield. She was quiet for a moment, and then she started to laugh. The noise startled me. Her laugh bubbled and grew into something hysterical. She tried to say something, but she was laughing too hard.

I stared at her. "What's so funny?" I asked.

"Sorry." She tried to take a deep breath. "Sorry, it's just—" She laughed harder, and then she got control of herself. "It's just such an *American* question." She was wiping her eyes with one hand, the other still on the steering wheel.

I wasn't sure if I should be offended or not, couldn't tell if she was making fun of me. She saw my expression and started to laugh again, shaking her head. "It's not you," she said. "It's just this place. We'd never ask that. It's—"

But she had lost it again. I started to laugh too. All the tension and fear burning off us like smoke, rising up into the air. I laughed until my sides hurt, thinking of how tense and quiet the house was, thinking of all the things that nobody had said, the things hanging over us like ghosts; it was the same release as crying.

I saw the sign for Giant's Causeway. It leaped out at me like an omen, and I was back in my elementary school classroom, discovering the place in the pages of a book.

"Can we go?" I asked. "Please. I want to see it."

"Why not?" She turned the car, followed the signs.

We took a bus down a steep mountain road, broke free of the rain just in time to see the rocks come up before us. Perfect hexagons, so geometrical that they looked man-made. The same shape as the pills I'd taken.

"Isn't it gorgeous," Mom said, though *feral* was closer to the word I would have used. Alien, wild, strange. It looked nothing like the placid pictures I'd shown Mia on my phone. It looked like the edge of the world.

We were the last tourists of the day. The driver waited in the bus. We went out onto the rocks alone, facing the wild, seizing mass of the ocean. The rain started up again, hard and insistent. The wind was turning the waves like dancers, making Mom's and my hair fly wild as birds. I felt like we were on the edge of something vast and infinite. Like we were getting ready to jump together into some unfathomable depths. The rocks at our feet were like some devil worshipper's symbol, some holy place. I felt the salt and wind against my face, the shocking realness of this, the truth blinding and tumultuous and new.

I took out my phone, took a picture. The image on the screen was darkened by the storm clouds and the lashing rain, but you could still see some of the wonder: the light breaking through, the symmetry of the rock edges, sharp enough to cut. I sent it to Mia. The bubble of her response appeared immediately. It's beautiful, she said. Another bubble appeared. Come home.

I felt the words like an electric current. The way I imagined it felt to have your heart shocked back into beating, a procedure I'd seen on TV. I read the words again and again. *Home, home, home.*

And then, just when I had forgotten about what was inside me, just when I could believe that none of the past mattered, the cramps came.

They were bad immediately, cinching my insides. Pain like mallets, striking the metal keys of me. I put my hand to my stomach, tried to push hard enough to soothe them. I felt like crying out; my resolve to remain neutral and unaffected, to do everything in my power not to let my mom see, was fading fast.

"Bernie?" Mom turned to look at me. "Are you okay?" The rain was hard enough that she had to squint.

My eyes were filling with tears. The sharp, hot pain. The fear and the shame. I wasn't sure if I could speak.

"Mom," I said. It came out like a gasp, like a drowning child fighting for air.

She was beside me in a moment, steering me to the bus, telling the driver to go, with a command in her voice that she saved for emergencies. Out the window, the scenery blurred behind the tears in my eyes.

I thought of the night I'd told Mia I loved her, the night Riley had tried to die. Mom's Atlantic Ocean eyes looking into mine. "It's going to be okay, Duck," she'd said. And it hadn't been, and it hadn't been, and, still, it wasn't. I was going to have to tell her. It was either tell her or have her realize it herself. I didn't know which she would hate me for more.

She was standing up, next to the driver, directing him as if this was a route she knew. She came back to me, squeezed my shoulder.

"Are you sick?" she asked. "Are you nauseous?"

I shook my head.

"Hey, hey." She saw that I was crying, wiped my eyes for me. "We're almost at the car."

We got off the bus. The change in position eased the cramps, and I felt better momentarily, taking big breaths of the rain-soaked air. She guided me to the passenger seat, got in on her side. We were both soaking wet, and she started the heat.

"Take off that jumper," she said. "You'll catch cold."

I got it over my head, wet fabric against my sweaty forehead. I had stopped crying.

"Bernie," she said. "What hurts?"

Like I was a child again, after a fall.

I shook my head.

"Mom," I said. "I have to tell you something." The words in my throat as hot as the pain. I took deep breaths.

"Mom," I said again. And for a moment, everything faded: the pain, the fear, the shame. For a moment, I felt as brave as Damon had been the first night he got to the shelter and asked for a bed. As brave as Mia had been as she kept her hand from shaking and dialed 911. As brave as Riley had been to come back from the hospital and try to stay alive. As Kaleb had been to quit drinking, as my mother had been to come home. As brave as Ina had been to go dancing.

"I'm having an abortion," I said.

Chapter Thirty-Two

2016, County Tyrone

It was an hour-and-a-half drive from Giant's Causeway to Coalisland, and I drove it in fifty minutes. The acceleration beneath my foot as smooth and sweet as it had been all those years ago. But what I was carrying now was more precious, more brutal. I thought of being stopped, of the police noticing the blood that was soaking the crotch of Bernie's jeans, like bright-red flowers blooming there. Women could be sent to prison here for doing what Bernie had done.

The word hung in the air like the sound of a shot. A word that had, all my life, made me go cold with fear and disgust. To choose to endure what that woman in Donegal had suffered, to choose yourself over your own child. The deadliest, most despicable sin. And my daughter's pale face to my left, her cheeks wet with tears, and her hands pressed to her stomach to stop the pain. I asked her if she was okay, again and again. Apart from that, we said nothing.

There was blood on the passenger seat when we got out of the car: two spots where it had soaked through. I helped her up out of the seat and into the house.

"Let's get you to the bathroom," I told her.

She nodded, the movement of her head rubbing against my chest where I was holding her to me. I thought of what was happening inside her, the war that was occurring. I tried to keep my face neutral.

She took off her wet clothes in the bathroom. Piece by piece. They clung to her, tight and sticky with rainwater. When she removed her jeans, I could see the blood down her legs. The pad in her underwear was heavy with it. She sat on the toilet. She was pale again.

I ran a washcloth under hot water. Began at her knees, wiping off the blood. Going slowly so I wouldn't hurt her. I moved up her thighs, where it was thicker. Finally I reached the edge of her underwear. The washcloth was dark red, and she was shivering.

I helped her take off her underwear, folded them over themselves quickly so she wouldn't see the size of the blood clot, threw them in the bin with the washcloth. I went to our room, found a fresh pad—her bag was full of them, I saw with a pang—and a fresh pair of underwear.

She was still bleeding. I could see the blood in the toilet when I knelt beside her. I gave her the clean underwear and pad. She put them on slowly. I could see how exhausted she was. She was crying again.

The bathroom door opened. Ma stood there in black trousers and a black blouse. She looked like the woman in mourning that she was.

"Ma, Bernie isn't well." I stood up, trying to block her view. But Ma pushed past me.

It took her twenty seconds to take in the scene, to understand. And then she was kneeling beside Bernie, wiping stray hairs off her sweaty forehead. Saying, "Aye, what a brave girl."

She looked back at me, and she was not the mother I had grown up with at all. She was a woman made of soft things, the mother I had always wanted her to be.

"What are you waiting for?" she asked, a hint of the old sharpness. "Let's get her to bed."

It was the Aoife who had existed when Ina was sick or hurt: suddenly soft, like something you could rest your head against. It was the Aoife who had never been at my bedside. I felt like I was falling in two directions at once: the anger that she could be gentle with everybody except me and the realization that she was right. That, in this moment, she was being a better mother than I was.

Chapter Thirty-Three

2016, County Tyrone

The abortion was not any of the things I had expected. It was not my mother's disappointed gaze and the regret of lost life washing over me. It was not a gory mess that sent me retching into the toilet. It did not make me angry or sad; it made me tired. It made me feel at peace.

It was a quiet, civil war, a fight for autonomy. It was lying in the sheets that Mom had slept in as a child. It was recognizing my own body: my need to protect it, the love I had for it.

It was my grandmother beside me, with a wet washcloth pressed to my forehead. It was my mother helping me change my pad and underwear, rubbing my back as I sat on the toilet. It was the blood that was just blood, the miscarriage like the childbirths they had both borne.

In the end, I was with them. In the end, I was alone. Nobody could love me out of the pain or forgive me from the burden. I had to do it myself, let the medicine take its course, lay back and trust my body to survive the suffering. But it was good to know that my mother was there anyway, hushed whispers on the periphery of consciousness when I finally fell asleep. It was good to know that, even alone, I had her.

In the end, I felt lucky. To have been given the choice, the ability to go back in time and unmake my mistakes. Lucky to be in control of my body, self-governing and whole. It was what we all wanted. To choose our own freedom, to choose our own pain.

Chapter Thirty-Four

2016, County Tyrone

"What happened to my father?" Bernie asked.

We were walking in the fields behind the house. I had told her we were leaving that day, but we had not done anything to pack. Ma's words from the day before kept playing in my head. "Will you be staying?" Like a child asking their mother not to leave them to their nightmares. I thought again about the classroom where I had spent my days from age seven to age seventeen. I thought about how I had pounced on Tad's friend. How I had played soccer outside the schoolyard. How I had meant to take my A levels.

Bernie looked like herself again, a little pale still but quicker to laugh. She looked more like herself, I realized, than she had in a long time. I still couldn't believe what she had done. Kept remembering the feeling of her soft legs under the washcloth. The smell of the blood and the way her knees had shaken.

The day was warm, the air so sweet smelling, I felt intoxicated. It felt like a dream, a memory. The grass was rich and luscious below our boots. Wildflowers bloomed.

"He left," I said.

"You mean he enlisted?"

I didn't answer.

"Mom. Did he enlist?"

"No," I said. "No. He wasn't a soldier."

"You lied."

"Yes."

"Why?"

"I was happy he was gone. I was happy there was no one except you and me. I didn't want you to think that you'd been left."

She didn't say anything for a minute. Then she asked, "What was his name?"

"Dean," I said. It was strange how this was what it had come down to: telling her what things were called. In some ways, she had known the truth her whole life. The fear, the violence. She just hadn't known its name.

"Does he know about me?"

"He was there for the first year," I said. "I don't know—I don't know why he left exactly. But it wasn't you." I remembered his soft skin, the way he insisted on holding her against his bare chest when her immune system was strong enough to risk it. The smell of him, like honey and cayenne pepper, his aftershave. "He couldn't stand to live with me anymore, I think. I was angry all the time."

"Does he know where I am now?" she asked.

I shook my head. "I wouldn't know how to contact him. I've tried a couple of times. When we were really low on cash." I tried to laugh, but it came out bitter and hard as unripe fruit.

She looked at me, searching, like she might be able to look through me and see the past.

"Do you want to find him?" I swallowed. Looked off at the hazy line of the horizon, still cloaked in morning fog, and then back at her.

She was smiling slightly, like I had surprised her. It was not a question I would have ever asked her, one week ago in America. But we were not the same women we had been then.

"What was he like?" she asked, instead of answering my question.

"He was clever like you," I told her. "He loved to read. And he loved you, Bernie."

We kept walking. She was quiet for a moment, and I played another question over in my head. What I wanted to ask. We had not spoken much about what had happened, but I wanted to know about the child we had lost. My granddaughter, born dead.

"Was it Avery?"

She flinched; she'd been expecting this. "I thought the past didn't matter," she said.

I wanted to retort, tell her I needed to know. But I didn't. It was her secret to keep, if she wanted it that way.

After a minute, she stopped. "Look at me," she said.

I looked at the house and the field, not wanting her to see how I felt: frightened, uncertain. Then I looked at her.

"It's just me," she said.

"I didn't want you to be like me," I started. "I didn't want you to regret—" But the list was so long. I didn't know where to start. "I didn't want—"

She moved toward me, held me. She was, for a moment, my daughter again. I felt her belly against mine, both of ours soft and empty. What I felt for her was stored there, in my stomach. All the anger, all the love. And I knew in that moment that it was the same for her. That our two bodies had been made to hold each other.

Chapter Thirty-Five

2016, County Tyrone

The birds chirped in the morning light. Fog hung on the horizon like a cape. Mom was wearing her leather jacket.

"Where are we?" I asked.

She'd stopped the car by the side of the road. Our suitcases were in the back seat, and there was a hint of lipstick on my cheek from when my grandmother had kissed me goodbye. I was still spotting, the last pieces of my child coming out of me. But I felt lighter, emptier, freer.

Mom didn't say anything as she got out of the car and shut the door. I followed her. She stood a little off the road, looking out in front of her at water running over rocks: a small stream.

I looked around; there was nothing special about this clearing, this stretch of ground. Nothing special except her. After a minute, she sat down on the bank of the stream, took off her boots and socks, let her feet dangle in the cold water. She still hadn't said anything. I found a place next to her and sat down too. She gave me a small smile and then turned back to the stream. I put a hand in the water, felt how bracing the cold was.

"It's beautiful," I said. "The whole country—it's so beautiful."

"Yes," she said. "The whole country."

❖ ❖ ❖

"I don't know if I can go."

We were standing in the white-walled bustle of Dublin Airport, by the ticket counter. A strong Irish sun streaming through the floor-to-ceiling windows. Over the loudspeakers, announcements were pronounced, left unheeded.

I had not been expecting this.

"What do you mean?" I asked.

"I don't know if I should leave again," she said. "All my life I've run away."

I could feel the watch on my left hand. It was heavy with the time we were wasting. We had a plane to catch. It was time to go home.

"It's not running away," I said. "It's going home." Except that this was her home, too, where her mother was. I felt again the washcloth against my thighs as she wiped the blood off me. I knew she should not stay, knew that her mother, that house, would devour her if she did. But it was not my decision to make. I was only her daughter; I could not save her.

We stood there for a long moment. People jostled us as they passed, dragging suitcases, carrying distended backpacks filled with their lives, their secrets. Two points make a line segment, but I felt the circle of the two of us. The intimacy that separated inside from outside.

I thought of Kaleb's car, Tupac playing on the stereo, driving slowly in the hot summer air. I thought of the village, of the homeless shelter, of Foothill Boulevard. I thought of Mia putting M&M after M&M in her mouth and sucking on them until they dissolved. The two of us at the mall and in her backyard and lying on our backs to watch the stars. I thought of her texting me: Come home. How the words made my heart move in my chest. It would end up broken again. It would be worth it.

"I'm going to go, Mom," I said finally. "Even if you're not. I'm going to go home."

It was true, I realized. I would go, with or without her. With or without her, I would be all right. I turned away from her; my hand, behind me, searched for hers. For a moment, I waited, ready to drop my hand, to walk away.

But through the bodies churning within the daylit space, through the exchanges of boarding passes, the goodbyes and good wishes, the baggage wheeled and carried, held tightly to backs and chests, and across the vast chasm between us, a span of time that had built a border wall, I felt Bríd Kane, my mother, take my hand.

ACKNOWLEDGMENTS

I owe enormous gratitude to the novelists, poets, activists, journalists, and survivors of the Troubles. I am also deeply thankful for those who defend, support, and provide abortions.

Much of this book was written at Trinity, with the guidance of Eoin McNamee, Claire Keegan, Kevin Power, and Harry Clifton. Thank you to my fellow writers who talked through drafts ad nauseam: Molly McNally, Tory Dickerson, Virginia Evans, Will Rockwood, Thomas Pool, and Paul Dunne. Thank you to Bríd and Brónach McGuinness, with whom I spent many weekends in Belfast. The character Bríd, though nothing like the real Bríd, is named for her.

Early readers of this novel include Eoin McNamee, Virginia Evans, Tory Dickerson, Jonathan Lethem, Daphne Klein, Helen Reeves, Geraldine Clarke, Megan Barnard, Bríd McGuinness, Helena Essex, Tiger Kaplan, and my parents. I have enormous love and gratitude for each of them.

Thank you to everyone at the Book Group and Lake Union. To the agent of my dreams, Nicole Cunningham, I am infinitely grateful for your support, acumen, and grace. To my incredible editor, and a brilliant poet, Erin Adair-Hodges, thank you for seeing Bríd and Bernie and for your encouragement and inspiration. Michelle Li, thank you for reading with empathy and insight.

This book would not exist without my family: my mother, Maura; my father, Mino; and my sister, Antonia. They taught me what it is to love, as Bernie says, at "full speed." Thank you to Tiger, who has been my home for as long as I have been writing this novel. Finally, my grandfather Xavier McDonnell died before this book was published. He was tethered to the country of his mother and is present throughout these pages.

ABOUT THE AUTHOR

Photo © 2023 Beowulf Sheehan

Francesca McDonnell Capossela is a queer writer and Irish American dual citizen. She grew up in Brooklyn and holds a master's in creative writing from Trinity College Dublin. Her writing can be found in the *Los Angeles Review of Books*, *The Point*, *Banshee*, *The Cormorant*, *Columbia Journal*, *Guesthouse*, and the anthologies *Dark Matter Presents Human Monsters* and *Teaching Nabokov's Lolita in the #MeToo Era*. Francesca lives on the Lower East Side of Manhattan with her dog Lyra. For more information, visit francescamcdonnell.com.